The Dalethorpe Chronicles

by

Lionel Ross

ISBN: 978-0-9560369-7-1

The Dalethorpe Chronicles

by

Lionel Ross

ISBN: 978-0-9560369-7-1

Dedication:

To my own dear Luise,
always by my side to encourage me

By the same Author:

Fine Feathers 978-0-9552404-2-3

(Originally published by **PublishAmerica 2005**)

(i2i Publishing 2006)

Hidden Heritage 978-0-9552404-1-6

(i2i Publishing 2006)

The Baghdad Declaration 978-0-9552404-3-0

(i2i Publishing 2007)

Men of Conviction 978-0-9560369-3-3

(i2i Publishing 2009)

4

CHAPTER ONE

THE NEW OCCUPANT

2010

The Old Vicarage that stood on the edge of the small Lancashire town of Dalethorpe had been empty for many years and its overgrown garden and shuttered windows gave the house a forbidding, if not a sinister appearance. Many of the local children were convinced that it was haunted and it was a suspicion secretly shared but never admitted by most of the adults. The news that a gentleman from London was to live there was greeted with great surprise. And when they heard that he was a man alone, with no family to share the large building, their surprise was transformed into astonishment.

The new occupant of the Old Vicarage was obviously a person of considerable means as a veritable army of tradesmen had been employed to transform the dilapidated house into an elegant and luxurious home.

Unusually, while the house was being made ready, its new owner never appeared and the curiosity of the neighbours was generously fed by this absence. Then the day after the last workman had departed a late model Jaguar car arrived and virtually glided up the drive to deposit its sole occupant at the front door of the house.

The man was just a shade less than six feet tall with a lean, well-proportioned figure. He looked active but not athletic. He had dark hair that had turned to silver grey at the temples. He was clean-shaven and his penetrating grey/blue eyes needed the assistance of light-weight rimless glasses. He was dressed in a city style Navy blue overcoat with a velvet collar. All this was reported to their parents and to other townsfolk, by the thirteen year old

Mottershead twins, Jessica and Adrian. These young people were fortunately blessed with an unusual talent for observation and detail.

From their vantage point they saw the new owner of the Old Vicarage fish into his pocket for his key as he bounded up the steps to the front door of his new home. A few seconds later the show was over as the large glass panelled door closed behind him.

The twin's mother Rosemary shared her children's curiosity and insisted the following morning that she and her husband Roger should visit the new arrival and welcome him to Dalethorpe. Roger had been far from willing to participate in this venture. It was a Sunday and therefore a 'golf-day.' He told his wife that he had no interest in meeting the new owner of the property just three hundred metres away from their own comfortable detached home.

"I have to say, Rosemary," he told her with a mischievous smile, "I know that it is nice to be neighbourly but I suspect that your main interest is in seeing what he has done to the place."

Needless to say, after a quick phone call to his golf partner, they were on their way down the lane to call upon their new neighbour.

There was a video entry phone alongside the huge front door with its beautifully restored stained glass windows. Somehow this piece of technology jarred with the early Victorian splendour of the house but it was an efficient contraption and pressing its button summoned the new resident who opened the door.

Rosemary undertook a quick tour of inspection of their new neighbour and was gratified and proud of her children's powers of observation and description. The gentleman who had opened the door was exactly as they had related and a very attractive man indeed.

"Hello," he said, as he smiled broadly, showing perfect white, teeth. "Can I help you?"

"No, no," Rosemary replied. "It is we who hoped that we might be able to help you. Are you settling in alright? We are your neighbours, Roger & Rosemary Mottershead. If there is anything you need, please do not hesitate to ask us."

Roger had remained silent during his wife's speech but now proffered a hand to be shaken, and shaken it was, with apparent enthusiasm, by the new arrival.

"That is so kind," the owner of the Old Vicarage replied. "Won't you come in?"

"My name is Carl Oliver," he informed his visitors as they entered the panelled entrance hall.

Carl led them to the huge lounge at the rear of the house from where they could see the extensive garden.

For as long as anyone living could remember, the braver of the village children had played in the long grass and inside the undergrowth of wild shrubs. They had also climbed the steep mound at the end of the garden. Rosemary had been one of these brave children some thirty five years ago. Roger, on the other hand, had never been among the legions of the brave in those days and was totally convinced that the 'jungle,' as most children called it, was inhabited by ghosts and vicious wild animals. It therefore came as a shock to Rosemary to see a beautifully planted and manicured garden where the jungle of her childhood had stood. The large mound however, was still there with its uneven surface that seemed totally at odds with the landscaped area.

Carl courteously indicated to his guests to be seated.

"Now, how about a little drink?" he ventured. "You are my very first visitors and I hate to drink alone."

Rosemary had removed her gaze from the garden and was busily eyeing the furniture and attendant décor in the elegantly furnished room.

Roger, on the other hand, had unexpectedly decided that he was enjoying the visit. *He is a really nice chap,* he decided. *I must invite him to the golf club.* And when the host offered him a glass of his favourite single malt, he was more than delighted that he had joined Rosemary on this exploratory visit.

As soon as the three were settled in the comfortable armchairs, Rosemary decided that the time had come to embark on a journey of investigation.

"Are you going to be living here alone?" she enquired.

Carl had been expecting an interrogation by the neighbours, whoever they turned out to be. It was thus something of a relief that the first visitors were such a pleasant couple. He decided to supply a minimum of information but dressed it up to sound like far more than he was actually confiding.

"Yes," he replied. "There is or was a Mrs Oliver but I am afraid we went our separate ways a few months ago."

"Ah," Rosemary responded, a little surprised at the apparent openness of the new owner of the Old Vicarage. "It is always hard for the children when marriages break down," she ventured.

"We had only one son," Carl replied, adding graciously, "And he is in banking. What children do you have?"

"Oh," said Rosemary, surprised that the tables had been turned so easily. "We have a nineteen year old daughter Fiona. She is away at university and we have thirteen year old twins."

"Ah," said Carl, "would those be the children I noticed peeking through the hedge when I arrived yesterday?"

"Oh really," Rosemary answered, trying to sound annoyed. "I really must tell them not to spy on people and to keep their curiosity to themselves."

"Please do not say a word to them," Carl replied. "They meant no harm."

"Now tell me, Roger, what do you do for a living?"

Rosemary did not like this turn of events. Suddenly the interrogation was being aimed at them. She had nothing to hide but that was not what she was there for.

She decided to change the subject.

"You have done a wonderful job with the garden," she congratulated him. "You must have seen how it was when you decided to buy the house," she continued, "a jungle, just a jungle!

"Can I make just one comment?" she continued smiling.

"Comment away," their host replied.

"I would have thought that after making the garden look so wonderful, you would have flattened out the mound at the end."

Suddenly the whole demeanour of their new neighbour changed.

"That is really none of your business," he snapped. Having said that he ostentatiously looked at his wristwatch and all but asked them to leave.

At the front door he bade them a frosty goodbye and the Mottersheads found themselves outside the Old Vicarage completely unable to understand what had so upset their host.

CHAPTER TWO

KARL OLAFSEN'S INFATUATION

893AD

It was said of Karl Olafsen that he was forced to leave the settlement becoming known in the Norse language as Wid Næss, (wide promontory) as a result of his dalliance with a slave girl. It was his erstwhile friend Asmund who had arrived with the girl from Ireland. He had given her the Norse name of Runa as no one knew her real name.

The girl was totally different in appearance from all the other women, not only in Engla Land but even in Karl's old country. Norse women were usually blonde with blue eyes. They were also quite tall whereas this girl was short. Karl had been captivated by her unusual beauty from the first moment he saw her.

On his travels he had occasionally seen people whose skin was jet-black. He had been told that they came from a huge country across the southern sea. This girl however, was neither black nor possessed of the pale skin of the women of the north lands. She had light brown glistening skin, dark brown eyes and a mass of dark curly hair and her white robe did little to conceal the wonderful womanly shape it was designed to cover. Most slave girls were sullen and rarely smiled but Runa was always happy, smiling and humming strange tunes in a language that none of them recognised.

Karl was becoming increasingly obsessed with her. At night, when he should have been making love to his own woman, Hildr, he lay awake dreaming of the passion and tenderness he could show Runa, if only she was his.

Wid Næss was a settlement that was expanding. Most of the population were Vikings which was to be expected in a small town in the far south-west of the area known as the Danelaw. However, many of the other inhabitants of the area were Saxons who had chosen to remain after the invasion of the Norsemen rather than move over the river Maeres Ea to their own Kingdom of Mercia. As a result, together with a sprinkling of the Celtic aboriginal residents, Wid Næss was becoming more and more, a melting pot, fusing together the different peoples who would one day constitute the population of north western England.

Then Karl saw his opportunity to approach Runa. She was working in the fields by the river and seeing that none of the other women were within earshot, he sauntered towards her.

"Where is my friend Asmund today?" he began. "What is he thinking of to leave a beautiful girl like you alone in this field?"

Runa returned his interest with a dazzling smile that showed glistening white teeth.

"My master has departed today for Ireland," she explained, "and I must work with the other slave girls to bring in the harvest."

Karl took hold of the girl's hands.

"If you were mine, I would never let you work in the fields and roughen these beautiful fingers. Where are you from?" Karl continued.

Karl knew that such a beautiful creature as this Runa would have a voice to match; soft warm and musical. He was not disappointed. Just the sound of her answering his questions was more exciting for him than the act of love with any other woman.

"I came from Ireland but that was not my real home," she told him with a tiny smile gently gliding over her moving lips.

"Then where is your real home?" Karl gently enquired.

Suddenly the girl realised that the other women had stopped work and although they were too far away to hear the conversation, they were staring at the two of them. In the well-ordered society of the Norsemen it was improper for a man to start a conversation with the slave girl of another man, especially when she was supposed to be working for her master.

Karl realised that to continue talking to this goddess would cause her serious problems.

"I must see you again," he declared urgently. "Meet me this evening, after our supper, in the woods further up the river."

Runa looked deeply into Karl's eyes. She liked this handsome, blonde giant of a man and felt that he wished her no evil. She had spent most of her life, certainly from the age of puberty, avoiding men who just desired her body and she sensed that this man was different. He seemed to be genuinely interested in her as a person, and as a slave that was not something to be lightly discarded.

"You are going to cause me problems with my master," she pointed out, "but yes, I will meet you after our meal."

Karl spent the rest of the day in a state of great excitement. His simple cart, the main means of transportation, had been damaged the previous day when it had hit a rock on the road. He had to repair it and although he was slowly completing the task, his mind kept wandering to what he would say and learn from Runa. He longed to take this vision of loveliness into his arms but he felt that this should only happen when and if he had established a bond of friendship.

Then he thought to himself, *what am I doing? Asmund is my friend and second only to the head man in this settlement. He would be well within his rights, under our law, to have me killed if he discovers that I am trying to steal his slave-girl.* But his desire to become acquainted with Runa overwhelmed his normal caution.

At supper that night, he hardly spoke to Hildr. They had been together for five winters but the gods had not blessed them with children. Until his recently acquired obsession with this girl, the lack of sons to carry on his family, grieved him but now this was pushed to the inner recesses of his mind.

Karl ate quickly and rose to leave their wooden hut with just a mumbled apology to Hildr. She had noticed that he had not been his normal bright self for some weeks now and could discover no obvious reason for his preoccupation.

Leaving behind the last buildings in the small town he felt his steps become lighter and quicker as he made his way towards his tryst with Runa.

Chapter three

Dalethorpe

An outburst regretted

As soon as they had closed the front door of their home, the Mottersheads, who had remained in a stunned silence on the short walk home, turned towards each other and gasped.

"What on earth caused that outburst?" Rosemary wondered.

"Don't know!" Roger replied. "It's beyond me! All you did was to mention the bloody garden and the fellow responded as if you had insulted him."

"Well," Rosemary continued, "I don't think we will be adding him to our list of friends."

"Absolutely not," Roger agreed, "The man was so bloody rude and just when I was beginning to see him as a potential new friend."

"Well," Rosemary continued, "I am just sorry we bothered. Are you going off to golf now?"

"May as well," her husband replied. "I am really annoyed by that ignoramus's behaviour in throwing us out. I will take out my frustration on a golf ball."

The Mottersheads were having a dinner party that evening and Rosemary put on her overall and busied herself, preparing the meal. She had just placed the roast in the oven when the doorbell rang.

"Jessica! Adrian!" she called. "Will one of you please go to see who is at the door?"

She could hear the 'fairy footsteps' of her twins as they ran down the stairs to open the door. Then she could just make out quiet conversation in the hall, followed by the twins running into the kitchen.

"He is here," they told her breathlessly.

"Who is here?" she demanded.

"The man from down the road," Jessica told her.

"What man from down what road?" their mother replied, not a little exasperated by the lack of clarity in the information provided.

"You know," Adrian explained. "The man we told you about last night; the man with the Jag; the one from the Old Vicarage!"

"Did you say I was in?" Rosemary whispered.

"Yes, of course," Jessica said. "Why? Don't you want to meet him?"

"Alright," Rosemary answered. "Take him into the lounge and tell him I will be there in a minute."

Having quickly removed her overall, patted her hair and repaired her lipstick, Rosemary entered the lounge with a rather less than friendly expression on her face.

"My dear Rosemary," her visitor said, "you really must forgive me for being less than courteous to you and your charming husband. Moving home is always stressful and I had just remembered that I had an important phone call to make. It was kind of you to make contact. I know your sole object was to welcome me. Sorry!"

Rosemary, always or nearly always the lady, smiled, just a touch less sincerely than at their previous meeting and said,

"I am afraid Roger has gone off to play golf but please sit down and have a drink."

"Thanks but no thanks," her apparently contrite guest replied. "I just wanted to apologise and now I must be on my way. Loads to do, you know!"

Rosemary closed the door behind him and immediately phoned her husband to relate the latest happening with their new neighbour.

Roger was in the middle of a swing on the ninth hole when his mobile rang and as a consequence he clipped the ball which rolled just a few agonising feet.

"What do you want now Rosemary?" he demanded. "First you drag me off to see some boorish fellow who happens unfortunately to have moved into our lane and now you have ruined my stroke."

Rosemary ignored the outburst and quickly related the details of the visit and conversation with the said boorish neighbour.

"There is something very strange about him," she told Roger.

He had now mastered his irritation and replied soothingly,

"Don't worry, dear. We can talk about it when I come home."

CHAPTER FOUR

WID NÆSS

ASSIGNATIONS

Karl walked quickly towards the spot where he had agreed to meet Runa. He felt as if his feet were almost floating above the rough surface of the path as he made his way down to the river. This wide waterway was the boundary between the Kingdom of Mercia to the south and the area known as the Danelaw to the north and to the east.

He arrived at the spot before Runa, the girl who was dominating his every thought and deed. It was dark now but, in those days, they enjoyed warm, balmy nights throughout the island known as Engla Land, at least until some time after the harvest when they began to count the days to the festival of Yule. The temperate climate was just one of the many attractions that this land held for the Norsemen.

Karl was waiting impatiently. He was beginning to think that Runa had decided that the planned assignation was far too dangerous. He was deeply disappointed and turned from gazing at the dim lights of Saxon torches across the river in Mercia when he heard footsteps approaching. And there she was, looking lovelier than ever.

Runa approached him with a little smile dancing along those delicious lips.

"I am sorry to be so late. I nearly did not come. I do not want trouble from Asmund when he comes back but I do so want to talk to you."

"And I desperately want to talk to you," Karl told her.

"Tell me, my dear," he continued. "Where do you come from?"

"I was born near a place called Paris, in the land of the Franks and the Gauls. When I was still a girl of only twelve summers, your people the Norsemen came up the river in large numbers and attacked the town. Just a few of us were taken captive before the siege began and I was taken by Asmund when he returned, first to Ireland and then to this place that you call Wid Næss."

Karl had heard many similar stories and had himself participated in many raids further down the coast of this island in the Kingdom of Mercia. Now, however, the Norse people were settling down to peaceful lives as farmers inside the Danelaw and most of them had experienced more than enough of fighting.

"I have seen many people from the lands of the Franks and the Gauls but they do not look like you," he commented. "You are much more beautiful."

"Ah," she replied, "that is because my grandparents came from the East. Have you heard of the land called Judea, Israel or Palestina? It is where the Christian prophet Jesus came from."

"Yes, of course," Karl answered. "I have met many Christians and indeed some of our own Norse folk are deserting Thor and Odin to worship this new god.

"But I have never met a Christian who looked as beautiful as you."

"Please may I explain a little more," Runa said, feeling for the first time, since she was snatched from her family, that here was someone who was really interested in her as a person.

"Of course," Karl answered.

"I am not a Christian but Jesus, the man the Christians follow, was from my people. We are known as Judeans or Hebrews. We also worship the one true God that the Christians worship but without including Jesus in our prayers. "

"So your people too have given up sacrificing to Thor and Odin, but what about Freya, the god of fertility, marriage and growing things? A lovely young woman like you must want the blessings of Freya to make her have children and to bless her harvests in the field?"

"We have only one God and he looks after everything in our lives," Runa explained.

"Only one God, he must be very powerful," Karl exclaimed.

Runa suddenly realised how late it must be.

"Thank you for talking to me, you do not know how wonderful this has been for me," Runa said, "but I must return to my hut or the other girls will tell Asmund when he returns."

"Meet me again tomorrow night and we can talk again," said Karl.

"I will try," Runa said and ran lightly off, back towards the settlement."

For the next twenty five nights, until the new moon was visible once again over the lands to the east of the Danelaw, Runa and Karl met secretly, by the river and once they had finished exploring each others history and personality it would have been strange if they had not started to explore each other physically. Their love making was everything that Karl had dreamed of but unlike previous conquests; there had been many, he only yearned to be in her company and his love for the slave girl grew stronger and stronger. However, they both knew that all this must end. Asmund was due back from Ireland and Hildr was complaining continuously about Karl's mysterious evening absences.

They resolved to meet just once more and that evening Karl made his way with a heavy heart towards their usual meeting place. Suddenly he heard a man's voice behind him.

"Greetings, friend Karl," the voice exclaimed. "And where are you off to at this time of night?"

Karl instantly recognised the voice as that of his friend Asmund who had returned a day early from his voyage to Ireland.

"I do not suppose that you have seen my little slave girl Runa have you?" Asmund enquired. "She is not in the longhouse with the other girls and they tell me she has been going out for long walks every night."

"No, I have certainly not seen her tonight," Karl replied truthfully but feeling very uncomfortable. "Anyway, how are you my friend? Did you have a good voyage and visit to our settlement in Dubh Linn?"

"Yes fine." Asmund replied irritated by this attempt to change the subject. "Are you sure you do not know where she is. I know you liked her. I often watched you staring at her as she went about the settlement."

Karl knew that somehow he had to bluff it out and he had never realised how obvious he had made his fascination with the girl.

"Look I only came up here for a breath of air," he lied, "and now I must return home to Hildr."

Eventually Runa, down by the riverside, realised that something had happened to prevent her lover appearing and she slowly and dejectedly returned to the hut.

When she saw the longhouse in the clearing she could just make out the figure of a man pacing up and down outside. Then with a shock she realised that the man was Asmund. He had obviously seen her approaching as he stood there glaring as she ran quickly towards him.

Before she could utter one word of greeting Asmund launched into a veritable tirade of accusations.

"Where have you been? I know you have been out every night until late while I have been away. Been meeting a lover, have you? And I thought you were to be trusted. So who is this lover? I just met Karl and he looked very guilty when I questioned him."

Runa was shocked. Asmund had been good to her ever since he had captured her in the land of the Franks. She had worked hard in the fields for him, cooked his meals and lay with him in the Longhouse where his love-making had not been cruel and violent like many of the other Viking men. Some of the other women had told her of their experiences. She knew she must deny his accusations and she also knew that he had been denied the loyalty that he deserved.

"I missed you," she lied. "To pass the evenings I went for walks down by the river. Now you are back, my master, I am happy again."

Asmund grabbed her hand and started to drag her towards the longhouse. He had never treated her this way before and his anger was obvious for all to see.

"I do not believe you," he muttered, "but we will get to the bottom of all this tomorrow afternoon. There is a meeting of the Vapnatak (council of the settlement) and I will bring you and your friend Karl Olafsen before them. We will soon find out the truth."

Asmund pulled her by the arm over to their mattress and flung her down there. Other members of this longhouse heard the commotion but thought better than to interfere. It was not the first time that foreign and even Norse women had betrayed their lords and masters.

CHAPTER FIVE

DALETHORPE-1852

A FAMILY SECRET

Carl Joseph Oliver was born in 1825, the son of Carl Isaac Oliver and Emily Johnson. Sadly, all Emily had to show for seven previous pregnancies was one frail daughter, Dorothy, a sickly child of eleven years, who was possessed of some unknown illness that sapped her vitality. Carl Isaac was well-to-do and could afford the fees of the best doctors from Manchester and London, but to no avail. This poor creature had only one pleasure in life and that was to nurse her china doll. Outsiders often commented secretly that the doll looked healthier than its owner. Now he had the son he yearned for, to follow on the family tradition and the boy grew in to a handsome and intelligent young man. Sadly, these attributes, of which he was personally well-aware, resulted in Carl Joseph being somewhat arrogant and self-opinionated.

There had been Olivers in Dalethorpe for as long as anyone could remember. They were considered as aristocracy by the local people and the family was well-known and respected in towns as far away as Accrington, Blackburn and Burnley. In earlier times they had been farmers and had quietly ridden out the many changes that had occurred in their native land over the centuries. Whether the Roman Catholics were killing the Protestants or the pendulum was swinging the other way, the head of the family had always managed to indicate peripheral support for whichever religion was in the ascendancy at that time. This tightrope policy had also ensured the family remaining unaffected by the wars between the Republicans and the Monarchists, the Roundheads and the Cavaliers, as they were called.

Carl Isaac Oliver was possessed of sound business acumen and observing the rapid growth of the Lancashire textile industry, at that time virtually a 'cottage' industry, he invested in the latest equipment money could buy to enable his workers to efficiently produce fabrics of good quality and competitive price, albeit in their own homes. The workers owed their 'benefactor' the cost of the latest looms and he allowed them to re-pay his generosity by supplying the finished rolls of cloth to him at a fraction of their value. Sadly, very few of these hard-working souls were ever cleared of their debts to the Oliver family, but they still held them in high esteem.

This accumulation of wealth enabled Carl Isaac to move his family to a luxurious suite in the Mitre Hotel in Manchester while the old farmhouse was demolished and a beautiful elegant home was built, far more in keeping with their position as virtual squires of Dalethorpe. A rough road already acted as the main and in fact the only street in the village at the time and Carl Isaac instructed the builders to construct the house with a wide path for carriages and well-planted gardens to the frontage and to the rear. Between the old farmhouse and the farming land there was a large mound and the builders were told that in no circumstances must this mound be disturbed in any way.

The building foreman was one Patrick O'Reilly and he had tried to argue the point with Mr Oliver. This had produced an outburst of anger unprecedented in one of normally even temper.

"Do as you are told or I will get someone else to oversee this job that will," Carl Isaac had snapped.

Not surprisingly Carl Joseph Oliver joined his father's thriving enterprise as soon as he left school. All of his compatriots at King Richard's School in nearby Bartley were from wealthy families, many involved in the rapidly expanding textile industry. Most of them went on to Oxbridge but business was the life blood of the Olivers and Carl Joseph was no exception. He could hardly wait to leave school and start a career as a captain of industry.

In 1852 Carl Joseph was summoned to his father's room to be told that the elder Oliver was seriously ill and unlikely to survive for more than another few months. Carl Joseph had of course noticed the steady decline in his father's health that resulted in most of the day to day business being left in his own capable hands. He was therefore far from surprised to receive this sad piece of news.

Having told his son of the serious nature of his health problems, the father indicated to him to sit near him as he had some other confidential information to impart.

Carl senior was sitting on a chaise-long in the bedroom and patted a space alongside for his son to occupy.

"What I have to tell you now is for your ears only. Neither your mother and certainly not your poor ailing sister must ever know what I am about to tell you."

Carl junior looked appropriately serious which was hardly difficult when he had just been told that his father was dying.

"Take this key and go to the cupboard door in the corner. There is only one item inside. It is quite heavy so carry it carefully and put it on the floor in front of us."

What on earth is going on, Carl wondered as he unlocked the heavy wooden door with the large key.

Inside, as his father had said, there was just one item, a brown paper parcel standing on end. It was quite large, maybe three feet high and two feet wide. Carl Joseph bent to pick it up and was surprised, although warned of the fact, that it was quite so heavy.

He placed the parcel on the floor in front of his father and undid the string to remove the paper. He could not believe what now lay before him; it was a lump of rock with strange etchings on it.

"Father, what is this?" Carl junior exclaimed.

"That is our family secret and I have a long, long story to tell you," Carl Isaac answered.

CHAPTER SIX

WID NÆSS

ACCUSATION

The monthly meeting of the town council or forum, the Vapnatak, was always attended by the majority of people in the settlement. The proceedings were conducted in the Norse language. As the Vikings had settled down in Engla Land, they had adopted the way of life in their old countries and become farmers. Many of them also had families and business interests in Ireland from where the Norse inhabitants of Wid Næss had come. So voyages between the two countries were frequent and relationships friendly, as denotes people of the same origin. Once the boundaries between the Viking area called the Danelaw and the Kingdom of Mercia had been delineated, those Anglo-Saxons who remained north of the river began to integrate into this society.

The town leader was Gunnar Spakisen, a man who had survived over sixty summers and who had the respect of the entire community. To start the proceedings of the Vapnatak, Gunnar would announce the matters to be discussed. These were mainly routine and primarily related to farming and the general welfare of the settlement. Any additional items were proposed by other senior members of the community.

On this occasion, as was usual at the end of the routine business, Gunnar invited any other matters to be raised.

Asmund rose and Gunnar said,

"Ah, Asmund Eriksen, you have something to bring to the attention of the Vapnatak?"

"Yes, Gunnar, this is a personal matter," Asmund replied. "However, if my problem goes unresolved I feel this kind of behaviour will spread."

"So what is this problem that warrants the attention of the Vapnatak?" Gunnar answered.

"I have a girl slave who I brought here some time ago from the land of the Franks. You will all know her; her name is Runa," Asmund explained.

"While I was away in Ireland she was missing from the Longhouse every night. This can be confirmed by everyone in our Longhouse," he continued. "I suspect that she has formed an association with another Norseman, my 'friend' Karl Olafsen."

Everyone present gasped. Karl was well-known and well liked. Surely he would not steal the slave girl of a friend.

"What evidence do you have of this behaviour?" Gunnar enquired.

"I have already told the Vapnatak that the girl was out on her own every night while I was away," he reminded the meeting.

"But what evidence do you have that Karl Olafsen was with her?" Gunnar enquired.

"I saw him walking in the direction of the woods by the river on my return from Ireland," Asmund replied. "And he looked quite shocked and guilty to see me there; and then Runa came back from the same direction."

"Were they together?" Gunnar enquired.

"No," Asmund answered.

"I have a question for you," Gunnar responded.

"It is a serious accusation that you are making against someone we thought was your friend. Why were you walking down there yourself?"

"I often take walks to relax. " Asmund explained. "And after the voyage with the constant noise of the waves crashing against the longboat, I needed a little peace and quiet."

"If you can take a walk to find peace and quiet, why cannot Karl?" Gunnar enquired.

"I still think he was on his way to meet Runa," Asmund said defiantly. "He is always staring at her. I am sure he desires her."

"Looking at a beautiful slave girl is not a crime in our law," Gunnar replied. "She is a very beautiful woman. Even at my age I could desire her but that does not mean I would try to take her from you. However, to be away from the Longhouse late, night after night, while you are away does sound suspicious. Bring her to the Vapnatak and we will question her."

Asmund quickly returned to the Longhouse and virtually dragged Runa to the open-air meeting.

"Why were you out of the Longhouse every night while Asmund was away?" Gunnar demanded.

"I like to walk in the woods by the river," she replied in a voice quivering with fear.

"Were you alone or did you meet someone down there?" Gunnar enquired.

"I, I was alone," the girl whispered.

"Your master Asmund suspects that you were meeting Karl Olafsen," Gunnar continued. "Is that true?"

"No, no I was alone," she wept.

"Very well," Gunnar announced. "You are forbidden to leave the longhouse other than with your master Asmund. He will take you to work in the fields each day and you must at all times do your work where you can be easily seen by the other women. If you are found in the company of Karl Olafsen at any time, you will die. Is that understood?"

"Yes, yes," she answered trembling as Asmund dragged her by the arm back to the Longhouse.

However, Asmund was far from satisfied and felt he could never again trust the girl.

As for Karl, usually an enthusiastic member of the Vapnatak, he had suddenly found urgent business in the east and only returned that night. He then discovered, not surprisingly, that his woman Hildr, his best friend Asmund and most of the people in the settlement were treating him as an outcast.

Some fourteen days went by during which time Karl came to two conclusions. He could not live without Runa and he could no longer live in Wid Næss. He felt that his future lay further east, still on the plain but nearer to the great hills that divided this part of the Danelaw from the Kingdom of Jorvik. To leave Wid Næss with his belongings was not difficult and not unusual. Many Norsemen left their first settlements and moved away to open small farms (Thorpes.) However, Karl could not and would not leave without Runa.

He started to announce to all and sundry that he and Hildr would be leaving Wid Næss. He told anyone who would listen to him that he was not prepared to stay in a settlement where his good name had been brought into question at a Vapnatak. This display of indignation did help a little to restore his popularity and even Asmund began to wonder if he had been too quick to condemn his old friend.

Four new moons had now risen in the sky and grown and waned in their fashion. Karl was on nodding and even smiling terms with Asmund although it was like a knife to his heart to see him about the settlement with Runa. And then Asmund spoke to him,

"I believe you are thinking of leaving Wid Næss," he said.

"Yes," Karl answered. "I plan to set up a Thorpe (a small farm) to the south."

"But to the south lies the Saxon Kingdom of Wessex," Asmund replied looking somewhat surprised. "You know these Saxons hate us and say we have stolen part of their land."

"That is true, but I intend to go to an area where we are welcome down near Scrobbesbyrig (Shrewsbury.) The Saxons there have no argument with us Norse people. Their problem is with the people from Waelisc (Wales) who attack the town frequently."

This was, of course nonsense. Karl had no intention of entering Wessex and knew as a Norseman that this would be an incredibly dangerous act.

Plans to leave proceeded and his farming land outside Wid Næss was sold to a new arrival for a goodly sum. Somehow, he had to let Runa know of his intention to take her with him and to leave Hildr behind in Wid Næss. And then his opportunity came.

Asmund had delayed visiting his farms in Ireland since the trouble with Runa. But now a messenger had arrived to say that he was needed urgently over there. He instructed the other women to watch Runa while he was away. Most of them were only too pleased to help as they were jealous of her incredible beauty and the effect she had on every man who saw her. However, a dispute developed between Meldun Runolfsen, who had bought Karl's land and three of his neighbours. Meldun was a violent, quick-tempered man and had killed one of the three in a fit of rage. Gunnar called the Vapnatak into session but Meldun refused to appear. He was a wealthy man and was able to persuade a number of the other Norsemen to take his side by offering them substantial inducements. Gunnar then called on all the uncommitted men to take up arms to drive Meldun and his supporters out of Wid Næss. A pitched battle ensued, in the midst of which the Longhouse of Asmund was set on fire. While there was so much confusion, Karl came face to face with Runa running away from the scene. She threw herself against him weeping and Karl just took her hand and said,

"Come quickly."

He had been ready to leave for some time now with horses and a cart containing his belongings hidden in the woods well to the east. So together the lovers escaped from Wid Næss and towards the new life they would start many miles to the east.

What eventually became of Hildr and all the residents of Wid Næss, after the fighting had subsided, was never discovered by Karl whose only thought was to have won the woman of his dreams to be his forever.

CHAPTER SEVEN

DALETHORPE

A HISTORY LESSON

Carl Joseph was mystified. What could be so special about an old piece of rock with what looked like a few scratched letters on it?

"You look puzzled my boy," Carl Isaac said.

"Yes sir, I certainly am puzzled," his son replied.

"Have you ever heard of Runes?" the old man enquired.

"Yes sir," Carl Joseph replied. "Were they some sort of Viking writing system?"

"Good man," his father replied. "The runic alphabet was used by generations of Vikings to write everything from poems and history to memorial stones.

"Now take a look at this stone and tell me what you can see," the old man continued.

"Sir, all I can see is squiggles and scratches."

"Now listen carefully to what I am about to tell you. This stone was originally embedded in the top of the mound at the end of the garden. When the farm was demolished and this house built, I removed the stone and sent it to the British Museum to try to discover its origin.

"They reported back that their experts had identified it as a Viking grave marker," Carl senior explained.

"They were able to improve the legibility of the letters on a wax-paper rubbing and they supplied that to me when they returned the stone."

The old man rose with some difficulty to go over to a drawer besides his bed. He produced a large roll of waxed paper which he spread out on the floor in front of the chaise-long. He seated himself again and pointed to the strange letters that were impressed into the wax paper.

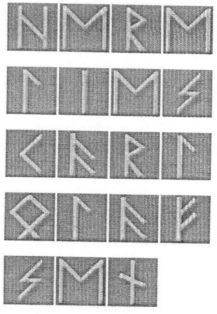

Carl Junior stared at the strange writing. He could clearly recognise the letters 'R' and 'I' and what looked like a letter 'M.' He tried to read it but it made no sense. *In any case*, he thought, *if it is written in a Viking language, I have no chance of understanding it.*

"Did the Museum people tell you what it meant," Carl junior enquired.

"Yes," replied the old man, "it is quite simple. All it says is, '*Here lies Karl Olafsen*'."

"And do we know who Karl Olafsen was?" Carl Joseph enquired.

"No. The Museum has no idea. There are many Viking burial mounds like we have in our garden but few of them had a runic memorial stone. The Museum people wanted to come along and excavate the mound but I forbade this."

"Why father?" Carl Joseph asked in astonishment.

"This is the other part of what I have to tell you," the old man continued.

"You do not remember your grandfather who was also called Carl Joseph, do you?" The son shook his head sadly.

"As you know he was only thirty eight when he died. However, on his death-bed he told me that the mound at the back of the old farmhouse must never be disturbed. If it was, he said, we Olivers would lose our claim to this land. I felt guilty for even removing the stone marker but with gangs of builders around I decided to take it away, as much for safety as curiosity.

"Of course my father had no idea what the mound was and neither did previous generations of Olivers going back for many hundreds of years. As I have told you many times, there have been Olivers living on this plot of land for as long as anyone can remember. We are even mentioned in the Domesday Book (1086) with this whole area then being allocated to Robert d'Oilly who had our ancestor Karl d'Olive as an important farmer-tenant."

All the talking had exhausted the old man and he sat back.

"Can I get you a drink or anything else, father?" Carl Joseph enquired. He was somewhat shocked to discover that just talking could have such an effect on the older man.

"No. I am fine. I will just rest a little. Please put the stone and wax-paper rubbing back in their proper places and you can go about your business.

"Can I rely on you to follow the ancient instructions regarding the mound and to divulge what I have now told you only to your own eldest son?"

"Of course you can father, now please rest."

Carl Joseph left his father's room intrigued by the knowledge of his family history that he had just received. But the young man also had other matters on his mind and they involved substantially increasing the family fortune.

CHAPTER EIGHT

A DEATH, A MARRIAGE AND A BIRTH

The soul of Carl Isaac Oliver was re-united with its maker on the nineteenth of October 1852. He was buried in the family crypt in the graveyard adjoining the Church of St Barnabas-by-Dalethorpe in the presence of his family, servants, workers and those from many miles around who felt it was fitting to attend the final journey and burial of a man of his calibre.

On the ninth of March in the following year, in the same church, Carl Joseph Oliver was married to Elizabeth Mottershead, his childhood sweetheart. Unlike the truly ancient clan Oliver, the Mottersheads could only trace their residence as a family in Dalethorpe, back to the late eighteenth century. This was when Joshua Mottershead, a master baker had arrived from Ancoats, a small township near Manchester. With the advent of more and more industry and the grinding poverty of those who laboured therein, Joshua had decided to sell his bakery and move to a country area where he could set up shop in a far healthier environment. He had stumbled upon Dalethorpe by accident and immediately fell in love with the place.

The wedding was a glittering occasion and was attended by local gentry from miles around. Jacob Mottershead, son of Joshua, the father of the bride, although certainly not considered a gentleman in the manner of the Oliver's friends, was well regarded as a man of substance (although the primary substance was flour!) Elizabeth quickly assumed the mantle of a gentleman industrialist's spouse and enabled her mother-in-law Emily, to withdraw from such a demanding role and concentrate her attentions exclusively on her poor ailing daughter Dorothy.

Carl now set about bringing his plan to fruition. There were at this stage large numbers of textile factories in the county; indeed it was said that *'Britain's bread hung by Lancashire's Thread.'* Most of these were in the towns where the workers lived in the most unimaginably appalling conditions. Carl however, was determined to build a mill on the edge of Dalethorpe and equip it with all the latest machinery. His workers in the cottages round about would then be only too delighted to transfer to the large airy building rather than spend their days in the midst of the claustrophobic domestic environment of their homes.

Lancashire at that time was not only the centre of the British cotton industry but in reality was the centre of the world cotton industry. A specialisation had occurred wherein, for geographical reasons, some parts of the county specialised in production of cotton yarn (spinning) and in the others places weaving was the main industry. The Oliver's were weavers or at least they employed weavers to produce the cotton cloth to be sold at a substantial profit all over the world.

The new factory opened in 1856. Carl ensured the news of its construction and of the latest and most efficient machinery installed within the large single storied building would attract the maximum possible publicity. The Lord Lieutenant of the county was invited to declare the factory open on behalf of Her Gracious Majesty Queen Victoria and he was delighted to attend. So were other industrialists and reporters from the Manchester Guardian and similarly prestigious journals.

Every one of the Olivers' workers accepted the change of location without protest. This was partly because of the improvement in working conditions and partly because they did not dare to refuse. There were no other textile employers in the immediate area and their only skill lay in the field of weaving. By the standards of the time Carl was a fairly benevolent employer but he still managed to reduce the weavers' wages once they were settled into the new mill. This was a recipe for trouble but that was to come later.

CHAPTER NINE

UP HILL & DOWN DALE

Karl and Runa had run all the way to where Karl's cart was hidden. They were convinced that they were being pursued but with the fighting and chaos now happening in Wid Næss, it would be many hours before the absence of the lovers was noticed.

Two horses were tethered in the wooded area. One was to pull the kartr (cart) with Runa and his possessions carefully on board while Karl himself rode in front on the other horse carefully herding the small flock of sheep which would supply an important ingredient of their diet in their new home.

The first night took them many miles to the north and east of the great river Maeres Ea. They camped in a valley near another Viking settlement Skjaldmarrsdalr and Karl went into the town to replenish supplies of food. Once he had sufficient for a journey that might last from this full moon until the next, probably about thirty days, he returned to Runa and the cart hidden in some woods outside Skjaldmarrsdalr. She was overjoyed to see him return and to have the opportunity to discuss their plans.

"Runa, now we can talk in peace, I want you to know that you will never be my slave."

She began to cry,

"So are you sending me back to Asmund," she said. "Now I have lain with you, he will kill me. Please take me with you."

"Of course," Karl replied. "But you will come with me, not as my slave but as my woman."

"By the laws of my people I should only marry a man who follows my God, the one God of heaven and earth," she replied still tearful.

"I do not know if I can forsake all my gods for your God but in time I may. Surely you would rather be my woman than Asmund's slave?"

"Yes, yes, of course," Runa answered. "I love you and I think I would now die if I could not follow you."

"Well there we are then," Karl replied. "Kiss me and I now declare that you are my woman. I will protect you so that, never again, will you be a slave.

"We have journeyed a long way north," he continued. When the sun rises in the east tomorrow, we must set off in that direction."

Like most Vikings, he was an experienced navigator and was well versed in the movements of the sun, moon and stars across the sky.

The sun rose early at that time of the year and the pair set off to travel across the plains and flat lands. Karl knew they must avoid the few settlements that there were in the part of the country they would be traversing. Some of these were Saxon and a warm welcome was far from guaranteed from people the Norsemen had been fighting fairly regularly for the best part of the previous century. Karl intended to reach the fertile valleys that lay before the great hills on the other side of which was the great Norse Kingdom of Jorvik. He had travelled this way only once before and had been impressed by the beauty and richness of the country.

After twenty five days their supplies of food were beginning to run low and Karl had still not found the place where he wanted to establish his Thorpe. They were certainly in the right location but, apart from a gently wooded and fairly flat terrain he would only build their Thorpe where there was a river or stream for irrigation. Karl was well aware that in Engla Land the climate supplied frequent bouts of rain but even in this damp land, he had experienced drought and was determined that their new home should be near a good supply of water.

Progress was slow as Karl had to find grazing for his sheep every day and travelling through the woods and forests to avoid the local population, made this more difficult. In the evening of the twenty fifth day he made camp in a gently wooded area and leaving Runa to prepare some food, he started to explore to find better grazing for the sheep. This was proving difficult and, against his own better judgement he decided to allow himself to be in full view by ascending a hill, naked of the cover of trees or shrubs, to see what lay on the other side.

The decision was vindicated by the fact that he had not only found grazing but exactly the right conditions to settle down and build their new home and life. In the valley below lay large areas of grassland with a stream dividing them so that the higher reaches would be ideal for sheep and the lower sections of the valley were flat enough for the construction of a wooden Longhouse. This lower area was surrounded by land that could be planted with crops from the seeds he had dried and brought with him from his old home.

Karl decided to take a closer look at the valley and carefully descended. He walked around the area becoming happier by the minute until he bethought himself to offer up a prayer to Wodin and Freya, the two gods he considered most appropriate to bless the new home he was about to build. Finally he realised that the sun was sinking in the west and he scrambled up the hill to descend on the other side to the wooded area where Runa and all their worldly goods were waiting.

As he strolled back in the dusk, happily dreaming of the Thorpe he would build with his beloved Runa, he suddenly became aware of voices, men's voices coming from the direction of his temporary encampment. He froze and strained his ears to try and identify the language that was being spoken but at that distance it was impossible. He now crept slowly forward, concealing himself behind large shrubs or tree trunks each time he stopped to listen. He was almost at the clearing where they had encamped and now the voices were totally recognisable. He estimated that there were at least three men and one woman speaking in the Anglo-Saxon language. He could also hear the voice of his beloved Runa speaking the Norse dialect that she had learned from Asmund. She seemed to be crying and then he realised that the Saxon woman seemed to be trying to comfort her.

Although the languages of the Norsemen and of the Saxons were very different both in word structure and pronunciation, they all derived from earlier Germanic tongues and had many words in common. When the Vikings and the Saxons were not fighting each other they were trading together and Karl had a reasonable working knowledge of the language spoken by the Saxons. However, he was far from sure of the intentions of the people who were now holding Runa. She had already been abducted once, from her old home in the land of the Franks and Karl was worried that these Saxons would abduct her again to be their slave. In addition, if they stole his small flock of sheep and all his possessions on the cart, all he would have left would be the gold coins that he carried with him, the proceeds of the sale of his land in Wid Næss. However, he could not imagine life now without Runa and that was his main concern. Somehow, she must be rescued.

Karl edged even nearer and could clearly see the people in the clearing. There were four men not three and dressed in the manner of Saxons peasants. They appeared to be unarmed which surprised Karl greatly. Runa was standing facing them and was trying to explain in the Norse dialect that seemed not to be understood by the intruders,

"My man, a mighty Viking warrior, will be returning very soon. Go away and leave me alone or you will be sorry!"

Runa was crying as she spoke and then Karl saw the Saxon woman approach her and stretch out her arms in a gesture of friendship.

"We do not understand what you are saying," the woman tried to explain, "but we wish you no harm."

Runa did not understand a word of this but the woman was smiling and the men were unarmed. Karl, however, understood everything and unsheathing his sword, he walked noisily into the clearing, sword in hand.

"Why are you holding my woman and my goods?" he demanded in the Saxon language.

One of the men stepped forward using the same gesture of friendship as the woman, by holding his two arms out in front of him.

"Sir, we wish you and your woman no harm. Nor do we wish to steal your possessions."

Karl examined the faces of them all and then slid his sword back into its sheath.

"My name is Karl Olafsen and I come here in peace to settle and farm. Look here is my flock of sheep," he explained.

"This is a big country. I am sure you have plenty of room for just a man and woman, be they Norseman or Saxon."

"That is true," the man who had stepped forward agreed. "It is just two summers since we arrived here from the south. We have a small settlement of just twenty five souls just two miles away. Have you a place in mind for you and your woman to settle?"

"Yes," Karl replied, feeling the obvious and unaccustomed warmth emanating from these people. Dare he tell of the valley he had just discovered? Would they feel that he was encroaching on their territory?

"But first, please tell me in which direction you have settled?"

Two of the men and the woman immediately pointed in the opposite direction to where Karl now planned to put down roots.

"Runa does not yet know as I have just returned after discovering a lovely valley over the hill that lies in that direction," he explained.

"Ah," said the man who was obviously the leader. "You mean the empty dale. You are right it is lovely but at this time of the year all this land is lovely. When you are settled you must come to visit our settlement."

"I must tell you," Karl said. "I have met many Saxons and some have even become friends. However, you know who I am, a Norseman, and yet you have received me with such warmth despite the bad blood between your people and mine."

"Jesus and our God tell us to love the stranger and we try to live by his commands," the leader again replied.

"Jesus?" Karl responded. "Then you must be Christians."

Karl turned to Runa who had understood almost nothing of the conversation but could tell by the demeanour of both her man and the strangers that there was nothing to fear from these people.

Karl now spoke to her in the Norse tongue that she understood.

"These Saxons will be our neighbours when we settle here and build our Thorpe. They are Christians. I think they must worship the same God as you. Is that right?"

"I think so although they also follow a man called Jesus who was born of my people," Runa explained.

Karl once again addressed the Saxons.

"Runa, my woman is from the same people as your Jesus and worships the same God as you. I am sure you will all be great friends.

"We have talked but not exchanged names," Karl added. "My name is Karl and as I just told you my woman is called Runa. What are your names?"

The leader replied smiling,

"I am Thomas and my wife is Mary. And these three are James, Matthew and John.

"Now we must go as it is almost night time. If you need any help from us, please let us know and do come to visit."

Karl and Runa ate their evening meal happier than they had ever been. They had found the right place to live near good people and tomorrow they would take all their possessions into the valley known as the empty dale.

Before going to sleep Karl once again thanked his Viking gods for leading them here to this place and Runa thanked her God for his blessings.

CHAPTER TEN

1856-A YEAR OF GREAT CONSEQUENCE

The year 1856 marked the closing of an era for Great Britain with the end of the Crimea War. It was a hard fought contest with allies Britain and France in support of the Sultan of Turkey and against the Empire of the Russian Czar Nicholas. It also marked three far more personal events in the life of Carl Joseph Oliver. These were the birth of Carl Isaac Oliver; the opening of the Oliver Weaving Company and the discovery of another mysterious stone marker near the top of the burial mound.

Carl had kept his word to his father. He was profoundly curious to discover more about the Viking mound but he would neither undertake excavation himself nor allow anyone else to explore it on his behalf. He felt this promise to his father to be a sacred vow but this did not stop him climbing the mound, as his father had done before him and peering down as if his eyes could penetrate the layers of rock, shale and soil to expose the mounds secrets.

The owner of the new Oliver weaving shed was in a particularly happy frame of mind. The factory was in full production and orders from the cloth merchants in Manchester were arriving thick and fast. His baby son had been baptised the previous week and in the warm glow of these events Carl paid one of his frequent visits to the mound. This entailed scrambling up the fairly steep sides which was not an altogether easy operation even for young healthy man like Carl. The loose shale always tended to slide as his stout boots ascended. He decided to ascertain if it would be easier try to climb it from the far side, away from the house. His decision appeared to be vindicated as this side of the mound was totally exposed to the elements and the mixture of soil and shale appeared to be more firmly embedded by centuries of exposure to wind and rain. However, just as he approached the top, a large chunk of covering gave way under his foot and slid down towards the ground. Fortunately he easily recovered his balance and looked down to where his foot had been, to find another suitable foothold. There was now a gap in the surface covering of the mound of about eighteen inches by twelve. This was only two or three inches deep but enough to expose a panel of rock similar to the one his father had found years before. He managed to sit down, somewhat insecurely, alongside the gap and peered in at the rock. Again there was evidence of some kind of writing and Carl slid down the side of the mound to fetch a garden trowel with which to gently expose the entire face.

This rock turned out to be smaller than the one his father had found and after levering it out of its ancient home he carefully washed it before bringing it in to the house. Elizabeth his wife was resting in her room and ignoring the curious glances of the servants he carried the rock into the same room where his father, just four years earlier had told him the story of the first rock.

Carl now laid the 'new' smaller rock on a stout table that he used as a desk and brought, from the cupboard the older rock to lie alongside it. The colour and substance of the two rocks appeared to be identical and fetching the wax-paper rubbing of the writing on the older rock he tried to identify and recognise similar letters. This, however, proved to be impossible as this script was entirely different. He puzzled over it for some time but was making no progress. On the first rock there were two or three recognisable letters but on the one he had just unearthed there was nothing bearing any relationship to the standard Latin alphabet that he used to write English. He resolved to write immediately to the British Museum and instead of having to arrange for a messenger to deliver the entire rock to them he decided to do his own rubbing on paper to show the mysterious letters. Fortunately, he mused, at least the letters are in a far better condition than on the earlier discovery.

The paper rubbing was duly mailed from the post office in nearby Accrington and Carl put the matter to the back of his mind as he concentrated on current business and family matters.

CHAPTER ELEVEN

1857-A WEDDING

From time to time Carl puzzled over the lack of response from the British Museum to the letter and rubbing he had sent from the newly discovered stone. Eventually, after many months had passed and a new year, 1857, had long since arrived he decided to make a personal trip to the new post office over in Accrington.

"Can you give me the date when this package was sent?" the clerk enquired.

"Certainly," Carl answered delighted that in his usual methodical way he had written down this information. "It was the eleventh of August last year."

"Sir," the clerk replied with a worried expression, "did you say the eleventh of August?"

"I certainly did," Carl replied, beginning to feel mildly irritated. "Why is that important?"

"Sir," the clerk replied. "As you know our new postal service is the envy of the civilised world and to my knowledge mail en route from this office has only once gone astray."

"Good, good," said Carl, now quickly losing patience with the man. "So?"

"Sir," the clerk said making an effort to look authoritative, "on the eleventh of August last, all the post from this office was stolen on its way to the sorting office. I will never forget that date as it was my birthday and some birthday present, I don't think!"

Carl was now exceedingly annoyed. He had no interest in listening to this clerk prattling on about his birthday.

"Why was I not told at the time?" he demanded.

"Sir," replied the clerk feeling somewhat out of his depth with this important man. "We had no way of knowing who had posted letters that day except of course for the new 'registered' service. Was your letter registered?" he enquired feebly.

"No it was not," Carl snapped.

He was wasting his time and would just have to do another rubbing and this time he would make sure it was delivered by a messenger. *What use is this new postal service,* he brooded, *if it cannot be relied upon!*

Without another word to the hapless post office clerk, Carl turned on his heel and marched out of the post office.

Carl returned to the mill to find that unlike the eleventh of August 1856, the Royal mail was performing efficiently and among the envelopes containing cheques, invoices and orders there was one that looked like a wedding invitation. He put it aside to open last and only late in the afternoon did he decide to see what the envelope contained.

It was indeed an invitation to an event and one totally outside his experience. A new and very beautiful synagogue had been opened earlier that year on Cheetham Hill Road in Manchester. One of his best customers, Simon Levi, a German Jewish cloth merchant had been involved and was justifiably proud of his personal involvement in the project. Carl had been supplying Simon with 'grey cloth' for some years and had found him to be a perfect gentleman and a close friendship had developed between the two men. Now Carl and Elizabeth were invited to the wedding of Simon's daughter Sarah.

Elizabeth was delighted when, that evening, Carl showed her the invitation.

"Oh, we can go, can we not?" Elizabeth exclaimed. "I have never been to a Jewish wedding and I am sure it will be both interesting and enjoyable."

"Of course we must go," Carl replied. "Simon is one of my best customers and I hold him in high regard."

Elizabeth became pensive.

"Why is it that some people do not like the Jews?" she enquired. "I could not imagine nicer people than Simon and Leah. They live like us, dress like us and although Simon came from Germany years ago, he has hardly any accent. The only difference is that they pray in a synagogue and we pray in a church.

"Do you think it is something to do with Jesus?" she continued.

"Maybe," Carl replied, anxious to avoid a theological debate with the wife who he considered a great asset but deemed, in his overbearing masculine way, not to be over intelligent.

Carl picked up the invitation again and read it carefully. The wedding was to take place on Tuesday 18th August 1857 at the recently finished Manchester Great Synagogue followed by a reception and dinner at the newly built Cheetham Town hall. The entire invitation was written in English except for some strange block characters on the top which Carl surmised must be Hebrew. He resolved to show the invitation to his vicar, the Rev James Johnson as he suspected that he may well be able to read this biblical language and could tell him what these words meant. He gazed at this unfamiliar script and wondered where and how he had seen such writing before. Then suddenly it came to him and he was dumfounded. *This lettering looked very much like the script on the stone he had unearthed from the mound last year!*

Without offering any explanation to his wife he jumped up from his easy chair and ran out of the room. Elizabeth looked up shocked and called after him,

"Carl, what on earth is the matter? Are you unwell?"

Her husband however was now running up the wide staircase taking the individual stairs two at a time. Then he ran along the landing into his private study where he grabbed the heavy stone from a cupboard and back down stairs again to the drawing-room where they had just three minutes earlier been sitting quietly and gently discussing the wedding invitation.

"What on earth is that?" Elizabeth said, wondering if her sober and sane husband had suddenly taken leave of his senses.

Carl was now quite out of breath and placing the stone on the floor he grabbed the invitation and started to compare the letters. *Yes,* he decided, *they certainly look the same.*

Suddenly Carl remembered his poor wife who was becoming increasingly alarmed by his behaviour.

"It is alright, Liz my dear," he told her soothingly. "I just thought of something and I needed to ascertain if my assumption was correct or not."

"So what is that?" Elizabeth replied pointing to the large stone tablet lying on their best Chinese rug.

"It is just an old family heirloom," Carl answered condescendingly. "It's a long story and one day I will explain it all to you; nothing to worry about in the meantime."

Tuesdays and Fridays were the days when Carl attended the Royal Cotton Exchange in Manchester to obtain contracts from merchants to supply the cloth, woven in his weaving shed. Tomorrow was Friday and Carl resolved to take the stone with the strange lettering with him in his carriage to show to his friend Simon. The carriage took him twice a week to Accrington where he had his first class reserved seat on the Lancashire and Yorkshire Railway 8.55am express train to Manchester.

Carl wrapped the rock in some old dust-covers and insisted on carrying it himself to his carriage, despite the protestations of the driver. Then he repeated the same operation to board the train in Accrington station. He found himself virtually diving through a rugby scrum of railway porters all determined to help him when did not wish to be helped. There were six reserved seat holders in his compartment and the other five all looked up in surprise to see him carrying this obviously heavy object himself.

His friend Tim Hesketh surveyed him in astonishment and eventually commented,

"Can't afford a porter, then, Carl?"

The response was a watery smile as if Tim had just told a bad joke. Carl made it abundantly clear to his fellow passengers that he was definitely not open to questions as to what the strange package contained, as the train made its way, first to Bury and then on to the magnificent Manchester Victoria Station.

A cab conveyed Carl and his mysterious parcel on the short journey to the Royal Exchange on Cross Street. Fortunately, Carl had recently rented a small office in the building from where he could negotiate the sale of his cloth with more privacy. The parcel was duly and securely locked in this office and Carl made his way on to the floor of the Exchange to seek out his friend Simon Levi.

CHAPTER TWELVE

THE EMPTY DALE

The next morning, by the time the rising sun was visible far off in the east, Karl and Runa were busy coaxing the horses and driving the sheep up the slope that would eventually mark the boundary of their new home in the Empty Dale, as the Christians had called it.

Once they reached the top, Runa could see with her own eyes the beauty of the place and how it was absolutely ideal for them as a home. There was lots of grazing for the sheep and land to spare for planting seeds for crops. There was a fast flowing stream of clear water for drinking and irrigation. Runa remembered her father, from whom she had been so cruelly snatched, telling her stories from her own people's past in the land of Israel. In particular she thought of Adam and Eve in the Garden of Eden and she tried to imagine herself as Eve and Karl as Adam. But, unlike Adam and Eve, they would have to work very hard to turn the Empty Dale into a flourishing settlement. In the Norse language a small farming settlement is called a Thorpe. She turned to Karl and with smile lighting up her lovely face, she said,

"Now we must change this Empty Dale into a dale with a thriving Thorpe. Then we can call it Dalethorpe."

Karl smiled back at her.

"Dalethorpe it shall be, so come my woman, let us get to work in building Dalethorpe."

The next few months flew by. By the time of the first winter snow, they were happy and warm in a traditional wooden Viking longhouse. The sheep were well fed by the excellent pasture and seeds had been planted for the first crops that would appear early in the spring. Their Saxon friends had been as good as their word and were delighted to give assistance to Karl in a variety of different ways. Mary had become a close friend of Runa and she had visited her and met the other women of the small community.

In spring the lambing took place and this coincided with a human 'lambing' when Runa gave birth to their first son. After much discussion he was called Olaf after Karl's father and Yosef after Runa's father. And so a tiny scrap of humanity came to be known as Olaf-Yosef Karlsen.

Runa prayed to her God every morning and had long since explained to Karl that it was Asmund who had given her this Viking name. Her real name, given to her by her father Yosef ben Hayim, was Rachel.

Karl had resolved to call his beloved woman by her real name of Rachel and this announcement, after the birth of their son, gave her more pleasure than any gift could ever impart.

Rachel had learned about circumcision from her father and had watched mesmerised from a discreet distance when Yosef had performed this operation on two of her younger brothers. She longed to have this ancient biblical commandment carried out on her own son but there was no-one capable of performing the rite. She discussed the matter with her Christian friend Mary and was disappointed to find that they had given up this and many other laws kept by their saviour or prophet Jesus.

Another ten years went by and the flock of sheep was now large enough to supply many of their needs both directly and indirectly. Their diet consisted of lamb and mutton together with a rich assortment of home-grown vegetables and fruit. They wore woollen clothing carefully spun and woven by Rachel. They sold surplus flocks of young lambs to Saxons in a wide area. Life was good and Olaf-Yosef now had the company of two sisters and a little brother.

Karl saw his wife praying every day to her God and that her prayers were answered and he too began to see the truth that gods such as Wodin and Freya could not be responsible for their good fortune.

Karl also noticed that their Saxon friends were prospering and he recognised that, although they involved Jesus, they prayed to the same God as his woman Rachel.

"I am only going to pray to your God from now on," he told Rachel.

Their first-born Olaf-Yosef was a bright boy. Karl was able to read and write in the runic script which he proudly taught to his son. Rachel still remembered the letters of the Hebrew alphabet and the words she used in prayer every day.

"If you are teaching the boy to read and write in your language, maybe I should teach him mine," she tentatively suggested to Karl.

Karl by now even knew a few words of the Hebrew they used in prayer and he readily agreed.

As a result Olaf-Yosef was able to read and write in both languages although Norse was the everyday language of Dalethorpe and neither the father nor the son could remotely converse in Hebrew. But then even Rachel had hardly what could be described as a working knowledge of the ancient tongue.

This tiny family settlement was a Norse island in a sea of Anglo-Saxons. All the other villages in the area were Saxon; some Christian and many pagans. To trade and to keep on good terms with the neighbours meant speaking their language. Karl already had a good working knowledge and

Rachel learnt enough to pass the time of day with her friends.

From the age of twelve, Olaf-Yosef often accompanied his father on trips to sell their sheep and the produce of their fields to other settlements in the vicinity. As a result he became increasingly fluent in the Anglo-Saxon tongue and little by little he found himself addressing his father, mother and siblings in this language rather than the Norse of his childhood.

It grieved Karl to think that their Norse heritage would probably disappear within another two or three generations but he was a realist. If they were to live within the Kingdom of Mercia rather than under Danelaw, this was inevitable.

Karl pondered on this and decided to spend a little time each evening chiselling out the story of their family history on a series of stone Runes. The language was of course Norse and the script Runic. He then decided to bury these Runes under a mound which he knew, in accordance with his Norse tradition would one day house his, his wife's and his family's remains.

And then tragedy struck. Karl and Olaf-Yosef were returning from delivering a small herd of sheep to a farmer in Brun Lea, a Saxon settlement some distance from Dalethorpe. As they approached home, Gustav, then a lively boy of twelve summers came running towards them, obviously in a highly agitated state.

"Come quick," he shouted. "Mother is ill and I cannot wake her."

It quickly transpired that Karl's beloved Rachel was dead. The body of a prematurely born baby lay between her legs and she had bled to death alone in the longhouse. The three younger children had been working in the fields at the other end of the dale and had only returned minutes before their father and brother.

Rachel's body was buried inside the mound which until then had only housed the runic stones. Karl was a broken man. He became obsessed with writing a Rune in praise of his wife and this was lovingly buried alongside her last remains.

Olaf-Yosef decided that the best tribute to his mother would be a stone engraved with her names in her own Hebrew language. This he lovingly completed and embedded in the side of the mound.

Just a year later saw Olaf-Yosef, a young man of just sixteen summers, engraving another runic stone but this time in the Norse language in memory of his father. Poor Karl could not bear to live without his beloved Rachel. He had truly died of a broken heart.

The children, who had been so well trained by their parents, continued to look after the farm and at the age of twenty one, Olaf-Yosef asked Eliza daughter of their close friends and neighbours, Thomas and Mary to become his woman and move to Dalethorpe. A Christian priest was brought from nearby Whalley and he married the young couple in accordance with Christian rites.

A hundred years after these events, when the area was under the stewardship of Anglo-Saxon King Edward, Dalethorpe was a small town of some one hundred and thirty people, all engaged in agriculture and sheep farming and mostly descended from the Viking Karl and his beloved Hebrew wife Rachel.

CHAPTER THIRTEEN

THE SECOND STONE

Apart from the small office that Carl rented as a member of the Manchester Royal Cotton Exchange he was also entitled to a permanent location on the floor of the exchange hall. Most of the Mill owners had business cards printed that stated not only the names and addresses of their factory premises but also their position in the exchange hall. These were identified by the series of numbered pillars that had been used in the construction of the building. Thus Carl's address on the floor of the Exchange was by Pillar 5 and it was there that he met customers and suppliers and transacted most of the business of the Oliver Weaving Company.

On this particular Friday Carl, after leaving his mysterious parcel in his office, had returned to his usual spot alongside Pillar 5 to await the usual approaches of Spinning Mill owners and yarn merchants. They were anxious to sell him fine cotton yarn to be woven into first grade cotton cloth at the Oliver Weaving Company. This was where he had initially met Simon Levi whose huge warehouse was located just a short distance from the exchange on Princess Street. Two other customers approached him to enquire about his prices and deliveries for different specifications of fine cambric. He promised to let them have quotations by the following Tuesday and it was then that he spied Simon busily talking to another mill owner by pillar twelve. Carl waited patiently until Simon was free and then approached him.

"Good morning," he began. "It is so good of you to invite my wife and I to your daughter's wedding."

"My pleasure, sir," Simon replied. "I do hope you can grace the occasion with your presence."

"Wouldn't miss it for the world, my dear fellow," Carl answered reassuringly. "Tell me, any tips about protocol that we should know. Never actually been in a synagogue before, don't you know!"

"Well yes, seeing that you have enquired there are just a couple of things you should be aware of," his friend told him.

"Firstly you keep you hat on inside the building. I know in church you take yours off but our protocol is the opposite."

"That seems a little strange but hardly difficult," Carl replied grinning, "anything else?"

"The service will be in Hebrew but I am sure you will be able to follow in the English translation that is in our prayer books."

"So is that it?" Carl enquired.

"Yes," Simon answered, "except for the fact that the ladies will be seated separately from the men and in their own gallery upstairs."

"Right," Carl responded. "I will warn Elizabeth about that."

After a brief pause Carl changed the subject to the one that was really uppermost in his mind.

"Simon," he ventured. "I want to show you something in my office before you leave to return to your warehouse. It is something I would like your advice about."

"Certainly my dear fellow," Simon responded. "I have finished my business here for today. Just lead the way to your office and I will try to help if I can."

When Simon saw the large heavy article wrapped round in an old dust cover he was understandably puzzled. And when the dust cover was removed and all Simon could see was a dirty old rock, he was intrigued.

"Is this what you wanted to show me, my dear fellow?" he enquired laughing. "An old lump of rock wrapped in a dust cover; it seems somewhat unusual to put it mildly?"

"Look Simon," Carl replied, "this is not a joke. Just take a look at the markings on this rock. Does it remind you of anything?"

Simon was beginning to wonder about his friend's sanity but he nevertheless peered down at the face of rock to where Carl was pointing. Certainly something was chiselled into it but in the dull light of the office he could not make out what it was.

"It is far too dark in here," he told Carl. "If you really want me to look properly at this, whatever it is, can you please light the oil lamp and bring it over here."

A minute later Simon was gasping, "It is Hebrew, strangely shaped letters but definitely Hebrew! Where does this come from, some old cemetery?"

"I cannot tell you where I found this," Carl answered gravely. "Can you read it? That is what I need to know."

Simon bent down and then straightened up again with a somewhat shocked expression on his face.

"Dammit," he exclaimed, "this is a gravestone. You must tell me where you obtained it."

"What does it say?" was Carl's reply. "Just tell me what does it say?"

"If you must know all it says is a name, the name of a lady; *Rachel bat Yosef* which means Rachel the daughter of Joseph."

"And that is all?" Carl demanded.

"Yes that is all," Simon replied. "Now tell me how this gravestone came into your possession?"

"That I cannot do," Carl replied. "Suffice it to say that it comes from a place that is sacred to our family."

"Sacred to your family," Simon replied. "But you are not Jewish. How can an old Jewish gravestone have anything to do with your family?"

"Look," Carl replied. "I am sworn to secrecy about everything associated with where this stone was found. It was a solemn promise I made to my dying father and I cannot tell you any more. Please do not press me and I do thank you for identifying the engraving and translating it for me."

Simon glanced at the troubled expression on his friend's face and nodded gravely.

"All I can say is that one day I hope you will be able to explain. In the meantime I will be patient."

"Thank you," Carl replied. "Now about this wedding of yours; who is the chap who has won the heart of your daughter?"

Chapter fourteen

Industrial Action

The Levi wedding was a glittering affair. Carl had found the proceedings somewhat difficult to follow but the English translation, in the books provided, did answer many of his questions. He was seated on the front row towards the rear of the building and from this vantage point he could not only see Elizabeth sitting opposite to him upstairs in the gallery but he also had a wonderful view of the bride when she entered the elegant new synagogue. And what a beautiful daughter his friend had produced.

The reception, dinner and ball afterwards were in a similar format to those at upper class Christian weddings. Among the guests were many prominent members of Lancashire and Manchester society most of whom, at least the Christian ones, seemed to have been absent from the ceremony. Carl, however, was pleased that they had done the right thing, in his opinion, and attended the Synagogue first. There were of course large numbers of Simon's co-religionists, who Carl had not met before but that only made the occasion more interesting. All in all, Carl and Elizabeth thoroughly enjoyed the occasion and they returned home later that evening, a good two hour's journey in their carriage, in the best of good spirits.

The following day Carl arrived at the mill a little later than usual and as was his custom, his first duty or pleasure, according to content, was to open the post. There were a number of cheques and this never failed to put in a good humour. He then went into the weaving shed. This also was a habit he had developed since the weaving shed had opened last year. It was important to show his workers that he was there, in the mill, ensuring that they produced the required tally of woven cloth. He had a daily inspection regime and that involved checking the mechanical clocks attached to the looms to see how many yards of cloth had been woven. In addition, Carl stopped at a number of randomly chosen looms each day to inspect the fabric as it slowly completed its journey from the point where the shuttle had created cloth out of yarn, to the growing roll of woven fabric in front of the machine. It was woe betide any weaver who fell below his target production or allowed faulty cloth to go forward. Carl had invested a large sum of money in the project and he was quite capable of summarily dismissing any weaver who fell below standard. Even slight falls in production or higher than average faults would lead to financial penalties in the form of fines that would be levied on the poor workers who were hardly overpaid in the first place. Carl considered himself to be a model employer and maybe, by the standards of day he was better than many. What consolation that was to a poor man with a large family whose wage packet had been reduced to almost starvation level was difficult to appreciate?

On this particular day he returned to his office and started to calculate how much yarn he needed for a new order that he had received in the post that day. He had only just started this important task when there was a knock on the office door and three of his weavers entered. They were all large burly men with faces that were red and blotchy and overhanging stomachs that indicated an over-fondness for the local brew. They were, however, first-class weavers.

The oldest of them, Fred Higginbotham had worked for the Oliver family, originally in his own cottage and then in the new mill, for many years.

"Excuse me, Sir," Fred began.

"Yes Fred, what is it? Cannot you see I am busy and why are three of you leaving your looms at the same time? I must tell you that I will be looking at the production figures from you three very carefully this week."

Fred looked more than uncomfortable. "Sir," he again ventured.

"Well what is it man? Spit it out," Carl answered becoming increasingly irritated.

"It's about Meg Watson," Fred said, shifting uncomfortably from leg to leg.

Ah so that is what this deputation is about, Carl realised.

Meg Watson, one of the few female weavers in his employ, had been sacked the previous week for absenteeism and bad time keeping. She was a woman of about forty years of age and had been left alone to look after seven children when her husband had died of pneumonia.

"Sir, we think you should give her back her job," Fred ventured.

Carl had no need, in his own estimation, to even consider such a request and he was outraged that three of his workers should approach him, especially in factory time, on such an errand.

"I cannot and will not put up with bad time keeping and shoddy workmanship and I must tell you three," he said, his eyes blazing with anger, "that I will not have my workers telling me how to run this factory. Get back to work and the next man who comes in here on such an errand will follow Meg straight out of the door. I have a business to run here."

Needless to say the three men turned tail and left the office muttering what Carl took for apologies for having disturbed their employer. He was however, to soon discover how wrong he had been about the subject of the men's conversation.

Carl continued his calculations until it suddenly dawned on him that the normal clatter of the looms from the weaving shed had ceased. He rose from his chair and made his away down the corridor leading to the shed. He flung open the double doors and was horrified to see that the place was empty and every one of the looms was stopped. He looked for the foreman, Bill Watkins, but he had disappeared with the weavers. Carl was livid with rage. *How dare they do this to me?* He brooded. *My family have looked after these people for years and this is how they repay me.*

He decided to return home although it was still only mid-morning. After the large banquet of the previous night he had decided to walk to the mill that morning and he had enjoyed the pleasant stroll. Now, he found himself, striding back to his house in the most furious of tempers.

Carl considered Elizabeth, his wife to be a lady of limited intelligence and in any case, Carl, a typical Victorian industrialist, would never have dreamed of discussing or consulting her on any matter of business.

He marched straight to his study, lit a cigar, poured a glass of whisky and pondered on what he could do to get the weaving shed working again. To give in to the demands of his workers and to re-instate Meg Watson was unthinkable. Equally unthinkable was to lose even one day or one hour of production when demand for his cloth was so high. However, Carl could see no way out of the situation and decided to try to obtain a new set of workers from the nearby towns and, as he put it, let this ungrateful rabble go to hell.

Elizabeth eventually realised that Carl was in the house at a time when he was normally at the mill and came to see what ailed him.

"I am fine," he told her reassuringly, "just a business matter to sort out."

However, Carl had totally underestimated the determination of his employees and within days, the news of the strike had spread throughout the area. In virtually every other mill, workers donated, from their own pitifully small wages, enough money to save the Oliver weavers from complete starvation.

As for Carl's efforts to secure an alternative workforce, these were disastrous.

Posters inviting applications for thirty two weaving jobs, a foreman, a cloth-looker (inspector) and a tackler (loom maintenance man) brought responses but mainly from inexperienced or careless workers. When production resumed, the cloth being woven was full of faults and complaints began to pour in, from his customers.

Carl's largest customer Simon Levi arrived at the mill unannounced and told his erstwhile friend that, unless something was done and done quickly, he would be obliged to cancel his contracts and he might be forced to sue for damages.

"I really do not know what has happened to you," Simon told him. "You had a first class mill here and suddenly everything has gone wrong. You are taking first quality yarn and turning it into substandard cloth. If you carry on this path you will soon be bankrupt."

Carl told Simon the story of how he had sacked Meg Watson and how his workers had walked out in solidarity.

"Look Carl," Simon told him. "I am going to give you until next Monday to sort this out. If you can't do it then I will have another suggestion for you when I return next week."

Carl had been delighted with the way his new mill had been performing. He saw it growing and he had plans, or at least dreams, of opening a number of similar factories in other parts of Lancashire. He did, however, have other business interests. There was still the production from the farm and his father had acquired property in London and Manchester earlier in the century. He was not going to let a bunch of workers dictate to him about whom he employed and who he dismissed.

On the Friday after Simon's visit, Carl travelled down to Manchester as usual. He took up his position by pillar five but because his labour troubles were now the talk of the industry, he received no new enquiries and the only visitors he had were two Spinning Mill representatives worried whether Carl would be able to pay their accounts for cotton yarn supplied.

"Don't worry about that," he told them condescendingly. "I will see that cheques are sent out to you next week."

Three other mill owners made it their business to stop by. On the one hand, they had considerable sympathy for one of their own, who now found himself in such a situation. On the other hand they hoped, secretly, that they would pick up lots of new business if the Oliver enterprise folded.

The elderly Sir Thomas Gartside, whose family ran three weaving mills, told him,

"We know how ungrateful these people can be. We give jobs to them and they repay us with shoddy work and rebellion," he said patting Carl on the back. "Best of luck, my boy, show 'em who is boss."

Just as Carl had decided he was wasting his time at the Exchange, Simon arrived.

"Well, have you sorted things out?" he enquired in a rather sharp tone. He had relied on the Oliver mill very heavily during the last few months and this new situation was putting his own business in danger.

"I am trying to," Carl replied.

"Sorry," Simon said. "That is not good enough. I will see you next Monday and tell you what I have in mind."

Simon then turned on his heel without as much as a 'Goodbye' and walked quickly away from him.

Carl caught the train back to Accrington and hired a cab to take him back to the mill. As soon as he arrived he went into the shed and was horrified to find two of his new weavers in an advanced state of inebriation. In addition, all his instruction and threatening had made no difference to the standard of work. The cloth on the machines was totally substandard.

"You are all sacked," he told them, "just get out of here."

"What about our wages?" one of the most disreputable looking men demanded.

"What wages," Carl replied. "You get paid for turning out good cloth and all you have done is to waste all my cotton yarn and lose me business."

The man who had now become a spokesman took a step forward.

"We ain't leaving here without our money, are we lads?" he shouted.

Men of Carl's class were not often intimidated. The workers knew that they would starve without the likes of Carl. They usually treated their employers with great deference and that was the behaviour Carl expected.

Carl took a step towards the burly man and poked him in the chest with his fore finger.

"Now just get out of here before I call the police to have you removed," he replied.

His old workforce would have behaved differently. They had walked out in support of one of their number who they felt had been wronged but they would never have dreamed of doing what this man did now. Carl had exchanged good hard working people for the dregs of the Lancashire labour force. Men who had drifted from job to job and through indolence and drunkenness had never held down decent employment. The ruffian took a swing at Carl that connected with his jaw and knocked him to the ground. He lay there unconscious while the rabble he had hired, ransacked his office for valuables before scattering to the four winds away from Dalethorpe.

An hour later a dazed Carl scrambled to his feet, saw that his office had been ransacked but his safe, at least, was still securely locked. Returning to the weaving shed he disconnected the drive shaft of the huge steam engine that powered the entire factory and staggered home.

CHAPTER FIFTEEN

A WISE WOMAN

Elizabeth was shocked and horrified to discover the condition of her husband when he lurched into the family home in Dalethorpe.

"Oh my love," she exclaimed, "what has happened to you? Are you hurt?"

Suddenly Carl needed to confide in someone about all that had transpired over the last two months. He had men he called friends but they were really only social acquaintances. He had, in the past, discussed many work related problems with Bill Watkins, the foreman but he had walked out with the weavers in solidarity with Meg Watson. He used to rely on Bill when there was any problem at the mill but now he had gone. Then there was his close business friend and customer Simon Levi. He had made it perfectly clear at the Exchange, that very morning that he was totally unimpressed with Carl. He was no doubt coming the following week to be highly critical of the way Carl had handled the walk-out and strike and goodness knows what he would have to say.

So Carl took the unprecedented step of telling his wife the whole story.

Carl had always looked upon Elizabeth as the pretty little lady who would supervise the nanny employed to look after young Carl Isaac; instruct the cook as to what meals to prepare for the family; complain to the housekeeper if the housemaids were not keeping the place clean. She was, of course, also expected to grace Carl's bed with a view to increasing their family. In addition she was a graceful adjunct on his arm on social occasions. However he had never, until this moment, looked upon her as a life partner and confidante but to whom else could he turn?

Carl invited his wife to sit down and after assuring her that he was none the worse for the injury he had just sustained to chin and ego he proceeded to tell her the whole story.

Elizabeth listened to every word of Carl's story intently, without comment.

"So am I right in thinking that just because you dismissed this Meg Watson, you have lost all your workers; workers whose families live in the Dalethorpe area and have been employed by your family for many years?"

Carl nodded.

"And am I right in thinking that you brought in casual labourers, people who had been thrown out of almost every mill in east Lancashire and you were surprised when their shoddy work was destroying your entire business?"

Carl nodded again.

"And am I right in thinking that you seem to have destroyed your relationship with Simon Levi, a good customer and a good friend?"

Carl nodded again and started to speak but his wife gently placed her forefinger over his mouth and shushed him to remain silent.

"I am only a woman and have not had your education. And my family were hardly of the calibre or antiquity of yours, but surely this whole thing could be resolved by going to see this Meg Watson and asking her to come back to work."

Carl had secretly been aware of this for some time but he did not know whether he could force himself to retract the dismissal of the woman. The loss of reputation entailed in such a step would make him a laughing stock not only among his original workers but among his peers and colleagues at the Cotton Exchange. He could just imagine what Sir Thomas Gartside would have to say. But then, it was Carl's mill and Carl's future in the textile business that was at stake.

"Look, Elizabeth," he replied. "Let me think about it until Simon comes next week."

"Very well," his wife replied with an air of gravity that he had never known she possessed. "But I am sure the only way out of this is to re-employ Meg."

Chapter sixteen

The Vicar to the Rescue

Carl spent most of the weekend agonising over the disastrous situation at the mill. In his heart of hearts he knew that only the re-instatement of Meg Watson could conceivably repair the damage done to his business. She had always been a good worker but because of her widowhood, she was constantly juggling the responsibilities of her work with the demands of her large family of young children. That meant that she was frequently late for work and if one of the children was seriously ill, she did not come at all. However, Carl had to recognise that when her looms were running she was among the best weavers he employed. On the other hand, to go to her, cap in hand, was to show weakness. *If I do that,* Carl brooded; *they will all think they can do what they want with me.*

The weather had been unusually reliable that summer and at eight o'clock in the morning Carl decided to walk to the mill rather than have the carriage take him. Elizabeth had spoken very little since their conversation about the walkout. At mealtime she was unusually quiet, even for her and to his relief she did not raise 'the subject' in the few exchanges they did have.

The mill was of course locked and Carl had to use his own key to open the huge door to the building. He went in to his office to await the arrival of Simon Levi and was relieved to hear the sound of a horse-drawn cab outside at about a quarter past nine. *Thank goodness he has come early,* he thought as he made his way back to the door to let in his best customer.

Simon had a plan and as soon as he was settled opposite Carl at the large mahogany and leather inlaid desk, he wasted no time in explaining his proposition.

"I want you to sell me a half share in the mill," he said. "I will then get your workers back for you and after that I will only become directly involved if there is another problem. I will see you in Manchester every Tuesday and Friday at the Exchange as usual and every Wednesday I will come here with my own cloth looker (inspector) to check the quality of the cloth you are turning out."

Carl had not even considered that Simon would make such a proposal.

"This is the Oliver mill. My family has been weaving and selling cloth in this area for the last half century. I know you want to help but I cannot sell my heritage to you," he replied.

Simon rose to leave.

"If that is your answer I am wasting my time here. You know, Carl," Simon continued, "I used to think you were a clever businessman but recent events have changed my mind."

He strode towards the door of the office and turned back once more to Carl who was sitting in stunned silence.

"Carl," he said in a voice showing outrage at Carl's stubbornness. "You owe me many thousands of yards of well woven cloth. You have one month to get back on track and fulfil your contracts with me. Otherwise, you will be hearing from my lawyers."

Carl sat there in stunned silence. Now what was he going to do? After sitting there, head in his hands for over an hour he decided that the only option was to take his wife's advice and to visit Meg Watson and offer to re-instate her as a weaver.

He locked up the empty mill and set out for Meg's house at the other end of the small village, beyond the parish church of St. Barnabas-by-Dalethorpe. He walked slowly as if all the world's troubles were heaped on his shoulders; indeed he thought they were. He was living through a nightmare, a self-created nightmare, but a nightmare nevertheless. As he walked past the church, his head bowed like a man on his way to be executed, a voice called out to him and looking round he saw the Vicar, the Rev James Johnson.

"Ah, Mr Oliver, could I have a word?" the vicar said.

That was all Carl needed but however much he despised the lower orders of his fellow men, he had been brought up to respect men of the cloth.

Carl tried to smile but what he achieved was more or less a grimace. However he managed to make his voice sound affable as he replied,

"Certainly Reverend; I was on my way somewhere but I can always spare time for the church." As he said this he was feeling that chatting with the Vicar was the last thing he wanted to be doing at that moment but then, the visit to Meg Watkins was hardly going to be a social call.

"Please come in to the church Mr Oliver," the Vicar said in an unusually cold voice.

As soon as they were seated the minister spoke.

"I know nothing of business and much of it is totally beyond my comprehension. However, I gather it is your mill that is responsible for half the village living off charity. What has gone wrong? Please feel free to speak to me in confidence."

Is there no end to my misery? Carl thought. His former friend and customer had just threatened to sue him. His wife was very cool with him. His colleagues at the Exchange were distancing themselves from him. His suppliers were suspicious of his ability to pay them and now the Vicar, of all people, wanted to become involved and all because his unreasonable workers had decided to withdraw their labour.

"Vicar, with the greatest of respect, I do not think you could or would understand the problem," Carl replied.

"Try me," the Minister answered. "You may be surprised."

Suddenly it occurred to Carl that he was hardly blessed with a wide circle of confidantes and advisors. He had not liked his wife's advice although he had been on the way to put it to the test. In addition, he had summarily rejected the suggestion of Simon Levi.

"All right," Carl said. "It is quite a long story."

The Vicar listened carefully and as the tale developed he began to feel a little sympathy for this man whose world seemed to be collapsing about him. He had always considered Carl to be an unduly proud man and he remembered the old proverb to the effect that pride go'eth before a fall.

"And were you on your way to see Meg Watkins when I saw you just now?" the Vicar enquired.

"Yes I was," Carl admitted.

"Well then," the Vicar said, "would you like me to come with you? I do know the poor young woman quite well."

Carl accepted the suggestion with enthusiasm.

"Well now," the Vicar continued, "if you want my support there are certain conditions."

Carl nodded. He did not know that men of God imposed conditions but in his world, the world of business this was normal.

"When we enter Meg's cottage you will let me speak first. I will tell her that you have something to say and then you will have to admit that you were wrong and hasty in dismissing her. Then you will invite her to return to work with all her fellow weavers. Finally you will say that you want to forget the whole incident and that you hope she will also do so."

For Carl this was eating humble-pie with a vengeance. However, having the Vicar with him was a great comfort and just a few minutes later the two men left the Church and walked briskly down the lane to Meg's poor cottage.

The Vicar knocked on the door and it was opened by one of Meg's daughters.

As soon as she saw the Rev Johnson she called out,

"Mum, the Vicar is here to see you." Then she saw Carl standing behind him and added, "And Mum, he's got Mr Oliver from 't mill with him."

Within seconds Meg appeared at the door hastily wiping her hands on a food-stained apron.

"Hello Vicar. Tis always good to see thee but thou is in strange company today."

"Can we come in Meg," the Vicar said.

"Thou art always welcome in my poor cottage but I don't know about thy companion."

"Please let us come in Meg, Mr Oliver has something to say.

Carl wished to be anywhere else but where he was at that moment but somehow, once inside he managed to say everything the Vicar had suggested.

Meg listened politely enough and then said,

"I have my children to feed so yes I will come back to work. But you must understand that they have no one but me to look after them and sometimes I might be late or not turn up but that would only be with good reason."

Carl nodded. "Understood," he said, "and what about all the others?"

"Well," Meg said. "I know Sam and John have just got fixed up with work at the Boardman mill across the valley but I will ask the others. Shall we start work again tomorrow morning?"

"Yes, yes," Carl replied almost in tears.

Carl thanked the Vicar and told him that he would always be happy to help him and the Church in any way he could. He then returned home to tell Elizabeth of all that had transpired.

The following day Carl arrived at the mill before clocking-on time at seven o'clock. He sat in his office waiting and wondering if he still had a business until at five minutes to seven he heard the sound of many footsteps and the hum of conversation as all the weavers, the foreman and the tackler made there way into the shed. Carl followed them and smiling broadly, he listened to the 'music' of the looms chattering away as they wove cloth for his customers.

CHAPTER SEVENTEEN

MADEMOISELLE MARIE

The next fifteen years had not been uneventful for the Oliver family. Carl's mother and sister had both died. Carl Isaac had grown in to an intelligent and handsome young man and had been offered a place to read law at Christ College, Oxford. A second son had been born in 1860 and with the knowledge of the names on the ancient runic stone; Carl had decided that he wanted him to be christened with the name Olaf. Elizabeth was far from happy,

"That is a Swedish name," she told her husband. "Why on earth do you want to give him such a foreign sounding name?"

"I think it sounds distinguished," he explained. "Olaf Oliver is the name for someone who will be noticed."

And Olaf it was. He was fifteen years old and with a quiet and studious if somewhat surly nature. He did however show a deep interest in Christianity and seemed destined for a career in the church. His father's secret dream was to see him appointed one day, to the highest office in the church, that of Archbishop of Canterbury. However, the unfriendly and withdrawn character of the boy made this a highly unlikely outcome.

Neither Elizabeth nor their two sons had even the remotest idea of the existence of the two engraved stones. Carl knew that one day Carl Isaac, as the first born, must be told, just as Carl's father had told him but he bided his time. In the meantime they were transferred to a dry locked cupboard in a bedroom in the house.

As for the mound at the end of the garden, the boys had been instructed that this had a very special sanctity in the family and must never be disturbed or terrible disasters would be visited upon them all.

After the events of 1857 the Oliver Weaving Company had achieved a period of steady growth. The factory now numbered some of the largest and best-known firms of Cotton Merchants among their customers and Simon Levi, just recently retired to a large house in Bowdon, Cheshire, had quickly re-built his bridges with Carl and resumed their friendship.

Carl still attended the Exchange at least once a week but now employed a mill manager, one Fred Eccles, who was more than capable of running the mill on his own. This gave Carl the opportunity to expand the property portfolio his father had left him and to invest in stocks and shares.

Carl now visited London regularly and remained there for sometimes two or three weeks at a time. He was investing heavily in properties in the East End. These were mainly blocks of terraced houses and his tenants were poor artisans newly arrived from country areas together with immigrants from Ireland and Eastern Europe.

Since the days of the workers walkout, Elizabeth had decided that she owed it to herself and to her family to insist on becoming involved in all major decisions relating to the family and to its businesses. It was she who suggested that the time had come to move to London.

"Carl," she had said. "You are away so much now in the capital. Don't you think we should move down there? Carl Isaac commences his studies in Oxford in October and Olaf will be at Theological College next year."

Curiously Carl was not impressed with the idea.

"Look Liz," he replied. "Our family home has always been here in Dalethorpe and I still need to keep an eye on the mill. Fred is very good but you would be surprised how much I still need to be there to keep an eye on things. And, of course there are our Manchester properties down in Red Bank."

Red Bank was a similar area in Manchester to the East End of London and the tiny terraced cottages there were attracting similar immigrant peoples to those in London.

Carl knew that what Elizabeth was proposing made complete sense but he had other private reasons for keeping his family well away from London. These reasons involved a young lady by the name of Marie.

Marie claimed to be the daughter of a French count and Carl had met her at a dinner party given by a business associate.

She was tall and shapely with regular features framed by cascading dark curly hair. She dressed in the height of fashion and the musical timbre of her voice was enhanced by her strong French accent. Carl had been seated between Marie and an elderly spinster lady of aristocratic extraction and it took literally no imagination to guess who would be the beneficiary of Carl's wit and conversation during the evening. Indeed the spinster lady became increasingly disgusted by Carl's manners in completely ignoring her and begged leave to retire from the table with a migraine, before dessert.

By the end of the evening Carl was presenting his card with the address of the small apartment he rented in London to Marie who quickly agreed to visit him the following evening.

Marie, of course, did not quite possess the pedigree she claimed. Her father's only claim to be a count was based on the minor position he held as a bank teller where he was employed 'counting' the coins. Her mother had been born in Paris and by thirteen years of age could be found plying her trade on the streets of Montmartre. At the age of eighteen she had met Marie's father, Claude, who she had persuaded to 'take her away from all this' to his home in a village just outside the small town of Croissy-sur-Seine. Soon after their marriage in the village church Claude had discovered that his new wife Francine was six months pregnant. Three months later she gave birth to a little girl who they called Marie.

Marie at the tender age of twelve had realised the power her good looks gave her over men and launched herself as a high-class prostitute. Unlike her parents, she was determined to raise herself from the gutter. She saved her money, other than investing in fashionable clothes to enhance her appearance, and decided in her early twenties, after being the subject of a duel in Paris between two admirers, that she should transfer to London. There, with the claim to be the daughter of the Compte de Croissy she quickly made her mark on London Victorian society.

Carl's first evening with Marie had been everything he had imagined it would be and more. It never occurred to him that her prowess in the bedchamber was the result of years of experience in pleasing men. Carl, in his usual over-confident way, was convinced that Marie had only consented to make love to him because she had fallen head over heels in love with the head of the Oliver family. Marie of course, scenting lots of money, had made sure that Carl was totally entranced. It took just two weeks before Marie was installed in a much larger apartment that Carl had taken to be their love-nest.

And so the family home remained in Dalethorpe with the head of the family frequently absent in London.

Chapter eighteen

A Violent End

Carl made it a point to regularly visit his elder son Carl Isaac in Oxford. From time to time the younger Carl had suggested that he should come up to London to save his father the trouble. Carl would never hear of this.

"You have your studies and your friends here in Oxford. It is no trouble for me to come here as I usually take the train back to Manchester and break my journey in Oxford to see you."

Eventually Carl Isaac graduated with a first class honours degree in law and Carl arranged a post for his son as an articled clerk in a large firm of solicitors in Manchester. The senior partner there had assured Carl that once his articles were complete there would be a partnership available, in exchange for an appropriate sum from Carl senior.

It was then that the father felt it was time to tell his elder son all he knew of the mound and the two engraved stones in the cupboard of the house in Dalethorpe.

However, fate had other intentions.

Carl was in Manchester and one of his rent collectors reported to him that a new tenant in Red Bank, one Patrick Hagan, refused to pay and was making the lives of other residents in the street a misery with his drunken behaviour late at night.

Carl sent a note to his property agent, James Jackson, telling him that he wanted this man to be evicted from the house. Jackson however, was ill and Carl decided in an unprecedented move, to evict this fellow himself. He took the rent collector with him and they arrived at number 23

Gordon Street, Red Bank, at eleven o'clock in the morning. Carl, for all his faults had never been a coward. In fact there had been occasions when his bravery could be better described as foolhardiness and the incident, all those years ago, when he had poked in the chest, the ruffian weaver he had just dismissed, fell into that category.

Carl knocked on the door, eviction order at the ready. The rent collector stood back partially concealed by his employer as he was already terrified of this Patrick Hagan.

The door opened and a huge fellow stood scowling in the doorway.

"And what would you be wanting?" he said.

"Are you Patrick Hagan?" Carl began.

"And what is that to you?" the Irishman replied.

Carl repeated the question and Hagan repeated the answer.

"I take it that you are Patrick Hagan and you are hereby evicted from this property."

"That is what you think," the Irishman answered.

Then everything happened so fast that the rent collector had difficulty afterwards in describing the scene to the police.

In simple terms Hagan grabbed Carl by the lapels, not a simple task as Carl was tall and well-built. He then hurled him onto the street just as a brewers dray was passing. The huge shire horses reared up in fear at the sight of a man being thrown through the air towards them and their massive metal shod hooves abruptly terminated the life of the head of the Oliver family as they came down on his head. As for the rent collector, he ran from the scene and kept running until he found a patrolling policeman who accompanied him back to the gory scene.

The funeral took place just a week later in the small cemetery that lay alongside the family church of St

Barnabas–by-Dalethorpe. Elizabeth was broken hearted. Carl had been an arrogant self-opinionated man but once she had the measure of him after the incident of the weavers' walkout, she was able in her own quiet way to keep him calm and under control, or so she thought. He was her husband and the father of her two sons. She believed that she loved him, despite all his faults.

After the funeral Elizabeth told the boys that there were important decisions to be made about the family future. She insisted that they must continue and complete their studies just as their father would have wished. She told them that she would remain, at least for the time being, in the family home in Dalethorpe. Carl Isaac could also continue his residence there until he was a fully qualified solicitor. He could easily travel from there to Manchester by train each day. Then, his mother told Olaf that he must continue his studies at his Theological College near Warwick.

The boys listened in silence and then Carl Isaac spoke.

"Who will run the mill and the property business?"

"I will," his mother replied. "We already have an excellent mill manager in Mr Eccles and if he needs more help we will hire it. As for the properties, the same will apply. I will discuss with the property agents in London and Manchester if they will continue and report to me instead of to your poor father."

Her son's had always seen Elizabeth as a quiet lady, very much in the shadow of their father and the resolute, businesslike person they now saw before them came as something of a surprise.

For the next nine months their lives continued exactly as Elizabeth had suggested until a thunderbolt in the guise of a letter, with a London postmark, arrived addressed to Mr Carl J. Oliver. The envelope was heavily scented and written in green ink; *thoroughly bad taste,* Elizabeth thought.

She opened the letter and was deeply shocked, not to say broken-hearted, when she read the contents,

My darling Karl,
Ver hav you bin, mon chere. Ve ver so good togeser. My English ees not gud and I haf never written in English befor. I haf bin vorried for months. Don't you luv me anymore?
Your adoring Marie

She sat looking at the letter and read and re-read it over and over again. There was no doubt now that Carl had been having an affair. For all his faults she had thought him to be trustworthy and loyal. How wrong she had been. No wonder he never wanted the family to move to London. She remembered how she had suggested this and how Carl had instantly dismissed the idea. The big question was what, if anything to tell her sons. Finally she decided that although his memory did not deserve this, she would keep the letter from Marie, to herself.

That night she hardly slept. By the morning she had decided what she must do. The letter had an address on it; Flat 3, 27 Grove Street, Hampstead and she resolved to call upon this Marie. She had intended to go to London to see her Managing Agents the following week anyway, so there was no need to make a special journey.

As soon as the train from Manchester Central Station arrived at St Pancras she disembarked from her first class carriage and signalled a porter to carry her luggage. She hired a cab to then take her to the flat they had used for years when on business trips. She asked the cabbie to carry her luggage inside and then to take her on to the Hampstead address.

Marie had long since given up on ever seeing Carl again. She wondered at first if she had offended him in some way when he failed to return but at that stage she had no way of contacting him. Since renting the flat they shared, he had often absented himself to travel north to look after his business affairs up there and he had always refused to leave her an address for his northern home. Each time previously he had returned, however. Apart from dining out in some of the best restaurants in London, other than when he was working, their time was spent in rapturous love-making. Eventually she received a visit from the landlord who explained to her that Mr Oliver had paid the rent for six months but next month a further sum would be required to keep the flat.

By this time Marie had already started to socialise with other men although this had proceeded no further than dining out and the occasional theatre trip. Now, suddenly she needed money and she quickly selected a gentleman as a target who she knew would provide large sums of money in return for her favours. She obviously entertained him at the flat but on no account would she let him move in with her.

Her new sponsor was paying the rent and enough in addition to allow for her not immodest requirements in terms of fashionable clothing. Marie regarded him, however, as a means to an end. *After all*, she conjectured, *a girl has to eat.* Carl however was different. She had genuinely enjoyed his company and if Marie could ever have been accused of falling in love, that was as near to that emotional state as she was ever likely to reach, with any man. She really missed Carl and was desperate to find him.

Carl had never been specific about when he would return. It was always,

"I shall be in the north for two or three weeks and then I shall return. The rent is paid and you have plenty of money to see you through."

She had always tried to discover when he would re-appear.

"Dahling," she had said on many previous occasions, "You know I miss you. Ven vill you be back?"

The reply was always,

"I will just have to see how it works out. But you can be sure I will be back as soon as possible."

Marie was certain that Carl must be married and that his wife resided in this mysterious northern area that he visited so regularly. As long as he paid the rent and fed and clothed her, however, she never felt it was prudent to ask too much about his other life. Now she was becoming despondent and had a strong feeling that she would never see him again. She had long since approached the host at the dinner party where she had originally met Carl but he had been no help. He told her that Carl had expressed interest in purchasing some property from him and he thought it would assist negotiations to offer him hospitality. The deal had not progressed after the dinner party and he had never seen Carl again.

She had always been careful to give Carl his space inside the apartment and indeed they each had separate dressing-rooms where her extensive and his somewhat smaller wardrobes were kept. After four months of absence she had decided to look for some information about Carl's 'other life' in his dressing room. She had methodically checked the pockets of all his coats and trousers, to no avail. She had also searched the drawers that contained such items as cufflinks, suspenders, braces and belts but not one piece of paper could she find, let alone one with an address.

It was now almost six months since Carl's disappearance. She had dined out with her new friend Robert Hastings in a small French restaurant that she always favoured and they had returned to the flat, as usual for an extra dessert of love-making. During the evening the weather had deteriorated and when it was time for Robert to leave it was raining very heavily. He had been out and about all day and as the weather earlier on had been dry, he had ventured forth without a raincoat. By the time he could find a cab to return home he knew he would be soaked to the skin. Suddenly Marie remembered an old raincoat of Carl's hanging in the guest cloakroom near the door to the apartment. She went to fetch it for Robert and almost instinctively checked the pockets for any of Carl's belongings; and there it was; a brown business envelope addressed to Mr Carl Oliver in Dalethorpe. She quickly stuffed the envelope under a cushion and returned to the bedroom, to Robert with the coat.

"You had better take this," she told him in a voice quivering with excitement.

"Thanks," Robert replied. "I will bring it back on Wednesday night."

Robert suddenly noticed her excited state. Had that been before or during their love-making, he would have understood but why lending him an old raincoat should make her eyes sparkle and involve her in an inability to stand still, was somewhat curious. Even more curious was the fact that she seemed to be ushering him out of the apartment as quickly as possible. Normally there were lots of kisses and confirmations of their next meeting, but now all she wanted to say was "Au revoir, Cherie."

As soon as Robert had departed wondering if he had said or done something to upset her, Marie recovered the crumpled envelope from under the cushion, found her writing paper and envelopes, her pen and the bottle of green ink that she considered to be so elegant, and proceeded to write the fateful letter.

Chapter nineteen

An Unexpected Visitor

Number twenty seven Grove Street was a large, three storey terraced house with imposing steps leading up to the heavy panelled front door with its stained glass windows. There were also somewhat less imposing steps leading down to the servants quarters below. Most of the houses were the dwellings of middle-class families but this house had been divided into three apartments.

There was a brass handle to pull the bell for flat number three and Elizabeth heard the bell clanging loudly from somewhere on an upper floor. There was however, no immediate response and she pulled the bell handle again. She was just about to leave when she heard light footsteps on the stairs. A minute later the door was opened by a good-looking young woman wearing a silk dressing-gown over what appeared to Elizabeth, to be little else.

"Can I 'elp you?" the young woman said in her strong French accent.

Elizabeth decided to go for an immediate identification.

"Are you Marie?" she enquired, trying to look as pleasant as possible but inwardly seething with anger.

"Oui, c'est moi, Madame," the girl answered with a smile.

How dare she be so good looking? Elizabeth fumed.

"Vot can I do for you?" the young woman continued.

Elizabeth had decided what she would say in this scenario.

"I have some news about Mr Carl Oliver. I believe he is a friend of yours."

Then the unexpected happened; the girl burst in to tears.

"Entréz, please Madame, I have been so vorried. Is he vell?"

"Can I come up to your apartment then," Elizabeth enquired.

"But, of course Madame," Marie answered.

The apartment was beautiful furnished with rich velvet drapes, elegant sofas and a collection of antique coffee tables.

"Please seet, Madame," the girl said. "A cup of tea or café?"

"No thank you Marie," Elizabeth replied. "Can I ask you a few questions about Carl?"

"Mais oui, but first tell me have you seen him and is he vell? You are a friend, Non? Maybe his sister?"

This interview was not now developing the way she had imagined. She was the one who was supposed to be asking all the questions. This girl certainly had been Carl's mistress and Elizabeth was sure she would instantly hate her for that. It was quite insane but somehow in the midst of her own sorrow and anger at being betrayed, she actually felt sorry for the girl. That was definitely not what was supposed to happen.

"I am sorry to tell you that Carl is dead," Elizabeth replied.

Marie let out a piercing scream and started to sob. Elizabeth had not shown that much emotion when the police had told her, all those months ago, what had happened to her husband.

Elizabeth sat there in silence watching this young girl, her husband's mistress trying to recover her composure.

Eventually the crying stopped and Marie asked what had happened.

Elizabeth told her the whole story and then said,

"Now do you want to know who I am?"

"Oui, Madame; a good friend or a member of the family maybe?"

Marie," Elizabeth replied. "I am his wife or rather his widow."

"Ah mon Dieu," Marie answered gasping. "Vous etes la marie? Ah mon Dieu!"

Elizabeth calmly produced the letter that had so radically changed her perception of her husband and handed it to Marie.

"It is because of this that I am here," she said gently. "Now you must tell me how, when and where you met my husband. I can see for myself that you a very beautiful young woman and that this is a most elegant apartment; paid for by my husband I assume."

Marie looked searchingly into the face of the older woman and saw no traces of anger. She had always suspected that Carl was married. Most of her previous 'friends' had also been married. In the shocking knowledge that Carl was dead, she wanted to talk and to answer Elizabeth's questions and she proceeded to do so. She told her how and where they had met. How she had always had gentlemen to look after her and how, for some indefinable reason she had fallen in love with Carl.

Some two hours had elapsed when Elizabeth realised she must return to her own far more modest apartment.

"Do you have money?" she enquired.

"Mais oui," Marie answered.

"You do realise you must leave this flat, do you not?" Elizabeth told her.

"I will be out of 'ere within the week eef that is alright?"

What Marie did not tell her was about her new 'friend' Robert Hastings. He just paid the bills but he could never be another Carl.

Elizabeth left her late husband's mistress, trying to understand her own reaction to the girl. Anyone else would have shown deep anger; even physically attacking the woman but all she felt was an overwhelming sadness for two women who in very different ways had loved the same man. As for her memory of Carl, it had been deeply damaged by her knowledge of his affair but life must go on; Carl had left her in a sound financial position and with two fine sons. She hoped they had inherited only their father's good points and not his bad ones and only time would tell.

Chapter twenty

1888-The Lawyer and the Vicar

Carl Isaac had recently become a senior partner in the same firm of solicitors where his late father had arranged for him to become an articled clerk all those years ago. He had been married for ten years to Olivia, the granddaughter of Sir Thomas Garside. She was a pretty, vivacious young woman with an outrageous sense of humour. They had been introduced at a ball given by the Bottomleys, another old mill family. Carl & Olivia were complete opposites. Carl Isaac was prudent by nature and quiet by disposition. He had the determination of his father but without his arrogance. He did however, have a quiet charm. Olivia was immediately intrigued to learn more about this young man. Then when she realised his surname was Oliver she knew he was the man for her.

"Can you imagine," she told on him at their second meeting, "if we were married, my name would be Olivia Oliver?"

She seemed to find this idea extremely funny and giggled when she said it. Carl, on the other hand, did not find this particularly amusing as at that time he had no intention of settling down with her or anyone else. However, he smiled courteously. That was not to say that was not attracted to the young lady and it only took a few months of her persistence for an engagement to be formally announced.

Elizabeth was more than happy with the match. Her future daughter-in-law treated her with a mixture of affection and good-humoured respect. She knew her older son was a sober, sensible person rather like herself and she judged correctly that a girl who could inject some joie-de-vivre into his life would be the perfect match for him. The fact that Olivia also came from a good family with a Lancashire textile background made the mother certain that Olivia was just what the family needed.

They were married eight months later and over the next seven years Olivia, always smiling and giggling, produced, with a little help from her husband, six lively healthy children.

By this time Olaf had become the vicar of a small country parish over in Yorkshire. He was still single and his mother always described him to her friends as being completely married to the church. This was of course the Church of England where many parishes preferred their religious leaders to bring with them a hard working wife who would strive tirelessly with the ladies of the community, in raising funds for the church and other good causes.

The year 1888 dawned with Elizabeth now approaching her half century. She had remained a widow after the death of Carl Joseph although there had been a number of opportunities to re-enter the portals of matrimony. A wealthy widow is always a target for adventurers and with her now, well-developed sense of independence she saw these occasional approaches as being highly suspect. The family portfolio of properties and investments forced her to spend a considerable amount of time in London. She still however preferred to remain in Dalethorpe where she shared the large family house with her elder son, his wife and their lively children.

Then two events occurred that forced her to re-consider their location. Firstly, the Rev James Johnson, vicar of St Barnabas-by-Dalethorpe died. He was deeply mourned by not only the village but the whole of that area of East Lancashire. A meeting of the Parish Council was called which Elizabeth always attended. A discussion then took place as to, who would be an appropriate successor for the much-loved now departed cleric. Much to Elizabeth's surprise the name on everyone's lips was the Rev Olaf Oliver. This had obviously all been whispered about in little huddles in the village, well before the meeting as there was not one dissenting voice, except for the proposed new vicar's mother.

"He is still very young," she proclaimed.

"Yes but we hear from Yorkshire that his ministry there is very well accepted."

"He is not married," she suggested.

"Yes but we are sure you will find him a suitable bride once he is living here."

"Don't you think the parishioners would prefer a stranger if they had to approach him on private and sensitive matters?"

"Not at all, to have an Oliver as our vicar would be a great privilege."

So Olaf moved back into his old bedroom in the family home and took up his position as Vicar of St Barnabas, a ministry which was intended to last him his entire lifetime.

While all this was taking place with Olaf, Carl Isaac was also facing a change. His firm of solicitors had been working with a larger firm of London solicitors on a number of matters and the senior partners of this London firm, Battersby, Wright and Green, all of whom were approaching retirement age decided they needed new blood and only one man would fit the bill. A family conference was called when it was decided that providing Carl would be happy working in London, after a trial period the family would all move to a suitable home probably in the Hampstead area.

This move would include Carl's mother Elizabeth who was delighted that, if all went according to plan, she would no longer be travelling between the North West and the South East of England with such frequency.

"I don't think we should sell the house," Elizabeth suggested. "We will still need a base here and the family have lived here for more generations than any of us know.

"That brings me to another point," she continued. "Carl Isaac and Olaf, you both know about the mound?"

"Yes mother," Olaf answered. "We know that it must never be disturbed which is why it would be better if we did not rent out the property while you are all in the south. If Carl does take up the London appointment I could stay on here and make this my vicarage."

"Why not?" Carl replied, "It would be very nice to make the old place the vicarage of St Barnabas."

"Let us remember that all this is dependent on Carl making the move," Elizabeth reminded them.

Then Elizabeth had a bombshell of her own to announce.

"It is strangely fortuitous that only last week I had an approach from a group of mills called, Combined Lancashire Weavers. They want to buy the mill.

"If I can come to terms with them, how would you boys feel about selling your father's old business?"

"I think that would be an excellent move, don't you Olaf," Carl answered.

"Yes, neither of us has any direct connection with the mill," Olaf replied.

"Mother, I assume you would like me to be involved in the negotiations in my capacity as your solicitor," Carl continued.

"Yes, of course dear," Elizabeth answered. "So that is as far as we can go today but I do believe we have started on a new path that should bring happiness and prosperity to our growing family."

This last remark was accompanied by a surreptitious smile to Olivia, now awaiting child number seven.

Chapter Twenty one

Dalethorpe 1903 A (Re)Discovery

Sadly, Elizabeth Oliver, the undisputed matriarch of the Oliver family, died in London, of a heart-attack at the relatively young age of sixty seven. In her class of society many of her contemporaries were living well into their seventies and eighties although for members of the lower (working) class to reach even sixty was considered to be an achievement, at that time.

Her last remains were transferred to Dalethorpe for internment in the family crypt in the church of St Barnabas-by-Dalethorpe. Since the tragic and violent death of her beloved husband Carl, the only men in her life had been her sons and grandsons. Now in death, she lay once again, besides her Carl, and the memories of his indiscretions, never to have been divulged to his offspring, went to the grave with her.

The funeral service was conducted by the Rev Olaf Oliver, vicar and younger son of the deceased. His older brother Carl Isaac was there, of course, accompanied by his wife Olivia and their ten offspring. Carl was now senior partner in the most prestigious and highly respected firm of London solicitors, Battersby, Wright and Green.

Despite the virtual procession of suitable young women, introduced to him by his mother, Olaf had never married and showed no interest in the opposite sex. He had closed off most sections of the old family home and lived a solitary life in his own quarters in what was now known as the Vicarage of St Barnabas. Until her final illness his mother had been the only frequent visitor to his home, indeed, except for old Mrs Hargreaves, who came in to clean his quarters every day and prepared his food, no other woman had set foot inside the vicarage for many years.

Olaf remained a remote figure to his flock. True, in times of trouble, his parishioners were always appreciated of his support when they needed him most, but otherwise he was a man alone and seemed to be happy in his chosen and almost reclusive existence. Indeed there were many in the village who not only found him unfriendly but they were nervous of being in his company. There was an indefinable something about the vicar that made many people feel uncomfortable when in his presence.

His brother Carl had purchased an impressive property on the edge of Hampstead Heath. The house was almost as large as the old family home in Dalethorpe and with ten children to house it was fully occupied. The oldest son, baptised Carl James, was now twenty five years old. His father had hoped that he would emulate his own career and opt for a law degree at Oxford and then join Carl senior in the firm of solicitors. However, Carl James, although highly intelligent, had neither the patience nor the inclination to submit himself to years of study. Much to the disappointment of his father, he had announced that he wished to follow a career in industry and being aware of the family links, in the previous century, to the production of textiles, he asked to be allowed to obtain an apprenticeship with a firm of cotton weavers.

Carl senior had retained a number of clients in the Lancashire textile industry and as Carl James was seen to be totally committed to the idea, arrangements were made with his uncle the Rev Olaf Oliver for a section of the old family home in Dalethorpe to be re-opened to provide living accommodation for his nephew.

Olaf had been living a solitary existence for many years and let his brother know that he was less than enthusiastic about the prospect of having a young man living in the house with him. Common sense prevailed however and Olaf was obliged to instruct his elderly housekeeper Mrs Hargreaves to unlock, thoroughly clean and prepare a room for Carl James.

The young man duly arrived and quickly settled into the house, now know as the Vicarage. The place fascinated him. When he was not at the mill, learning the intricacies of the weaving trade at Hardcastles, over in Accrington, he tried to explore the old family home and grounds where generations of Olivers had lived and died. The problem was the fact that most of the rooms were locked at the behest of his uncle and Olaf was determined that this was how they would remain.

The gardens, both to front and rear, were badly neglected. Once a year, Olaf employed two young farm labourers to clear the overgrowth with scythes, and to remove all the vegetation on a cart, for disposal elsewhere. It was October when Carl James arrived and the annual clearance had just been finished.

"Uncle," he enquired."The garden really looks forlorn. Wouldn't it be nice to plant some flowers in the front and vegetables in the back?"

"Look Carl," Olaf responded, knowing that this was just what he dreaded about having anyone else living in the vicarage. "It is fine just as it is. You will be here for a few months and then move on. I have no patience with gardeners or gardening so please let me hear no more of this."

"Uncle," Carl ventured. "There is one other matter regarding the garden that maybe you can explain."

"What is that?" Olaf replied wearily.

"What is that huge mound at the end of the back garden area? A few men could soon level it out as it spoils the view of the hills and stream beyond."

Olaf regarded the young man with an expression bordering on surprise.

"Has your father never told you about the mound? It is sacred to our family and Grandma told me years ago, that it must never be disturbed."

Then putting on his best preaching voice he continued,

"The bible teaches us that the last resting places of our ancestors are holy and if that is what is buried under the mound, we must always respect it."

"But do we know that the mound really is a grave site?" Carl enquired.

The vicar was fast losing patience with this impertinent young man.

"I have managed to live here very comfortably for many years and I would ask you to please refrain from making changes. Remember you are only here as a temporary resident and as my guest."

But Carl was far from satisfied and then he made another and even more intriguing discovery.

The bedroom he had been allocated, like most of the rooms in the house, was large and contained a double bed, large mahogany wardrobes, a dressing-table, a chaise-longue and had, quite obviously, originally been furnished for occupation by a married couple. There was also a large oak door on the wall opposite to the bed and this, Carl James assumed, was yet another cupboard or wardrobe. However, from time to time, during his sojourn there, he had tried to open this door and was mystified as to why it should be locked. When he had arrived he had found all the other wardrobes and cupboards in the room to be open and he had originally assumed that this one must house personal and private possessions of his uncle Olaf. However, he had quickly learned from the cleaner, old Mrs Hargreaves, that she had originally been instructed to re-open and prepare this entire room especially for his arrival. She told Carl that she doubted that the Rev Olaf had ever set foot in the room.

"Your Uncle, the vicar, keeps his self to his self," she told Carl. "When he comes back from church he goes straight to his own room and only goes back down stairs for his food. I don't think he knows a quarter of the rooms in this old house."

Carl was determined to avoid conversation with his uncle Olaf after the sharp way the vicar had reacted to his enquiry about the garden and the mound. He, therefore, had no intention of asking him about the locked cupboard door. However, his natural curiosity was slowly getting the better of him and when Olaf was out of the house Carl began to search the more obvious places where a cupboard key might be stored. The house was, of course huge and the possibilities seemed to be endless. He searched every drawer, every cupboard, every possible location where a key might be stored, in the kitchen, the larder, the scullery, the cloakrooms, the library, the hall, the dining room, the drawing room and the lounge; all without success. This took up odd hours after he returned from the mill on weekdays and a large part of a few Sundays when he knew Olaf would be over at St Barnabas all day. This was all to no avail.

Most of the rooms upstairs were locked and Mrs Hargreaves assured him that they had not been used for many years.

"Are they all bedrooms?" Carl enquired.

"No!" the old lady replied. "There is the master's study; that is the old master Mr Carl Joseph; he got killed you know!" she confided.

"Yes, yes, I am well aware of what happened to my Grandfather," Carl James answered, a touch impatiently. "Do you know which room it is and how to unlock the door? I suppose it is locked like all the other doors in this house!"

"Yes, of course Sir," the elderly lady continued. "I have keys to all the rooms but not to the cupboards and wardrobes. Them is private," she added.

"So give me the key and I will go and search for the cupboard key," Carl replied.

This conversation had taken place in the hall and at that point it was interrupted by the arrival from the church of Carl's uncle Olaf. He heard the last words and said,

"And what key might that be, Carl?"

"Oh, good evening Uncle," Carl replied as pleasantly as he could. In reality the older man and his nephew were from different worlds and after the conversation about the mound the relationship had become increasingly frosty.

"I could just do with some more storage space for my things," Carl continued. "There is a locked cupboard in my room and it would be useful if it could be opened. Mrs Hargreaves thinks the key may be in the study so I was just about to find out."

The vicar appeared to accept this story at face value and in an attempt to improve the relationship with his lodger, agreed to accompany Carl to the study.

The dark oak door opened easily enough in response to the large ancient key that Mrs Hargreaves had supplied. Heavy velvet curtains covered most of the windows but gaps gave just enough light for the inside of the room's contents to be seen. There were the shadowy forms of a number of high-backed chairs, a large desk and a chaise-longue all draped with dust-laden covers. The two men made straight for the desk and Carl pulled the cover away a little too violently. This led to uncle and nephew both being reduced to fits of coughing as they inhaled years of dust. If the vicar had been showing any sign of a thaw in his attitude to Carl, this situation hardly helped.

The exposed desk was a magnificent piece of furniture. It was constructed from dark brown mahogany and the surface was covered in green tooled leather with a gold leaf motif running all round the edge. The desk had five drawers, a large central one and two in the supporting pedestals on either side. Four of these drawers opened easily and proved to be empty. The fifth, the lower one on the right side, was locked and invited the insertion of a small key. The vicar had no idea where this might be and was now fast losing patience with what he no doubt considered to be a wild-goose chase.

"Look, Carl," he began. "I really cannot understand you young men. I would have thought that the wardrobes in your room would have been more than enough for your clothing. I have little experience of women but I am sure that the storage in your room would be more than adequate even for ladies clothing."

After that little speech the vicar turned on his heel and marched stiffly out of the study.

As soon as uncle Olaf had departed, Carl returned to the matter at hand; the location of the key to the cupboard in his room. He stood back gazing at the desk in desperation and wondering how he could open the locked drawer. Then a thought struck him. What an easy solution but maybe, just maybe, if he removed the drawer over the top of the locked one he might be able get his hand down into lower drawer and feel around at its contents for something that felt like a key. He quickly slid out the upper drawer and at first all he could see was a thin plywood panel that separated the two sections. He ran his hand over the panel and discovered it had split. A minute later he had prised up half the panel and there was no need to feel around inside the locked drawer. Even in the dim light he could see that the sole occupant of the drawer was a large brass key similar to the one that had opened the door of the study in the first place. Carl grabbed the key and ran from the study leaving the door wide open. He raced along the landing to his room, flung open the door and made straight for the locked cupboard door. Inserting the key he turned it and lo and behold, it worked. He opened the door and saw the expected cupboard. He had imagined that if this door was opened he would find the most priceless of family treasures but all that the cupboard contained were two old pieces of rock partially wrapped in cotton cloth. He uncovered them fully on the shelves on which they lay and in the dim light inside the cupboard that was all he could see; just two dirty, jagged pieces of rock. Who in their right mind would go to so much trouble to store such worthless items? He decided to try to open the matter again with his uncle, at a later date. However, the whole affair had now completely lost its sense of urgency.

CHAPTER TWENTY TWO

RACHEL

Carl was enjoying his apprenticeship in the weaving trade; not that he was actually being trained as a weaver. The mill owner John Hardcastle was a young bachelor and only a few years Carl's senior. John, together with old Bill Wainwright, the mill manager, was instructing Carl so that ultimately he would understand the intricacies of textile production and even more importantly, the business side of selling cloth.

Carl was also enjoying the social side of life in Lancashire for a wealthy young man about town. John introduced Carl to his own friends many of whom attended the wide variety of society events where young eligible men were introduced to suitably chaperoned young ladies of similar social standing. John also took Carl to the numerous theatres and music-halls that abounded in Manchester at that time. He was not averse to inviting some of the actresses, most of whom were definitely not of a similar social standing, to dinner with him after the show, and that is how Carl met Rachel.

John had been very impressed by Rachel when he saw her on the stage at the Hippodrome, singing with a voice like an angel. Her revealing outfit, however, was somewhat less than angelic. Unbeknown to Carl, he had sent her a note via the doorman at the stage-door inviting her to bring a friend and join him and his friend in the bar during the interval. The two young men were seated on the front row and to enable Rachel to recognise from where the invitation emanated, he had mentioned in the note, the numbers of the seats they were occupying.

The curtain had hardly descended when John whispered to Carl,

"Come on. I think there may be someone waiting for us at the bar."

The two young men made their way as quickly as possible to the back of the stalls. The majority of their fellow members of the audience were also endeavouring to reach the same destination to snatch a couple of quick drinks before the bell announced that seats should be resumed, for the second half of the show.

By the time they entered the bar it was absolutely heaving with a mass of humanity all intent on attracting the attention of the bar staff. Eventually John spied his quarry. She had donned a full cape that covered the frothy chiffon creation she had been wearing on the stage. Seated next to her on a bench in the far corner of the room, John saw an even lovelier apparition, at least in his eyes; this delightful creature had long blonde tresses and the most beautiful face he had ever seen.

"Come on, my dear fellow," he murmured to Carl, "let's say hello to these charming ladies."

Carl could not even see where his friend and mentor was heading, as he followed him through the throng of would-be drinkers. Finally he saw the two young ladies, both wearing full capes and sitting primly in the corner.

"Can we join you?" John enquired.

The dark haired young lady replied,

"Well considering you invited us to meet you here, of course you can."

This was said with a delightful smile that exposed perfect white teeth and sent strange shivers down Carl's spine.

"Look my dear ladies," John explained, "I must apologise. We had such a job battling through the crowd that it must be nearly time for you to return back-stage. Will you join us for dinner after the show to enable us to apologise properly?"

"I do not know what kind of girls you think we are," the dark haired beauty replied. "We do not normally accept dinner invitations from gentlemen who we do not know."

Both the young women seemed to find this statement amusing and promptly giggled in a manner that both the young men found most endearing.

John was quick to answer,

"So you will make an exception tonight and we can all dine together in civilised fashion at the Café Royal."

Once again the two girls giggled but this time they both nodded and arrangements were made for John and Carl to wait for them outside the stage-door. Carl was now even more impressed by the savoir-faire of John little knowing the effect this dinner appointment would have on his future life.

As soon as the show ended John sent Carl to find a hackney carriage while he strolled round to the stage door at the side of the large building. Carl and the carriage arrived quite quickly considering the demand for such conveyances at that time of the evening. A steady stream of actors, singers, dancers and acrobats were now making their way out of the theatre intent on either dining or returning to their lodgings. There was no sign however, of their dinner companions and when a full five minutes had elapsed without another member of the theatre group leaving the premises, John gave a resounding knock on the door with the carved ivory handle of the cane he always carried. The door was opened in response by the doorman who John knew quite well from previous similar expeditions. This man was always pleased to see John as he knew that John was a gentleman who was always happy to pay and to pay handsomely for assistance in arranging liaisons with the younger and prettier members of the cast.

"Hello sir," the doorman said with a wide welcoming grin. "Nice to see you sir; what can I do for you today?"

"Hello Henry," John replied. "We had arranged to see a young lady called Rachel and her friend here after the show but there is no sign of them coming out."

"I would invite you in but this manager is a right tartar; he would have my guts for garters, he would, if I did that."

"That is fine Henry, just do me a favour and find out if these two charming ladies are nearly ready."

"Certainly sir," Henry replied and walked briskly back into the dark cavernous interior to complete his errand.

He returned just three minutes later with Rachel.

"I have been trying to persuade Lizzie to come with us," she explained. "I don't know what has got into the silly girl but she flatly refuses to come. I know it is spoiling the evening but I can still have dinner with you both if you don't mind sharing my conversation between you."

A look of disappointment fleetingly appeared on John's face and then he reminded himself that it had been Rachel who had impressed him first; that was until he had seen Lizzie in the bar.

"Of course dear lady," John replied gallantly, "it would have been agreeable to have had the company of two young ladies, but when one is as charming as you, we really should not complain."

Just twenty minutes later the carriage deposited the three at the Café Royal where a table in a discreet corner was quickly organised.

It has to be stated that both gentlemen were more than a little impressed with Rachel but John felt his mind wandering from time to time as he thought about Lizzie, the delightful creature with the long blonde hair who had refused their invitation.

As for Carl, he was totally captivated. Rachel had long black hair that was a perfect frame for her beautiful face. Her lips were deep red and Carl, not being experienced with women in the manner of his older friend, wondered if this was a natural colour. Her deep brown eyes were almond shape and her nose slightly curved in a manner that only added to her beauty. Her skin tone was Olive which simply helped to increase her exotic appearance.

Carl could not take his eyes off her. He was painfully aware that the effect she was having on him was causing him to hesitate and almost stutter in the course of their conversation.

Apart from her physical appearance, Rachel's voice and accent were also fascinating him. She was, of course a singer and even her spoken words were full of music. Her English was flawless but Carl felt that that possibly it was not her first language or maybe not the language she spoke at home. Carl had met many French people, indeed at school one of his best friends had come over for an English education from Lyon. This goddess was certainly not French, he decided. He had also met many Irish and Welsh people but their accents were totally different to hers. Carl longed to ask her where she came from but was concerned that such questioning may not be welcome at a first meeting.

John was chatting away easily with both Rachel and Carl and did not seem to be even slightly overwhelmed to be in the company of such a wonderful young woman. John, however, knew Carl and could observe all the symptoms of a man smitten with the first stages of infatuation. He, for his part, still wanted to meet Lizzie but knew this would now probably involve a fairly extensive campaign to gain her trust.

Eventually John reminded Carl that they must be up early for work the following day and after depositing

Rachel at her lodgings their cab took them to Victoria station to catch the last train home.

On the return journey John had great difficulty in making conversation with Carl who seemed to be almost in a daze. Eventually he did speak on the only subject occupying his mind at that time.

"I would love to see Rachel again," he ventured.

"Yes, I rather gained that impression," John replied grinning.

"Do you mind? I rather like her," he stammered.

"Not at all, my dear fellow," John answered. "Look, if you must know I rather fancy the other filly-the one called Lizzie."

"So when could we pay another visit to the theatre?" Carl asked.

"Not sure, at the moment," his friend replied, "but soon as possible, soon as possible. Don't worry old chap. I can see you are smitten."

It was, however, to be some considerable time and in rather different circumstances when Carl was to meet Rachel again.

CHAPTER TWENTY THREE

AN EXCITING OPPORTUNITY

The following day a letter arrived at the vicarage in Dalethorpe addressed to Mr Carl James Oliver. It was from his father in London asking him to return before the end of the week, for a family conference. Carl was concerned and wondered why he should be required to return at such short notice.

He explained to John that he would be absent from the mill for a few days and on the Wednesday of that week, he caught the train from Manchester Central Station to London St Pancras. He had written back to his father Carl Isaac to inform him of his intended travel arrangements and to enquire if he could be met at the station by the family carriage, to be conveyed to Hampstead. He had added a PS to the letter stating that he hoped this summons was not because of any serious family problem.

On the journey, Carl's mind hopped alternately from one set of thoughts to another. He worried about the reasons for the mysterious summons to London. And he worried about how and when he would be able to see Rachel again, and this time without John being present.

On arrival at St Pancras, Carl James was delighted to see that his father, Carl Isaac, had come personally to meet him. As he approached the ticket inspector's cabin, where his father was standing, he studied the older man's face for any signs of worry or concern. All he saw, however, was a big welcoming smile.

"Hello Father," he began, "it is so good to see you. Is all well with the family?"

"Yes my boy," Carl Isaac replied, "your mother is anxiously waiting to see you and all is well, very well with us all.

"I received your reply and if my summons to come home alarmed you, I apologise. That was never my intention," he continued.

As the carriage made its way through the congested streets of London father and son chatted inconsequentially. Carl Isaac told his first-born son of the progress his siblings were making with their education and just before the carriage came to a stop he decided to explain the summons.

"Look my boy," he began. "There are three matters to be discussed. One is your progress in the textile world; second is your need to marry and settle down and thirdly there is the question of whether you should continue to live at Dalethorpe."

Carl James was somewhat surprised. The first matter troubled him not one iota. He was happily gaining knowledge about textile production and he was delighted to be working with John. His father would be pleased to learn of his progress. As for marrying, it had never occurred to him. John was years older than he and had successfully resisted all moves in that direction from his own family. Carl felt he was far too young to be settling down and thus denying himself the company of the Rachels of this world. Then there was the question of Dalethorpe and although his relationship with his uncle Olaf was far from ideal, he was happy to remain there, at least for the time being.

Olivia was waiting at the top of the steps outside the front door of the large house. As soon as Carl James alighted from the carriage she rushed down and flung her arms around him. Despite having produced ten children and being married to one of the most eminent solicitors in London, she was still the same happy, impulsive and positive young woman as the day she had married Carl Isaac. She still retained her girlish figure and apart from her hair now being speckled with a little grey, she hardly looked any older than on her wedding day.

Olivia flung her arms around Carl James and smothered him in kisses. This was exactly what Carl expected from his mother and when she linked his arm and piloted him up the steps into the hall of the house, he was more than happy. He had two wonderful parents. His father was grave, steady and gave him a feeling of security and his mother gave him her joie-de-vivre. What a wonderful combination, he decided.

Of his siblings, only the youngest and the oldest were at home. Baby George was two years old, a bonny little fellow who bestowed on his oldest brother a big smile. Carl wondered if he remembered him but after an absence of nine months Carl decided this was unlikely. Thomas, just eighteen months Carl's junior, came home in the evening and the older brother was surprised how much like their father Thomas was becoming. The fact that they worked together-Thomas was taking his articles at his father's firm-maybe had something to do with the growing resemblance. It was not just that they looked alike; they sounded alike and Thomas possessed that same gravitas from his father that Carl James neither had nor aspired to.

Dinner that evening was a happy affair and even the more serious members of the family Carl Isaac and Thomas were in excellent form. Carl James' only regret was that his other brothers and sisters were away at school and could not be there to see him.

After dinner Carl Isaac suggested that his first-born son and he could have their 'chat,' as he put it, the following morning before the father departed for the office. They agreed to meet in the drawing room after breakfast, at half past eight.

"Now my boy," the father began, "as I told you yesterday there are three items on our agenda so let us take them in order."

Carl James knew his father and his organised methodical way of approaching just about everything in life. The fact that Carl Isaac set out an agenda for a cosy father and son chat, was just the measure of the man. That is why he is such a successful solicitor and why I could never follow in his footsteps, Carl decided.

"Let us start with item one," the older man continued. "I gather Mr John Hardcastle is very pleased with your progress and that you now have a pretty good idea about the business of weaving cotton cloth."

"Yes sir," Carl James answered, thinking to himself that John had taught him quite a lot **outside** the mill, as well.

"Well Carl, I must tell you that the most amazing opportunity has presented itself in your field. I take it you know that your Grandfather originally had his own mill just outside Dalethorpe?"

"Yes sir," Carl answered. "I think he sold out fairly quickly didn't he?"

"Actually no!" his father explained. "Your Grandmother kept the business going after his death, until 1888 when we all moved to London. That was when the weaving shed was sold to Combined Lancashire Weavers."

"I see Sir," said Carl although he could not see what all this had to do with him.

"Now something very interesting has happened. As you know our war with the Boers in South Africa ended in May this year. Sadly Major Gordon Pilkington, who had only volunteered last year to go out to fight and finish off the Dutch rebels, was one of the last people killed before the ceasefire."

Carl was wondering why any of this should impact on his life but he waited patiently for his father's somewhat dry delivery to resume.

"Gordon Wilkinson was the son of Aaron Wilkinson who suffered a fatal heart-attack when he heard about Gordon. This is the point my boy," the father seemed to be arriving at a conclusion.

"The Wilkinson family owned Combined Lancashire Weavers and now they want to sell the business. And what's more, my lad," Carl Isaac explained, "that would include three weaving sheds and one of those is your Grandfather's old mill outside Dalethorpe."

"I see sir," Carl James repeated.

"Well, I think it would be a fine investment for our family to buy the whole lot. The two widows appear to be desperate to sell. Then you, my boy, with a little help and guidance from me on the business side, could run the business and what a money spinner that would be."

"Do you not think sir," Carl ventured, "that maybe I am a little too young for so much responsibility."

"Nonsense," the father replied. "You have a fine head on your shoulders and I must tell you that when your Grandfather opened the Dalethorpe mill, he was only about your age. You will be running three well-established weaving sheds each with their own managers. Your task will be to ensure that the units all turn out well-woven cloth; to be involved in purchase of yarn and above all to obtain plenty of orders from the Manchester merchants."

Carl was totally taken aback by the proposal but the way the entire matter had been presented meant that he could hardly say no. In any case, he pondered, this was a wonderful opportunity and took him in his chosen career to where he had eventually hoped to arrive. The difference was this could become a reality in just a few weeks and he would be running a large business having had little or no experience. Still his father had said he had a fine head on his shoulders and Carl Isaac Oliver was not given to mouthing undeserved compliments, especially to his own children.

After his long speech, Carl Isaac sat quietly watching his son and awaiting a reaction and after a few moments he had his answer.

"Well sir," Carl James began hesitantly, "if you really feel I am capable of running this business all I can say is 'yes' and thank you for showing so much confidence in me."

Carl Isaac smiled a deep warm smile. That was, in a fairly austere personality, an indication of deep satisfaction and pleasure.

"Right, young man, I will write today to the Wilkinson family solicitors in Quay Street, Manchester and make them a serious offer to convey to their clients."

After a pause he continued,

"Let's have a coffee and continue our discussions." He pulled the long sash to sound the kitchen bell and a young parlour maid appeared. He ordered the coffee and turned again to his oldest son."

"Now, item two on our agenda is marriage, your marriage."

"But sir, although I have attended many social events both here in London and in Manchester I have yet to find a lady with whom I would even consider spending the rest of my life."

"I think my boy, that if you are to become a captain of industry, you will need a suitable wife to entertain your colleagues and customers. Just leave this matter with your dear mother and with me and we will make some enquiries; now to item three!"

Carl James was far from happy. On the strength of one meeting he had fallen head-over-heels in love with an actress called Rachel and he knew she was definitely NOT marriage material for a man in his position. This was one matter that he needed to keep entirely to himself.

"Now Carl," the father said again, "Item three. Are you happy at Dalethorpe living with your uncle the Vicar?"

Carl James saw this as an opportunity to open up and tell his father about how difficult his present living arrangements were. He therefore told him about the way that his innocent constructive comments about the garden had been met with total opposition. He told Carl Isaac about the way the house was now run and about the hunt for the key to the cupboard in his room. He even explained about the disappointing contents of the cupboard.

"Carl my boy, what do you mean by pieces of rock?" his father queried.

"Well sir, one seemed to be about three feet long and maybe a little less than two feet in width. The other was slightly smaller. The edges of the rocks were jagged as if they had been hacked out of larger pieces of stone for some purpose. I suppose the best way to describe them would be as slabs."

Carl Isaac sat pondering all this new information. Why should anyone take two slabs of rock hacked from larger pieces, wrap them in fabric sheets and lock them in a cupboard in an unused part of the vicarage?

"Carl," his father asked, "did you take the pieces out of the cupboard and examine them in the light?"

"No sir," Carl James replied. "I really did not see much point."

"Well Carl, when you go back, please have a really good look at them either by a window or with the aid of a lamp."

"I certainly will," the son replied, anxious to please his father and to satisfy his own curiosity.

"You know, Carl," the older man continued. "I might have asked my brother Olaf if he could throw any light on this mystery but in view of everything I have heard about him today, I think I will wait for you to investigate. I must tell you Carl, and I do not want you to treat your uncle with any less respect, but he was always somewhat strange, even when we were boys."

"Now my dear boy, I think you should spend some time with your mother while I go off to court-nice big juicy case you know-but there you go, you did not want to be a solicitor. Is there anything else before I leave?"

"Just one thing," Carl James replied. "The mound in the rear of the garden, do you know anything about it? Do you really think it is a burial site or is it just Uncle Olaf trying to keep me away from it?"

"No, I don't think we can blame him this time," his father answered. "Your poor dear Grandmother Elizabeth gave Olaf and me strict instructions about the mound years ago. I am sure that one day its secrets will be revealed but in God's good time."

Carl James stayed in Hampstead for a few more days and was able to see six more of his siblings, returned from school for the long summer holidays. Only Henry and Giles were now absent as they were off on a school trip to Scotland.

He had really enjoyed returning to the bosom of his family and had certainly not missed his present home in Dalethorpe. He had only one anxiety as a result of being away from Lancashire. He constantly thought about Rachel and was determined to see her again, whatever his father may have said about finding him a suitable bride. But the time had flown and he would pack his suitcase that night and leave in the morning with his father whose carriage would deposit him at St Pancras, on the way to his office in nearby Holborn.

"As soon as I have some positive news about Combined Lancashire Weavers I will send you a telegram. I may need you back again in London fairly quickly if our negotiations proceed to a satisfactory conclusion," Carl Isaac told him.

Life was becoming very exciting, he pondered on the long train journey back to Manchester. He had probably been given the opportunity to make himself and his family into even wealthier members of society. Also, he had fallen in love with the most beautiful woman on earth but he knew there would be conflict ahead where Rachel was concerned.

However, his arrival coincided with yet another problem, a very serious one for the good name of the Oliver family. As the train sped northwards he could not have dreamed, in his own worst nightmares, of what was about to occur.

Chapter Twenty four

The Vicar disappears

Carl James was unpacking his suitcase when he heard the clanging of the door-bell downstairs. He glanced at his wristwatch and realised that Mrs Hargreaves would have left by now. Indeed, he reminded himself that she had her coat on, ready to depart, when he had arrived back half an hour ago from his visit to London. It was Friday afternoon and his uncle the vicar was normally home, writing his sermon for the next Sunday, so he waited for him to answer the front-door. Then there was a second ring and Carl realised he would have to go down himself.

Carl opened the front-door to discover two men on the doorstep. They were both dressed in the manner of functionaries or petty officials-bowler hats, shabby grey tweed suits and he immediately noticed that they had mud-stained, dirty shoes.

"Yes," Carl said, maybe a little sharply, "can I help you?"

"Are you the Rev Olaf Oliver?" the older of the two men demanded.

"No," Carl replied, "he is my uncle and he must be out at the moment."

"Are you expecting him back soon?" the younger man required.

"Look," Carl answered, "who are you? If it is Church business why not walk over to St Barnabas to see if he is there?"

"Are you expecting him back soon?" the man repeated.

"Listen," Carl replied. "I am not in the habit of supplying information to complete strangers, on the movements of family and friends, who are you?"

The older man pulled himself up to a more erect posture and almost standing to attention he announced pompously,

"I am Detective Sergeant Jackson and this 'ere is Detective Constable Hopkins of the Lancashire Constabulary; now kindly inform us of the whereabouts of the Reverend Olaf Oliver?"

Carl was more than a little shocked that two policemen should suddenly arrive on the doorstep of the Vicarage demanding to see his uncle. Furthermore, he was not accustomed to being addressed in such an impertinent manner by members of the police force. On the rare occasions when he had any dealings with them, it was in usually in circumstances where they called him 'sir' and treated him deferentially in the manner that the police usually used to talk to their 'betters.'

Carl tried valiantly to recover the upper-hand with these two men.

"I am Carl Oliver nephew of the Vicar of St Barnabas. My father is a highly respected solicitor in London and I must tell you men that I very much resent your tone. Why do you need to speak to my uncle, anyway?" He continued.

Once again the Detective Sergeant pulled himself up to his full height and intoned with just a touch more respect,

"Sorry, sir, I am not at liberty to provide an answer to that question."

Carl was becoming increasingly curious but realised he was not going to obtain any further information from the detectives.

"All I can tell you Sergeant is that I have just arrived back from London and my Uncle appears to be absent. You can rest assured that as soon as I see him I will tell him to contact you. Are you based at the police station in Accrington?"

"Yes sir," the Sergeant replied, "but we need to speak to him urgently. Can we come in to wait for him?"

Carl had decided that a serious matter involving the misbehaviour of one of the parishioners must be the reason for the visit and realising that the policemen were now making some effort to be courteous, he felt he must agree. He ushered them into the library and told them that as soon as his uncle returned, he would inform him that they were waiting for him.

After an hour with no sign of Olaf returning, Carl returned to the library. His unpacking was now complete and he was awaiting the return of Mrs Hargreaves to prepare and serve his dinner.

"Look," Carl began. "There is still no sign of my uncle. Do you want to come back in the morning?"

"No Sir," the Sergeant replied. "We would rather wait or at least, I will wait here while Constable Hopkins walks over to the church, to see if he is there." After a pause he remembered his manners and added, "If that is alright with you, sir?"

Whatever these policemen wanted to see Uncle Olaf about was obviously serious and urgent, Carl decided. And at least they were making an effort to be courteous.

"Very well," Carl answered. He then turned to address Constable Hopkins. "Please ring the bell when you return and I will let you back into the library to collect the Sergeant. Hopefully, you will then have had your chat with the Vicar and can leave."

However, Constable Hopkins returned after half an hour to say that there was no sign of the Vicar at the church and people in the houses near the church had not seen him in the village for the last two days.

"Well sir," the Detective Sergeant asked, "do you mind if we wait another half hour? If the Rev Oliver does not return then, please tell him, when he does come home that we need to see him urgently."

"Certainly Sergeant," Carl replied. "However, although I realise that much of your work is confidential, can you not at least, give me some idea as to why you wish to see the Vicar so urgently?"

"Sorry sir," the officer replied. "I am afraid that would not be appropriate; confidential you know!"

Carl was becoming increasingly intrigued but was forced to accept that he was not going to obtain any information from these men.

Mrs Hargreaves returned and seeing through the open door the two men sitting in the library, she asked Carl, now anxiously awaiting his dinner in the dining room, why they were there and was she also to prepare dinner for them?

"They wanted to see the Vicar," he explained; "must be church business!"

Carl then returned to the library and assured the policemen that he would tell his uncle that they needed to see him. He then ushered them out of the Vicarage and sat down to enjoy his meal. Mrs Hargreaves was an excellent cook and despite the fact that he now had three weighty matters on his mind, he still enjoyed his dinner as only the young, healthy and hungry can do.

By the following morning which was a Saturday, the Vicar had still not returned and Carl was becoming increasingly anxious as to what could have befallen his uncle. Then the door bell clanged and it announced a second visit by Detective Constable Hopkins.

"Good morning sir," he enquired. "Did the Vicar return last night?"

"No, not a sign of him and I must tell you I am becoming very worried. I think you should consider him to be a missing person and alert your colleagues, throughout the area, to look out for him. I am beginning to think he has either been attacked or involved in an accident. He has never once behaved like this during the time I have been living here."

Carl was somewhat shocked by the detective's reply.

"We have already notified all the police stations in Lancashire to look out for him and telegrams have been sent to our colleagues in Yorkshire and Cheshire."

"So do you suspect that something ill has befallen him?" Carl enquired.

"Not necessarily sir, but that is all I can say. If you do see him, tell him to contact us at once."

"That sounds as if you are looking for him as a common criminal," Carl replied.

"Sorry sir," the constable answered, "I am not at liberty to say any more."

As soon as the policeman had departed, Carl dashed round to the stables at the rear of the house, saddled his favourite horse and galloped off towards Accrington to send a telegram to his father in London from the post office.

Uncle Olaf disappeared-stop-*police looking for him*-stop-*can you find out what is going on*-stop-*Carl*

Chapter Twenty five

Disgrace and Disappointment

Carl Isaac Oliver was just about to climb into his carriage outside his home in Hampstead when a telegraph boy on a bicycle came pedalling laboriously up the steep driveway.

After signing a receipt for the communication and giving a tip to the perspiring messenger, he tore open the envelope to read the contents.

Carl Isaac had always had a difficult relationship with his younger brother Olaf. When they were in their late teenage years and early twenties, the two young men had already developed diametrically opposing views on just about every aspect of life. Carl Isaac was of course a committed Christian and attended church every Sunday, as he still did to this day. However, the Christianity of fire and brimstone preached by his brother was not the religion he loved. He had been quite surprised when the parishioners of St Barnabas had been so determined to appoint Olaf as their Vicar. He had hoped and wondered at the time if these good folk realised the stern, intolerant view of the world that their new shepherd was bringing to his flock. However, Carl Isaac was already heavily involved in his own career as a Solicitor and the father of a fast-growing family. That was, of course, another potential reason for heated disagreement between the brothers. Carl Isaac could no more understand his brother's rejection of all the potential brides suggested by his late mother than he could understand any of Olaf's other attitudes to life.

However, Olaf was still his brother and Carl Isaac was determined to discover what had become of him.

The new telephone system had recently been installed in Carl's office and he decided that his brother's disappearance was definitely a justifiable reason to use the new machine. He could not, of course, call the Lancashire Constabulary as they had not, at that time installed the facility. However, he could telephone the Post Office and dictate two telegrams, one to the Police and the other to his son Carl James in Dalethorpe.

Two hours later he received a telephone call from the Post Office in London who asked him if he would prefer to have the telegram, just received from the Lancashire Police, to be read to him before delivering the printed copy to him at the office. Carl Isaac was pleased with this new way of quickly gaining information and readily agreed to the Telephone operator's suggestion.

Regret to inform you that apart from finding said Olaf Oliver as a missing person we need to question him regarding possible offence of public indecency-stop- *as his solicitor will keep you informed* -stop-*DS Jackson-Lancashire Constabulary*

Carl Isaac sat back heavily in his chair and still grasping the mouthpiece of the telephone he said in a weak voice,

"Please deliver the telegram to me without delay."

Then he bethought himself to add sternly,

"Please understand that the contents of this telegram are strictly confidential and I will take proceedings against the Post Office and all staff involved in any breach of this confidentiality."

The Monday, after the first visit of the two detectives, Carl James returned to the Hardcastle mill to continue shadowing and learning from his mentor John Hardcastle. He was longing to discuss with John the mysterious absence of his uncle Olaf Oliver, but realised that, even for such a close friend and confidante as John, this would have been highly inappropriate. Equally, the possibility of his premature departure from Hardcastle's to run his own mills was a matter demanding absolute secrecy. Had John gained even an inkling of the fact that the mills of Combined

Lancashire Weavers were for sale, friend or not, he might have been prepared to bid against the Oliver family to obtain such a prize!

There was one subject, however, that Carl could discuss with John, one that was very important to him on a personal level. He was quite desperate, despite all the other matters in his life, to see Rachel again. He now knew that John was not a rival for her favours as his interest lay elsewhere with the elusive Lizzie.

John was of course curious to discover the reason for the sudden summons that had resulted in his protégé being absent from the mill the previous week.

"Everything alright in London?" he enquired.

"Yes fine," Carl replied.

"They asked you to go back rather expeditiously, did they not?" John commented.

Carl had been expecting this line of questioning and had his answer ready.

"My Mother is a very emotional person and was missing me," he confided.

"My Father thought it would be a wonderful surprise to arrange for me to return to the family for a few days," he explained.

John appeared to accept the explanation although secretly he suspected that there must have been more to it than that. However, he held his peace.

"Can we go to town this evening?" Carl enquired.

John laughed, "I thought you would want to go to Manchester and see Rachel again as soon as possible."

"Well can we go?" Carl repeated.

"Certainly, we can! You must be keen to want to go on a Monday when the theatre will be half empty," he commented, "but why not?"

It was a lovely evening and the two friends took the 6.35pm train from Accrington. The hills were bathed in the sunlight of the now fast-descending sun until, as they neared the ugly urban sprawl of the city, a murky darkness replaced the crisp views they had left behind. The two young men took a cab from Victoria station to the theatre, purchased tickets in the front row of the stalls and took their seats to await the start of the show. However, what they had both failed to notice on the billboards outside the theatre was that this was the first night of a new variety show by a new company and that there was no sign of Rachel, or Lizzie come to that. During the interval they slipped out to enquire from the co-operative doorman, Henry, what had transpired?

"Oh, that company left last week," he explained. "However, I do have a letter for you. Which of you is called Mr Carl?"

"I am he," Carl answered, his spirits rising at what appeared to be good news. *She has left a letter for me*, he thought. *Obviously she wants to see me again,* but when he read the letter, the contents dashed any hopes he had of developing a relationship with the delightful young lady,

Dear Carl,
When you receive this letter I will have left Manchester for our next venue. In any case I think it would be best if we now went our separate ways. I enjoyed your company and I could see that you enjoyed mine but I must not become involved, even with someone as nice as you are.
Yours sincerely,
Rachel.

Carl read and re-read the letter and turned to John who had been studying the change of his friend's facial expression as he finished reading.

"You don't look very happy," John commented.

"You may as well read this," Carl replied, thrusting the letter in to John's hand.

When John had quickly scanned the letter he turned to Henry the doorman.

"You must know the next venue for the company," he suggested. "Where have they travelled to?"

"Sir," Henry replied, "I truly do not know. I would like to help you two fine gentlemen but it is more than my job is worth to start making enquiries. You know what this new manager is like," he explained, raising his eyes heavenward.

Of course they had no idea what the new manager was like but they could readily see that there would be no further help from that quarter. The man Henry was obviously quite terrified and even a handsome tip was not going to change his mind.

So John and Carl repaired to a nearby restaurant for dinner and caught an earlier train back home.

Carl was deeply disappointed to have his hopes and dreams of a long term relationship with Rachel nipped in the bud but other and graver events were to occupy his life, at least in the immediate future.

Chapter twenty six

Helping Police Enquiries

It was not altogether surprising that Carl spent most of the ensuing night tossing and turning in his bed as he tried to accept the fact that he would probably never set eyes on the lovely face of Rachel again. He was glad when dawn came and he rose for a breakfast that he downed absentmindedly without a thought for the taste of the delicious piping hot porridge, prepared by Mrs Hargreaves. There was still no sign of the Vicar and Carl could not bring himself to believe that the police had any interest other than in finding him as a missing person. He did wonder briefly about the last remark of Constable Hopkins when he had called back the previous week but felt that this was just the policeman taking confidentiality rules too literally. He was hardly on good terms with his uncle but he still found his disappearance a cause for considerable concern.

Carl decided to ride to work on horseback that morning. He hoped that the fresh clean air in his face would blow away at least some of the worries that now beset him. In truth, this was the first time in his life that he had felt somewhat overwhelmed by serious concerns. He came from a happy family and had acquitted himself respectably, if not impressively at school. Now he felt the burdens of adult life had all arrived to assail him, at the same time.

Carl and John occupied separate but adjoining offices with a communicating door between them that was usually left open. The general office where the clerks worked was further down the corridor and apart from the senior clerk, whose job it was to record in a huge ledger all movements of yarn inwards and cloth outwards, there were three junior clerks, one of whom was a young woman. This young woman, Bessie, was employed to perform the most menial of office tasks including making the tea, taking the post to the local letter-box and answering the door to callers. And it was Bessie who knocked timidly on Carl's office door to tell him that two gentlemen wished to see him.

"What are their names," Carl enquired a little testily, breaking off from an important calculation he was doing for John.

"I will go and find out Sir," Bessie said.

"You know Bessie we do not see people without an appointment," Carl replied. "Yes, please at least discover their names and if possible why they wish, in particular, to see me."

Bessie was back in an instant.

"They are policemen," she stammered, peering nervously into Carl's face as if he had suddenly become a criminal. "Their names are Sergeant Jackson and Constable Hopkins."

"Well show them in," Carl said, getting up to close the door to his colleague and mentor's office.

"Sir," the Sergeant began, as soon as they were seated in Carl's office. "We have found your uncle the Vicar. He was sleeping in a shop doorway in Accrington and he was in a terrible state."

"Have you brought him home?" Carl enquired.

"No, Sir, I regret we cannot do that," the officer explained. "We have cleaned him up and given him some breakfast but we need to detain him to help with our enquiries."

"What do you mean to help with your enquiries?" Carl said. "You make him sound like a common criminal. He is the Vicar of St Barnabas, there must be some mistake."

"Sorry, Sir," the Sergeant continued. "I am not at liberty to give you any further information. We came to tell you that he had been found as you seemed to be concerned about his whereabouts."

"Thank you Sergeant," Carl replied. "However I would very much like to know why you are holding him."

"Sorry, Sir," the officer repeated, "may I respectfully suggest that you contact your father Mr Carl Isaac Oliver in London, he is your uncle's solicitor. Maybe he can help but I have told you as much as I dare."

The two men rose to leave and after formally shaking Carl's hand, they left the office. It then took only a few seconds, for John to re-open the communicating door and to stride into Carl's office.

"A visit from the police!" he said grinning. "What have you been up to?"

"It is not me," Carl explained frowning and proceeded to recount to John how his uncle had disappeared, had now been found and how the police, for some mysterious reason, were not prepared to release him. It was something of a relief to be able to share this anxiety with John but neither of them had the slightest idea why a pillar of the community, a man of God, should have been detained.

At lunchtime Carl rode down to the post office to despatch another telegram to his father.

I think you know the Police have found Uncle Olaf-stop-they say you know why they are holding him for questioning-stop-what is it all about-stop-Carl

He asked for the reply to be delivered to him at the vicarage that evening and he returned to work to await developments.

CHAPTER TWENTY SEVEN

DOMINIC

The O'Reilly family had arrived in Manchester in 1885. Patrick, Mary and their seven children had trudged all the way from their old home in County Kerry, with the sum total of their possessions on a cart pulled by their old and diseased donkey. Miraculously they had managed to complete the journey to Dublin where Patrick had used the last of his money, from selling his few livestock, to buy steamship tickets for them all to sail to Liverpool and a new and better life, or so he hoped.

On arrival in Liverpool, minus the poor donkey which had perished, worn out by old age and hard work, they were told that there were better opportunities for them in nearby Manchester. They stayed in a hostel for a week while Patrick worked as a casual labourer on a building site, to get together enough money for the short rail journey. They arrived at Victoria Station Manchester on the seventh day of June and Irish friends from their village who had arrived two years earlier, took them in to their already overcrowded home in Thompson Street in the Red Bank area, while Patrick went out to find work.

Over the following seventeen years Patrick worked hard, very hard and eventually they were able to rent their own family home farther down the same street. Their youngest son Dominic was born in Manchester in 1890 and had been a wayward and disobedient child from a very young age. In 1902 his father told him to either find some work to earn his keep or leave the family home. So Dominic left. He could neither read nor write but he did have two attributes. He was cunning and he was very good looking. Despite his poor diet he was a fine young man and living on the streets he quickly discovered that there were some 'fine English gentlemen' who would pay him handsomely for fulfilling their perverted sexual desires. The rewards for this service were more than his father earned in a few months and Dominic was quickly able to rent a room where, by the tender age of thirteen he was enjoying a comfortable if lonely life.

Dominic never allowed his 'clients' to know where he lived and his working address was in the underground public toilets in Piccadilly. There were a number of regular customers who visited him there by appointment and his client base was growing by way of recommendation. Then one day it occurred to Dominic that if he followed his clients to their homes after their sessions with him, he could threaten to report them to their families as the innocent victim of their perversions. He did think of complaining to the police but realised that could be counter productive. By now Dominic was making a good 'living' and he was not greedy. He just let the clients know that he knew who they were and where they lived and was able to double their fees without any objections from them for this fairly modest piece of blackmail.

He was sitting on a bench near his place of 'work' one summer afternoon when a stern-looking man approached him. He explained to him that another gentleman had told him that Dominic could look after him and was very versatile. A generous fee was agreed and the two descended the steep stone steps and entered a cubicle. The new client appeared to be satisfied but Dominic found it strange that on a warm summer day, he had a long scarf wrapped round his neck which he not only did not remove, despite the heat in the tiny area, but kept ensuring it was securely in place during their exertions. Afterwards, he asked Dominic to meet him again four days later and Dominic decided that he would, as usual, wait until the client was well settled in before following him to discover his identity.

The Rev Olaf Oliver was due at a diocesan conference the following Tuesday. He also had other 'business' to attend to in Manchester on that day and when the meeting finished he briskly made his way to his second appointment. Somehow on this occasion, in the heat of their proceedings, the scarf fell away from around his neck and Dominic saw the clerical collar of his client. He knew better than to comment but he was sure that the extra money he could extract from this client would be impressively large. As it so happened, all of this proved to be unnecessary, as just as the vicar was leaving the security of the cubicle closely followed by Dominic, a parishioner, one Charles Butterworth was just fulfilling a normal call of nature. Not immediately seeing Dominic behind the vicar he greeted him warmly by name. Then he saw Dominic who by this means learned the name of his client. The facial expression of Charles Butterworth changed in an instant. One second he was smiling broadly and greeting his spiritual shepherd and the next he was observing the man as the secret pervert he was.

Dominic was very quick to size up the situation and pretended to cry.

"This man," he wept, "has just made me do all sorts of awful things with him."

Charles Butterworth immediately took charge of the situation.

"Right," he said. "We are going off to the police."

However, other gentlemen wishing to relieve themselves caused the three to be separated on the way up the steep steps and by the time the elderly Charles Butterworth and Dominic had ascended on to the Piccadilly pavement, Olaf was nowhere in sight.

"I am afraid we have lost him," Charles commented. "It must have been awful for you. No one had any idea that the vicar was a pervert. Please come with me to the police station and we will tell them all about the activities of this disgusting man."

Dominic could hardly refuse. As it was, in just two sessions, he had already developed a strong dislike for the vicar. Other clients, once their needs were satisfied, usually smiled and thanked him. In fact a few of his clients, usually those he had not blackmailed, treated him almost like a young friend. This vicar, however, was cold and rough with him, never smiled and seemed to regard him as an object rather than a human being. There were others like him, but Dominic had already decided he was the worst, at least so far.

The unlikely pair made their way through the busy city streets and Charles told the desk sergeant that he wanted to report a case of Buggery 'against this poor child' and gross indecency.

Charles and Dominic were then interviewed separately by Detective Sergeant Jackson and Detective Constable Hopkins who both took extensive notes. At the end the sergeant said,

"There can be no doubt that the Rev Olaf Oliver is guilty of offences under the *Labouchere Amendment*, primarily *Gross Indecency between Males* in a public place. We will send a message to all Police Stations in the area to be on the look out for this man."

Turning to Charles Butterworth he continued,

"You told us that you live in the village of Dalethorpe where this Rev Oliver is the vicar. I must ask you to remain silent about this whole matter until we have this man safely locked up. If he knows we are looking for him he will go to ground. Can I rely on your discretion in this matter?"

Charles nodded gravely.

"As for you, young man," the detective continued, turning to Dominic, "you have given us your address and we will be in touch again as soon as we have caught this man."

Dominic thanked them profusely and left the police station. The address he had given was as false as his testimony and he decided to move his 'business' to the public toilets in nearby Albert Square. He knew his regular clients would soon find him there.

CHAPTER TWENTY EIGHT

TWO DEATHS

The Station-Master, replete in his high hat and black morning-coat stood on the platform, his pocket watch in hand, as the 8.14am train from London St Pancras rumbled into Manchester Central Station, like some huge smoke-belching dragon. Waiting on the platform, clutching his platform-ticket stood Carl James Oliver. He was anxiously surveying the alighting multitude looking out for his father Carl Isaac Oliver.

Eventually he spotted him striding purposefully along the platform, looking smart and dapper in his black jacket and striped trousers; clothing appropriate to a solicitor of his standing. He was accompanied by a porter who was carrying his suitcase while Carl Isaac's briefcase was clutched safely in his own hands.

"Hello Carl," his father greeted him. "This is a bad business, what? I brought some changes of clothing in case I need to stay on. Can we go straight to see your uncle in the police cells?"

"Yes, of course Sir," the younger Carl said. "He may be a difficult man but it is hard to believe that Uncle Olaf would be involved in anything really serious."

When they arrived outside the police station Carl Isaac turned to his son and said,

"You had better wait in the carriage. I am afraid I do not know how long I will be in here but it would not be appropriate for you to come inside with me."

"Very well Sir, don't worry about me. The important thing is to try to dispose of this matter with as little embarrassment as possible for the family."

"Absolutely my boy," the older man answered. "That is the one vital thing in all this-the good name of the Oliver family!"

Carl senior then jumped out of the cab and marched into the police station.

For the next three quarters of an hour Carl James sat in the cab awaiting the return of his father. Fortunately he had purchased a copy of the Manchester Guardian on the station and he tried to immerse himself in the numerous stories of the day. He was reading a despatch from the correspondent in South Africa about the aftermath of the Boer War when his father returned. He looked grave and shocked. Carl was used to his father's often serious demeanour but he had never before seen him look so angry.

"As Olaf's solicitor I should not be telling you this. In fact, as your father, I would not want you normally to have any knowledge of this most unpleasant subject, I will not go into any of the gory details with you or your mother but what you should know is that there are two witnesses to Olaf's behaviour and that there is a strong case against him for practicing *Gross Public Indecency*. Moreover, one of the witnesses is a boy only thirteen years old and the Jury will be horrified to listen to what he has to say."

Carl was, of course, well aware of what this all meant. He may have had a privileged and protected childhood but even at school, he had been warned by other older boys, to avoid the clutches of some of the teachers. Strange, he pondered, it seems as if Ministers of the Cloth are particularly tempted to indulge in this revolting behaviour. The two men at school who readily came to mind were both ones who were supposed to offer spiritual guidance. There was that nasty little old man, the Rev Simon Beckett. We all knew who his little friends were and tended to give him and them a wide berth. The other one, Carl remembered, was not a vicar himself but the son of one. He used to take two of the prettiest little boys on train-spotting expeditions or at least that was their story.

There was little conversation as the two men returned to Dalethorpe. Carl was shocked and his father deeply angered and offended by his brother's behaviour. It had been all very well to talk about defending the good name of the family but now there would be a trial and the press would have a field day. He could imagine the headlines- *Vicar accused of Gross Indecency-Member of one of Lancashire's Finest Families in Dock-Assignations in Men's Toilet.*

It was still only lunchtime when they arrived back at the Vicarage. Mrs Hargreaves was summoned to prepare a light snack.

"Also, please open up one of the other bedrooms for my father," Carl James instructed her.

"Sir," she replied. "Is there any news of the Rev Olaf?"

"Not at the moment," Carl Isaac replied a little sharply. "Now please can we eat?"

After lunch the two men discussed the situation.

"Whatever we do, this situation with your uncle is going to be dreadful," Carl Isaac commented. "I am probably going to have to persuade him to plead guilty, once I have thoroughly examined the evidence of the two witnesses. One of them is a gentleman from Dalethorpe, Charles Butterworth, and I only hope he will be discreet and not talk about what Olaf has done here in the village. I am sure the Judge will have Olaf locked up and on the face of it, he deserves it."

"Father," Carl James replied. "I know Charles Butterworth quite well. He is a decent old boy and he has a small cotton dyeing factory over on the Burnley road. Hardcastle's give him a little work now and then. If I could persuade him to withdraw his evidence, it would then be Uncle Oaf's word against the boy."

"Absolutely not," his father thundered. "If we start interfering with witnesses we will all finish up in prison with your uncle."

"Look Carl," Carl senior continued after a pause, "leave it to me. I am going to spend tomorrow making more enquiries about this sordid matter and then I shall return to London to await developments."

"Very well Father," Carl James replied. "I will steer well clear of Mr Butterworth for the time being."

"Yes, that would be best," Carl Isaac answered.

After a few minutes silence when the pair were engrossed in their own thoughts, Carl decided to attempt to change the subject to one of even greater significance to him and indeed to the Oliver family.

"Father," he began. "Is there any news about Combined Lancashire Weavers?"

"Well yes my boy," the father replied brightening perceptively. "I have made an offer and tomorrow I expect a reply from the solicitor acting for the Pilkington family."

"Let us hope it is good news," Carl answered. "We could certainly do with some at the moment."

Mrs Hargreaves then knocked on the dining-room door.

"Your room is ready Sir," she said.

"Excellent," Carl Isaac replied. "I will go upstairs and spend some time on other files I brought with me and I will see you Carl, at dinner."

It was now a half past three and Carl decided to ride over to Hardcastles and explain to John that his father had arrived from London on an urgent legal matter; perfectly true, he pondered as he wondered what his friend and mentor John would think about Uncle Olaf when the whole story was revealed to him.

Of course the first question John asked was,

"What is happening with your uncle?"

"All I can tell you is that the police are looking after him," Carl explained.

"What does that mean?" John asked, suspecting correctly that he was not being told the full story.

"Look John," Carl replied. "Please can we change the subject as I know little more myself and even that limited information, is strictly confidential."

"Very well," John reluctantly accepted, "but please be aware that anything I can do to help you and your family, I will do gladly; just say the word."

After that exchange the pair returned to their own desks until it was time to leave work to go to their respective homes for dinner.

Almost by way of light relief Carl decided to raise another matter with his father, over dinner.

"Father, do you remember that I mentioned two large pieces of rock in the cupboard in my room here?"

"Yes, of course I do my boy," Carl Isaac replied.

"While you are here, perhaps you would like to take a look at them with me?" Carl James enquired.

As soon as dinner was over the pair climbed the stairs to Carl's room and with the large key that Carl now kept in a drawer alongside his bed, the cupboard was opened.

The rocks were taken out and placed on a table. The wrappings were removed and father and son peered at the strange apparently valueless relics that had been stored so safely from some bygone age. The two men stared down at the rocks in puzzlement but in the dim light of the oil lamps they could see nothing that would indicate a justification for their retention until Carl Isaac ran his hand over the face of the larger one.

"You know my boy," he commented, "I think there is something chiselled into the surface. It is light now at six o'clock in the morning. I will come back to your room as soon as I awake and we can have a better inspection in daylight."

"Very well, father," Carl replied. "That sounds like a good plan."

But it was a plan that was not destined to come to fruition at that time.

They were descending the stairs when the front-door bell clanged.

"Who on earth can this be at nine o'clock at night?" Carl Isaac wondered.

Carl James took the remaining steps two at a time and flung back the panelled door to discover a somewhat scruffy looking youth of probably thirteen or fourteen years on the step.

"Is this the home of the Rev Oliver," the boy enquired.

"And who are you?" Carl James responded irritably.

"Never mind who I am," the boy responded impudently. "Are you the Vicar's son?"

"Indeed not and I suggest you leave at once before I call the police."

"I would not do that if I were you," the boy replied.

At that moment Carl Isaac appeared at the front door to see who was visiting so late at night.

The boy looked at the senior Mr Oliver and said impertinently,

"So you must be the brother. The police told me you would be coming to defend the Vicar."

"Are you Dominic?" Carl Isaac demanded with a look of thunder on his face.

"Yes, that's me," the boy replied. "I've got a business proposition for you gentlemen. Can I come in?"

"Indeed you cannot," Carl Isaac replied angrily. "I suggest that you get away from here as fast as your legs will take you or I will call the police."

"I would not shout at me," the youth answered, "not if you want to see your brother released from the lock-up."

"We have nothing to say to you; do you understand?" Carl Isaac responded. "Just go!"

But the impertinent youth held his ground.

"I came to tell you that I was sorry for the old Vicar and if you made it worth my while I would tell the police I made up the story about him messing about with me."

Carl James had been standing at the open door with his father. He could see his father was becoming increasingly agitated and he decided that it was time for him to take control of the situation. He stepped forward onto the top step and shouted angrily into the youth's face,

"You heard my father, go; just go!"

But still the youth stood there. Carl James may have thought he was taking control but in reality he was losing control of himself and raising both his arms he delivered to the boy a mighty push that sent him toppling down the stone steps until he lay at the bottom motionless.

"My God, Carl," his father gasped in a strangled voice, "what have you done?"

"He is just shamming," Carl replied and descended to where the youth's inert body lay. He kneeled down and shook the boy but there was no response.

"Father," he called back up the steps without turning his head, "Father, I think you had better come down."

But there was no reply from above so Carl turned to peer up the steps but could see no sign of his father. He stood up and then saw that Carl senior was sitting down on the top step by the door. Carl bounded up the steps to find that his father, his right hand clutching his chest and with a dreadful grey colour on a face that seemed to be drained of blood, was muttering over and over again,

"What have you done? What have you done?"

Then suddenly Carl Isaac's head dropped forward and he became still, very still.

"Father, Father!" Carl said as he tried to rouse him.

But there was no rousing Carl Isaac Oliver, solicitor of Hampstead London. He was as dead as the youth who had predeceased him by a few moments and whose visit had brought on his demise.

It was now nearly dark on what had been a lovely summer evening and Carl James Oliver stood motionless for at least ten minutes, on the top step weeping softly and looking from the body at the top of the steps to the body at the bottom of the steps in absolute horror, trying to take in what had just occurred.

Eventually Carl realised he must take some action. He knew that he was responsible, albeit unintentionally, for the death of the youth. He was all on his own. The house was on the edge of the village and at that time most of the neighbours would be sitting in their parlours or taking a well earned cup of tea before retiring to bed. The police would never believe that he had not intended harm to the boy. It was all too convenient. The lad was the prime witness in the case against Carl's uncle and without his evidence the case would almost certainly collapse.

Carl, although in a state of shock, was goaded into urgent activity when he considered his own personal safety.

He went down the steps once more, to the body of the youth and hoisted him on to his shoulder. He carried him round to the rear of the house, down the overgrown path until he arrived at the mound. The lad was not particularly heavy but Carl was panting hard when he arrived; whether from effort or fear, it was difficult to decide. He went round to the far side of the huge mound and dumped the body, like a sack of potatoes onto the dry earth. He then went looking for a spade and proceeded to dig away an area large enough to contain Dominic's body, at the base. He rolled the body into the grave and proceeded to cover it with the earth he had dug away. Finally he replaced the dry shale that was the outer cover of the mound so that it gave no hint of what was contained.

Carl then returned to the body of his father and dragged this much larger corpse into the hallway of the house. He laid him down, eyes closed on a large rug, his own eyes weeping copious tears as he did so. Then he locked the front door and saddled his horse to ride into Accrington to fetch a doctor and the police. The doctor had been able to confirm that the solicitor had died from a heart attack. It transpired that on a previous visit to Lancashire, Carl Isaac had complained of feeling unwell and this self-same doctor had warned him that his heart was not in good shape. It was well after midnight when all the formalities were completed. First thing in the morning he must send telegrams to his mother and to his father's office telling them the dreadful news.

Carl finally returned to his room exhausted but certain that sleep would elude him. The two large pieces of rock lay on the table and seeing them and remembering that he and his father were to examine them together the following morning, he unceremoniously re-wrapped them in their dirty, musty cotton binders and carried back them to cupboard which had been their home for so many years.

CHAPTER TWENTY NINE

SOME GOOD NEWS (AT LAST)

Carl Isaac Oliver was buried one week later, in the family crypt at St Barnabas-by-Dalethorpe. The service was conducted by the Rev Charles Rodgers who was sent personally by the Bishop with a special message for the bereaved family. Present at the funeral were the broken-hearted widow Olivia Oliver and all of her ten children. They all grieved for the loss of a fine father but the first-born son Carl James was inconsolable. Neighbours and friends present were aware that it was he who had found Mr Oliver and were more than sympathetic to him in his deep sorrow. Also present was the deceased's brother Olaf Oliver, accompanied by two men that only Carl and Charles Butterworth knew were plain clothed policemen. Mr Charles Butterworth was one of the witnesses to the vicar's downfall and fortunately was discreet. Only he, Olaf's escorts from the constabulary and Carl knew why Olaf did not conduct his brother's funeral and the reason for this was a cause of wild speculation by the assembled multitude.

After the committal proceedings were complete and the solicitor had been laid to rest with his forebears, close family and friends repaired to the Vicarage for drinks and snacks. Olivia and her other nine children had travelled straight to the churchyard on arrival in Accrington as the train from London had arrived an hour late. She had no idea about Olaf's problem as her late husband had been the soul of discretion and confidentiality; he never discussed legal matters with his wife, even those concerning his own family.

"Carl dear," Olivia said, once they were all back at the house, "do you know why Olaf did not conduct the service and who were those two rough looking men who seemed to be with him and where he is now?"

Carl however was not bound by the professional restraints of his late father and before retiring that evening, when the rest of the family had either departed or gone to bed, he told his mother the whole unpleasant tale. He did however leave out certain murky details and the visit of Dominic to Dalethorpe, on the evening his father died, was a secret he preferred to take with him to his own grave.

Carl had met Thomas Chichester, his father's friend and colleague on a number of occasions. He had travelled up with the family for the funeral and had intended to discuss matters relating to Carl Isaac's estate with the deceased's oldest son. Seeing how broken-hearted Carl was at the funeral he had instead checked himself into a hotel in Manchester. In any case, he decided, as the senior partner he now needed to spend a few days with the Manchester partners before returning to London.

Among the files he was handed was one relative to the proposed purchase of Combined Lancashire Weavers on behalf of the Oliver family. He opened the file and discovered that the offer made for the business by the Oliver Family Trust had been accepted. He sent a telegram off to Carl and hoped that the young man would be sufficiently recovered from the trauma of the previous day to reply. Sure enough, just an hour later a reply arrived.

I gather you are still in Manchester-stop-please come up to Dalethorpe for dinner this evening-stop-Carl

Thomas took the train to Accrington and a cab from there to Dalethorpe and arrived at half past six to find Carl in somewhat better shape than the previous day. He had insisted on sending his mother and siblings back to London and he wanted his life to continue just as his father would have wanted.

The two men ate their dinner in a fairly subdued silence. Thomas, before leaving that evening had read the file regarding Olaf and knew that this highly unpleasant matter must also be discussed with his late partner's son.

"Well, Carl," Thomas began when they were finally settled in the drawing-room. "We have two urgent matters to discuss and then your late father's estate."

Carl nodded. "Let us deal with the unpleasant stuff first," he suggested.

There was really only one unpleasant item on their agenda and that, of course, was the possible fate of Uncle Olaf.

"How much do you know about the trouble your uncle is in?" Thomas enquired.

"Most of it, I think," Carl replied grimacing.

"Then you will know that the police have two witnesses, a young man who was personally involved and a neighbour, Mr Charles Butterworth."

"Yes," Carl nodded. "My father felt that their evidence would be more than enough to send Uncle to prison for some time."

"Carl, I promise you that I will do my best to keep the family out of the limelight. Will you leave this matter with me?"

"Yes, of course and thank you," Carl replied feeling his eyes filling up again with tears.

"You have had a terrible time these last few weeks. Now would you like some good news?"

"Oh, yes please," Carl answered.

"Combined Lancashire Weavers have accepted your father's offer to buy the mills."

This was just too much for Carl and he started to sob out loud.

"I say, old chap," Thomas said, "That news was supposed to make you feel at least a little happier."

"Oh, it does," Carl replied, "It really does."

"So as you are now the senior trustee of the Oliver Family Trust, am I to proceed with the acquisition?"

"Yes, yes of course," Carl answered, pulling himself together.

CHAPTER THIRTY

A BIRTHDAY PARTY AND A WEDDING

A week later, Carl travelled to London to be present at the reading of his father's will. His late father's colleague Thomas Chichester and Carl were appointed joint executors. Generous provision had been made for his mother Olivia Oliver and educational trusts established for Carl's nine siblings. Carl Isaac had himself inherited a small fortune when his father had died prematurely and this he had transformed into a fairly large fortune. During his lifetime Carl Isaac had set up the Oliver Family Trust and this was the vehicle he used to ensure the future financial stability of the Olivers. And now the trust was to make its largest ever purchase, the business known as Combined Lancashire Weavers.

It took only a few more days for Thomas to confirm that the business was now theirs and Carl James returned to Dalethorpe to start work as the head of a large organisation. First however, he needed to acquaint his friend and mentor John Hardcastle about his new responsibilities. John took the news well enough although deep down he was a little jealous that his former pupil would now be in charge of a far larger business than that he himself controlled.

Then Carl visited the four mills and introduced himself as the new owner. The managers were all senior men and somewhat surprised to find that their new employer was 'little more than a lad' as they put it. Carl decided to base himself at his late Grandfather's mill just outside Dalethorpe. He worked tirelessly to build up the entire business and to show the managers that he knew exactly what it took to keep the weaving sheds running successfully. Little by little he gained their acceptance and respect and profits started to increase.

Carl was now, no longer, the carefree young man about town. Apart from his tremendous business responsibilities there were events in his recent past that had permanently destroyed his youth. He had seen his father, who he adored, die in a manner that made Carl feel personally responsible. The terrible guilty secret of how the boy Dominic had died and how he, Carl, had disposed of the body, lay heavily on his conscience. Indeed, every night when he went to bed, he glanced nervously through his bedroom window at the mound or at least its outline against the night sky. He had frequent recurring nightmares in which the boy Dominic appeared again covered in soil and shale and made his way towards the house. And then there was the second disappearance of Uncle Olaf.

The police had been obliged to release the former Vicar of St Barnabas when the main witness Dominic O'Reilly could not be found. The evidence of Charles Butterworth was excellent as corroboration of what the youth had to say, but on its own it was virtually useless. Olaf however, had not returned home, much to the secret relief it had to be said, of his nephew Carl. However Carl lived every day in the expectation of Olaf's return and this added to his discomfort.

Finally there was the memory of Rachel. Just one short meeting had ensured that her face, her smile, her voice and her entire demeanour were permanently engraved on his mind. He no longer thought of her every day but when he made a conscious effort to push all the other and unpleasant memories to the back of his mind, he would magic her image into his present and dream of meeting her once again.

Carl now lived to work rather than worked to live. He rarely took time off from the mill. It was not that the accumulation of wealth was the motivation; that was just a by-product of his single-minded devotion to business. It had been his father's dying wish that Carl should become a force to be reckoned with in the Lancashire textile industry and by the time he was thirty years old he was a vice-President of one trade association and treasurer of another.

Many of his friends and associates had taken to spending weeks away from their work either in Scotland, France or elsewhere to enjoy leisure activities. Carl only travelled if it was for business with the one exception of his birthday. Each year his mother insisted on making a family party in her Hampstead home to celebrate the occasion and Olivia was determined that when it came to her first-born son's thirtieth there should be a special celebration. By this time both Dalethorpe and Hampstead had installed the telephone and Olivia was delighted that now she could frequently hear her son's voice, all the way from Lancashire, coming down the somewhat crackly wire to her earpiece.

A month before his birthday his mother telephoned and told him, like it or not, she was organising a dinner and musical evening in her home to mark the occasion.

"Oh, come on Mother," Carl had pleaded, "what do you want to do that for?"

"It is because I am very proud of my oldest son and I want to introduce him to my friends," Olivia explained.

Carl could hardly argue. He tried to see his mother and siblings when he was in London on business but sometimes visits were months apart.

And so the day before his birthday found Carl on his way to St Pancras station in London. He arrived punctually and received an enthusiastic welcome not only from his mother but also from the three youngest siblings, still living at home.

The following day, Carl travelled into town to meet up with a customer from Italy anxious to place an order for cotton sheeting. One of his mills had installed wide looms capable of producing this fabric in quantity and Carl was delighted that the Italian had contracted to take the entire production for a year. He returned home to find that the servants had laid the table in the dining room for thirty four people. In addition the main lounge had chairs set out in two rows facing the piano where a musical entertainment was to take place after dinner. Carl had protested when his mother had told him of her plans over the telephone.

"Mamma, what do I need all this fuss for? I would be happy just to dine with you and my brothers and sisters, as we usually do on my birthday."

"Now Carl," his mother had said, "please indulge me. To have a son of thirty and one of whom I am so proud, is every reason to celebrate."

"Very well, Mamma," Carl had replied. Even a determined and successful man like Carl knew when he was beaten.

Carl dressed early for the formal dinner, in the manner that he knew his mother expected and arrived downstairs to await the arrival of the non-family guests an hour later. This was to enable him to spend a little time with his older siblings, now returned home for the occasions. The oldest of his brothers was Richard, just eighteen months his junior. He was now a qualified solicitor working in his late father's firm. He had married the previous year and Carl was glad to spend a little time with the couple. His sister, Clarice, was also married and although he knew his mother was not entirely happy with the choice of a son-in-law, Carl found the young man agreeable enough.

Eventually the guests began to arrive. They included a number of Olivia's best friends together with the new daughter-in-law and new son-in-law's parents. The last to arrive was his late father's colleague Thomas Chichester together with his wife and daughter Marjorie. She was a beautiful fair-haired young woman of twenty, dressed elegantly in the height of fashion. When the assembled party took their places at the dinner table, Carl found that his mother had placed him next to the lovely Marjorie. It must be said that no red-blooded young man could fail to be impressed and to enjoy the company of this delightful young lady. Carl was no exception and at the end of the evening he asked Thomas if he might have his permission to take Marjorie out for afternoon tea at the Ritz the following day before he returned to Dalethorpe. This was, of course, exactly what Thomas Chichester and Olivia Oliver had planned.

After his birthday party Carl suddenly found that visits to London were becoming more and more frequent. After a courtship of just four months Carl asked the delighted Thomas Chichester for the hand of his daughter Marjorie in marriage and not surprisingly the proposal was accepted with enthusiasm by the young lady and her parents.

Carl was indeed a happy man. All the problems of the last few years were fading to become just distant memories and with them the image of the entrancing Rachel ceased to be one to conjure up when he was in need of comfort. Marjorie was now his comfort and he knew that she would be a perfect wife for him. She was lovely to look at, a witty conversationalist and possessed of a kind and generous disposition. And both families were delighted with the match.

The wedding took place at the Church of St Ambrose in Hampstead and was a glittering affair graced by princes of industry and commerce, professional men of repute and a sprinkling of aristocracy.

Carl and Marjorie spent their wedding night in the fashionable Brown's Hotel in Albermarle Street in the district of Mayfair. This hotel had been enlarged by the acquisition of three additional neighbouring townhouses just three years earlier and was recognised as one of the best hotels in that most elegant area of London.

The following morning a cab collected them and drove them to Euston station where they caught the train to Bowness-on-Windermere. The new Mr & Mrs Oliver spent a rapturously happy week immersed in each others company and returned to Dalethorpe to begin married life together.

CHAPTER THIRTY ONE

DALETHORPE 1909-AN UNWELCOME VISITOR

Carl and Marjorie had been married for less than ten months when their first child, a daughter Alexandra Mary, was born. Although the old family house was still under-utilised, apart from the family of three, it now housed a nanny, a housekeeper, a housemaid and a cook. The old servant's quarters, not occupied for many years, were re-decorated and re-furbished to accommodate the additional members of staff. Mrs Hargreaves, who had so loyally looked after Carl and his uncle Olaf, was now a good age and she had been retired with a generous pension.

Carl had also instructed local trades-people to decorate the old nursery, the master bedroom and study. As a result the old house had not only come to life again but was now a most appropriate home for a mill owner, a man of substance and his family.

Six months later, Marjorie was again pregnant and seemed to be inheriting her mother-in-law's fecundity. Once again the Oliver clan was in expansionist mode.

It was a foggy evening in late November the following year and Carl and Marjorie had just finished dinner. Marjorie had two months previously presented Carl with a son to be christened Carl William. They had just finished their main course when the front-door bell rang. At considerable expense the electric light and electric door bell had recently been installed and instead of the clanging of the brass bell the family and servants were becoming accustomed to the high pitched ring of this new piece of modern equipment. Peggy the housemaid smoothed down her apron; patted her hair and trotted demurely to the front-door. A minute later she knocked timidly on the dining room door and entered to announce that there was a Mr Oliver at the door.

"Peggy," Marjorie answered a trifle irritably, "what do you mean Mr Oliver? You mean the caller wants to speak to Mr Oliver?"

"No, Madam," the girl replied, "he definitely said his name was Mr Oliver and could he see the master?"

"Did he look respectable?" Marjorie enquired.

"Oh yes Madam," Peggy commented. "Very smart indeed; nice overcoat and a nice coloured silk waistcoat."

Carl had been listening to this exchange and added his own interrogation of the increasingly nervous young woman.

"What age would you say this man is?" he asked.

"Oh, very old!" the maid replied. "He must be at least sixty."

Carl had a horrible idea that his growing suspicions regarding the identity of the caller would be confirmed and he replied,

"I will deal with this."

He leaped to his feet, almost spilling the cup of coffee that was all that remained of his dinner and he marched into the hall to discover a transformed Uncle Olaf standing in the doorway.

The defrocked former vicar of St Barnabas was dressed from top to toe in the latest fashion. He looked a picture of health and affluence as he strode towards his nephew. Carl could hardly believe what he was seeing; the transformation was frankly amazing. And when he spoke, his language and demeanour was almost unrecognisable.

"Carl, my dear boy," he began. "I have been meaning to visit you for some time now. Can I come in for a chat?"

Carl was an experienced businessman, an excellent communicator and he stood there wide-eyed and speechless until his natural good-manners forced him to a reply.

"Yes, yes, of course, please come in to the library. I will be with you in just a few minutes."

Carl called Peggy to take the visitor's coat and to escort the new arrival to the library.

"Peggy," Carl continued, "please offer Mr Oliver a cup of tea or coffee."

Carl strode back into the dining-room looking somewhat pale and shocked to see the unexpected visitor.

Marjorie studied him as he entered the room and said,

"Carl, what on earth is the matter? You look as if you have just seen a ghost."

Carl sat down heavily at the table and ignoring the almost cold coffee he poured himself a large brandy.

"Well my dear," he replied. "In a manner of speaking that is exactly what I have just seen-a ghost. The real life, flesh and blood ghost of my uncle Olaf, returned to haunt me."

"I doubt if I ever even told you that I had an uncle called Olaf. He behaved very badly some years ago and then disappeared, much to the relief of the whole family. Now, out of the blue he has turned up and I need to discover the reason for his visit."

"Shall I come in and meet him?" Marjorie enquired.

"No, finish your dinner in peace and I suggest you retire to bed. I will go and see what 'dear Uncle Olaf' wants," he finished, with heavy irony.

Marjorie looked at him anxiously.

"I trust he means you no harm," she said.

"No, I am sure he does not," Carl replied soothingly. "Please don't worry, he does not seem to be here to cause trouble and in any case I never gave him the slightest reason to do me ill; quite the reverse, in actual fact."

After downing the rest of his brandy, Carl made his way to the library.

Olaf was sitting comfortably in a leather armchair reading a copy of the Manchester Guardian. He looked up when Carl entered.

"Ah Carl my boy," he said. "It is so good to see you again. We have much to talk about."

"Have we, Uncle?" the nephew replied with heavy irony.

"Do you know that the shame and aggravation of what you did drove my father, your brother, to an early grave?"

"Yes, yes, was I not at the funeral?" Olaf replied. "However please do not blame me for his death. He was your father and he was also my brother. I would never have wished to harm him in any way."

Carl longed to tell Olaf the full story of the death of Carl Isaac but because of his own major part in the untimely demise of the young boy Dominic, that was impossible. Carl knew for certain that had the boy not been involved with Olaf, not only would the lad still be alive but also his beloved father, and Olaf would probably still be rotting in prison.

"I believe you are married to a charming wife and have a baby daughter and a baby son," Olaf continued.

"You are remarkably well informed for someone we assumed to be long dead," Carl answered.

"Oh, I have my sources," Olaf replied.

"And what sources would those be?" Carl demanded.

"Never mind that," Olaf responded.

Carl was having great difficulty in keeping his temper with this man; this prince of impertinence who had caused him so much agony and had now re-appeared with a totally uncharacteristic charm. What had happened to the boorish clergyman with his abrupt manners? However, Carl possessed normal human curiosity and needed to know how, where and when his uncle's life had been so changed.

CHAPTER THIRTY TWO

OLAF'S STORY

At the age of thirty five Olaf was still a virgin and he had long since realised that female beauty and allure held no interest for him. However, he had been aware of arousal when in proximity to young boys for some years before he finally succumbed. This event occurred in the same public toilets in Manchester which were eventually to be the scene of his downfall. It all started innocently enough with a call of nature. As he descended the steep stone steps he tripped and would have fallen to the ground if not for the presence of a young lad of about fifteen years.

"Hey, there," the boy said. "Bloody good job I was there to save you Reverend or you would have finished up flat on your face."

"Yes, yes, thank you," Olaf had replied

"'Ere, let me dust you down," the youth then said looking searchingly into Olaf's eyes and no doubt seeing fleetingly that this man seemed to be ready to welcome such attention. He proceeded to gently pat various parts of Olaf's anatomy to remove whitewash from the wall running alongside the steps until gradually the patting came nearer and nearer to the less relevant and more private and sensitive parts of the vicar's anatomy.

"Thank you, thank you," Olaf again muttered but, enjoying the attention, he made no attempt to terminate the encounter.

Then quite remarkably, Olaf allowed the youth to steer him into one of the 'spend a penny' lock up toilets where the vicar found himself enjoying an intimacy that he had previously never sought or understood. The lad was, of course, highly experienced and at the end of the event said,

"You seemed to enjoy that, Reverend. Maybe you would like to thank me with a little cash present."

From then on Olaf paid visits to a series of young men, at the toilets, whenever he had the opportunity. He knew that the bible said *'thou shalt not lie with mankind as with womankind'* but he convinced himself that as he was standing up (he could hardly do otherwise in the cramped space) this was not what the bible meant.

Detective Sergeant Jackson and Detective Constable Hopkins had both expended a considerable amount of time and effort to obtain a conviction in the case of the Rev Olaf Oliver. They both felt that the fact that he was a clergyman, allegedly a 'man of God' was all the more reason why he should be incarcerated for a considerable length of time in Strangeways Jail.

Sergeant Jackson felt particularly strongly for his own personal reasons. These went back to his own childhood when he had been betrayed by people who he should have been able to trust. He considered such evil to be the most despicable of all. Stealing the innocence of childhood was worse, in his eyes than the theft of any inanimate object and only murder itself was more reprehensible.

When their main witness Dominic failed to attend court to give evidence in a preliminary hearing against Olaf, both policemen feared the worst. Situations like this were not uncommon. They were relying on young boys from the dregs of society for help and frequently, in cases of this kind, the witnesses were virtually as guilty as the defendants. The address Dominic had supplied was a rooming house where the tenancies rarely lasted more than a few weeks. When they visited the house in the Hulme district, just as Sergeant Jackson had predicted, the 'bird had flown' the previous week. There was however, in the house another young man called Roger and he had known

Dominic from when the latter had been living at home with his parents in Red Bank. The two policemen quickly arranged a visit to the O'Reilly household in Thompson Street, but the father was unable to help.

"I've seen neither hide nor hair of that young rascal since he packed up and left two years ago," he told the policemen. Enquiries in the street confirmed that there had been no sightings of Dominic for that period so the trail ran cold.

From experience the two detectives knew that men like Olaf Oliver usually had more than one boy friend to look after their sexual perversions. The description of the vicar was therefore circulated through uniformed policemen on the beat who were instructed to interview boys, particularly in proximity to public toilets, who were known or suspected of acting as male prostitutes.

After four weeks of these enquiries the police were forced to release Olaf from remand and the details of the case were filed under 'unsolved crimes.'

Olaf was a free man. Somehow, during his time on remand, many of his fellow prisoners had discovered the details of his alleged crime and he had been forced to share a cell with another man guilty of similar behaviour. The two men, heartily detested by the thieves and murderers who made up the majority of the prison population, were thus protected from the undoubted physical injury that would have befallen them had they been allowed to mix with the other assorted criminals.

Olaf's cellmate was one Edgar Turner, a successful artist until convicted of an act of gross public indecency. He had been in prison for three years when Olaf arrived and was due for release two days before the police decided they could no longer hold the vicar. However, in the course of the few weeks when they had shared a cell they had become good friends and Edgar had suggested, without knowing how quickly this might happen, that Olaf would be welcome to visit him as a guest at his home in Victoria Park.

It was a matter of some surprise for Edgar, just a short time later, to discover Olaf on his doorstep, just as he was trying to pick up the threads of his own life. Edgar however, quite liked the quiet and normally unfriendly clergyman. Obviously they shared the same taste in young boys but apart from that, after years in prison surrounded by other and less well-educated dregs of society, Edgar had found it a relief to converse with someone, like himself, who had received a good education and had a good knowledge of the arts and literature.

"Olaf, my dear fellow, this is indeed a surprise; so have they let you go?" he wanted to know once they were seated in Edgar's elegant drawing room.

"Yes," he replied. "I am pleased to say that they seem to have lost their main witness."

"Well, that is good news. I hope he stays lost so that you can get on with your life," Edgar commented.

In the many hours they had spent together in the cell, completely isolated from every other human being, the two men had told each other their life stories. Olaf found this a new and liberating experience. As a child and growing up in Dalethorpe he had always felt intimidated by his older brother with his quiet charm and intelligence. He had more and more found his solace in the bible and the vast array of writings on the subject of Christianity. When his parents had suggested a career in the Church this seemed to be a way to make something out of his life. His older brother by that time was well on the way to becoming a brilliant lawyer and he expected that his parents would express similar pride in his achievements in Ecclesiastical College. He was certainly gaining knowledge about his religion and his chosen career as a clergyman but where Carl Isaac had been pleasant and friendly at Law School with staff and fellow students, Olaf, probably as a result of shyness, appeared gauche, unfriendly and almost rude.

When he was appointed Vicar of St Barnabas, he suspected, quite rightly, as it transpired, that it was because of his family connection to the village. In his new position he made little or no effort to communicate with his parishioners. When in the pulpit he gave excellent, erudite sermons that lacked humour and warmth. Outside the church he greeted his fellow villagers courteously but coldly and it soon became evident that the Parish Council had made a huge mistake in appointing him. They were, however, not about to offend the Oliver family who were to all intents and purposes the local squires and year in, year out, the Vicar and his flock continued to exist in a kind of unarmed truce.

His relationship with women was even more disastrous than with men. He had lost his father during his formative years and his mother appeared to be heaping all her love on his big brother. By the time he joined college, he had become a confirmed misogynist.

"So," Edgar continued. "Do you have somewhere to stay?"

"Actually, no," Olaf replied. "I can hardly go back to the vicarage. I will just have to find a cheap room in a lodging house."

"No, no," Edgar responded. "That won't do at all. You must stay here." He paused for a moment. "Actually I know someone who is looking for a clerk. It is a textile business in town and an educated man like you could do that job in his sleep."

So Mr Olaf Oliver joined the firm of Hartley and Abrahams, textile shippers, and sat at a large mahogany desk on a high swivel stool to enter the transactions of the company in a huge leather bound ledger. The two partners in the business were delighted to have such a well educated man as an employee and were so impressed at interview that they waived away Olaf's offer to obtain references, little knowing that had those been supplied, they would undoubtedly have been forgeries.

Hartley & Abrahams purchased their orders for cotton cloth from Lancashire mills. They then either shipped them in the grey (unfinished) state or had them commission dyed and finished for their customers abroad. Olaf's responsibilities included keeping ledgers and preparing invoices and most importantly keeping track of every yard of cloth received and processed until the order was shipped out.

Unbelievably it took Olaf some two years working there before he noticed that the name of the owner of one of their main suppliers, Combined Lancashire Weavers was Carl James Oliver. *Why had he never noticed this before* he wondered? *So this is my nephew and he must be a very wealthy man,* he decided and resolved to visit him. He chatted to the driver of the lorry that brought the next delivery of grey cloth from the mill to the warehouse and soon confirmed that Carl was married with two young children and still lived in the old family home, known, thanks to his domicile there, as the Vicarage.

Olaf's relationship with Edgar had now deteriorated as a result of the arrival of a young homosexual man called Peter Ashton. Edgar had originally made his acquaintance at a Picture Gallery on Portland Street. Initially the attraction was one based upon their sharing a love of oil painting but Edgar suspected that Peter was also interested in him physically and they started to explore each others sexuality. Then Edgar asked Peter to move in to his home in Victoria Park and quite understandably Olaf knew that his own relationship with Edgar was over. Naturally Olaf did not give in without a fight but Edgar made his lack of interest in the older man very obvious and started to drop broad hints about Olaf seeking accommodation elsewhere. It was then that Olaf decided he could no longer delay approaching his wealthy nephew with a view to returning to the old family house in Dalethorpe and obtaining well-paid employment with him.

He knew that he would hardly be welcomed with open arms but he had a few ideas about how he could 'persuade' Carl James to co-operate.

Chapter Thirty three

Blackmail

Carl James sat back in his armchair surveying his renegade uncle. *He has caused us all so much anguish; how dare he turn up here like this,* he pondered. Carl was now an experienced businessman and used to negotiating contracts with powerful men from across the globe but he was totally unprepared for what was to follow.

"Well!" He decided to take the proverbial bull by the horns, "what do you want?"

"Is that any way to welcome your old uncle?" Olaf replied.

"Look," Carl continued. "There is no question of welcoming you here. Please understand that as far as you are concerned, the word 'welcome' does not exist in my vocabulary. What you did was totally unforgivable."

Olaf looked grave and angry.

"You might be interested to know that I am the purchasing manager for Hartley & Abrahams," Olaf lied, "and even if you have no respect for me as an uncle, please be aware that I could easily ensure that you will receive no more orders from my firm."

Carl was now really angry. How dare this man who had so disgraced the family come here and start threatening him.

"I suggest you get out of here before I throw you out," Carl replied rising from his armchair and standing over the still seated figure of his uncle.

Olaf had only one more card to play and it was a complete bombshell.

"So you want to do to me what you did to Dominic, do you?"

In actual fact Olaf had discovered some time ago, from one of the other young male prostitutes, that Dominic had told this boy that he was going to see Olaf's brother and nephew on that fateful night. After that he was never seen again, a fact that saved Olaf from gaol. Olaf had wondered if his brother or nephew was responsible for Dominic's disappearance. The reaction he now received from Carl almost confirmed his suspicion.

Carl stepped back and slumped into his armchair. His face was pale and he felt a wave of nausea washing over him. However, he knew he must brazen this out.

"What are you talking about?" he eventually demanded. "Are you going out of your mind? And who on earth is Dominic?"

Olaf also was equally determined to carry on his bluff. Carl had certainly seemed shocked when he had made the accusation.

"You know quite well who Dominic is or was. I know he came here to see you while I was in prison and you must have murdered him to protect your wonderful family name."

"You are talking absolute rubbish," Carl replied regaining his equilibrium.

"Just get out of here. I never want to see you again."

"Sorry my dear boy," Olaf replied with deep irony. "I need a home and a good income and if you do not provide all this, you will find the place crawling with members of the constabulary."

"You have three days to come to some arrangement with me. I will come back again on Thursday evening."

Olaf pulled himself out of the deep armchair and strode out of the library and across the hall to the front door. Carl followed him. He opened the door and watched the defrocked vicar walk down the stone steps, and across the garden to a cab that had been waiting for him out on the road.

Deeply shocked and desperately worried, Carl returned to the library and poured himself a large glass of Scotch whisky. He then sat down and started to examine every word that had been exchanged in this selfsame room just a few minutes earlier.

How could Olaf know anything of the events of the night when both his father and Dominic had died? He anguished. The boy had definitely arrived alone. Olaf had been under lock and key in gaol and the only witness to the boy's death had been his own beloved father and he had died from the shock of seeing what had transpired. Olaf must be bluffing but he seemed so definite in his accusation. Dare Carl take the huge gamble with his own life of calling the evil uncle's bluff?

When he returned to the dinner table Marjorie was still sitting there with an anxious expression on her lovely face.

"I thought you said he meant you no harm," she ventured. "If I am to judge by your raised voice coming from the library that was certainly not the case!"

She peered into the face of her husband, normally so calm and controlled but the warm smile that he always had ready for her, was absent.

"I think you had better tell me what this is all about," she continued.

"Dear, dear Marjorie, I would love to tell you the whole horrible story but I feel I would be failing in my duty as a loving husband, if I burdened you with such information. It could even incriminate you."

She stared deeply into his eyes.

"And I feel I would be failing in my duty as your loving wife if I did not share your obvious pain."

Carl managed a sad watery smile and said,

"I must think this through. Let us have coffee in the drawing room and I will give you my answer. Please, my darling," he continued. "If I decide not to tell you, it will be for your sake and the sake of our family and I beseech you to understand."

They drank their coffee virtually in silence and it broke Marjorie's heart to see her dear husband so tormented.

Eventually Marjorie broke the silence.

"Please Carl, I cannot bear to see you like this; you must tell me what this is all about."

Carl looked into his wife's face. She was troubled, very troubled even without the information; what would it do to her to learn that her husband had killed a young man, albeit unintentionally? On the other hand, she was a sensible well-adjusted young woman and he knew her dedication to him was absolute.

"I am going to tell you the whole story," he said with a heavy heart. "Please try to listen and understand and only interrupt me for clarification of any point you do not understand."

Carl leaned forward in his chair and proceeded to tell Marjorie of all the events that had led up to tonight's confrontation.

He started with the visit of the police and tried to include every detail in the account of what had transpired. To say Marjorie was shocked to hear that Carl's uncle, a vicar, had been indulging in homosexual activities in a public toilet and with a minor, would be an understatement. She gasped and gasped again and then she shuddered as the tale unfolded. However, when Carl told her of how he had personally caused the death, albeit accidentally, of the young man Dominic, she burst into tears.

Carl rose from his seat and held her to him, to try and soothe her obvious heartbreak. Eventually she stopped crying and bade him to continue but when he explained how he had buried the boy's body in the mound, she again began to weep.

Little by little, Carl recounted all the facts including the demands that Olaf had made that very evening. When he had finished he poured himself a large glass of Scotch whisky and a glass of port for Marjorie. He sat back in his chair, absolutely drained and waited for some comment from his wife.

After just a few minutes she said,

"Together, we are going to beat this. We both need a good night's sleep and a clear head before we can decide on a strategy, but believe me my darling, we will beat this and send that evil man packing."

Marjorie may have suggested a good night's sleep, but that was now impossible. They both lay awake, turning over and over in their minds the huge problem they now faced.

At breakfast Marjorie suggested that Carl should go off to work as usual and they would discuss that evening what tactics they needed to employ to remove Olaf from their lives.

Marjorie spent the day in the nursery with her two babies and their Nanny. The latter, one Mrs Godfrey, found her mistress to be somewhat preoccupied but would never have considered it was her place to comment. Carl spent the day in meetings with a succession of suppliers and customers. This was a blessing as it enabled him to push to the back of his mind, the dilemma awaiting him at home.

He was now the proud owner of a Standard 30hp Model 'G' Cabriolet Motor Car which he normally liked to drive himself. However, today he was happy to let Kenneth, the company chauffeur drive the few miles from the office to Dalethorpe and he sat back in the rear passenger seat of the vehicle, agonising on the situation.

Carl reached home to find Marjorie awaiting his arrival on the top step outside the open front door.

He jumped out of the car and bounded up the steps to plant an affectionate kiss on her cheek. He studied her expression and was amazed to see that her usual serenity seemed to have returned to her.

"How are you my love?" he enquired.

"Very well thank you my dearest," she replied with a smile. "And how are you?"

"Much better for seeing you," he commented. "Shall we go inside?"

"Listen darling," Marjorie then ventured. "Let us have dinner and then we can talk. I have been giving the situation a lot of thought and maybe, in your shock, you have been over-reacting."

Dinner was eaten in silence punctuated by frequent little re-assuring smiles for Carl, from his dear wife. As soon as the meal was finished Marjorie suggested that they retire to the drawing room.

As soon as they were seated Marjorie said,

"First, my darling, I have a few questions for you,"

"Ask away," Carl replied.

"Do you have any idea why it is only now that Olaf has decided to demand money from you?"

"No," Carl replied, "but that is a question that would bear some investigation."

"Do you know if Olaf had pleaded not guilty to the charge that police brought against him? He must have done," she continued, "or he would have been locked up, with or without Dominic's evidence."

"Yes, that is undoubtedly so," her husband replied smiling as he realised the implication of what his wife had just said.

"Oh, you clever, clever girl," Carl continued. "So how can he go to police and accuse me of murdering someone, whose very existence in his life, he denies?"

"Exactly," Marjorie confirmed. "However, he is still, whether we like it or not, a member of the family. We do need find a way of removing him from our lives-I don't mean by murdering him!" She giggled.

"I would love to," Carl interjected, "but I would rather stay around to see our children growing up and enjoy our life together; one killing, although unintentional, is one too many for me."

"So," Marjorie continued. "We need to find out what this awful man is doing; where he lives and how he earns a living."

"I know the answer to the second part of that question," Carl volunteered. "He told me he works as a purchasing manager for Hartley & Abrahams, textile shippers. They are customers of ours and I have to say that I have never seen him in their office on Princess Street in Manchester, when I have called there."

"If he really is a purchasing manager, surely you would have had dealings with him?" Marjorie commented.

"Yes, I would have thought so," Carl confirmed thoughtfully. "So my first job tomorrow is to drive down to Manchester and call at Hartley & Abrahams."

Carl sat back in his armchair feeling relieved. The threats of Olaf had not yet been removed but, thanks to his dear wife, the situation now looked much more encouraging.

"I know your father is a brilliant lawyer and I can now see that apart from being a wonderful wife and mother, you have inherited a first class legal brain," Carl commented. "Thank you my darling, I think I will sleep tonight!"

CHAPTER THIRTY FOUR

CALLING ON A CUSTOMER

Carl decided to drive himself down to Manchester and by half past ten he was parking the Standard Cabriolet in Faulkner Street, just around the corner from the offices of Hartley & Abrahams. He strode briskly through the front door of the building and entered the ground floor suite of offices. A passageway led him to an enquiry window with a large, highly polished brass bell sitting alongside. He struck the bell briskly and the window opened. A young office boy who he had seen before greeted him.

"Mr Oliver isn't it?" the lad enquired.

"Yes that is right," Carl replied smiling. "Is Mr Abrahams available?"

"Yes, certainly sir," the boy replied. "I will just go and tell him you are here."

Within a minute a door further along the corridor opened and out came Jack Abrahams.

"Why, Carl," he greeted his supplier. "This is indeed a surprise. Did we have a meeting arranged for today?"

"No," Carl answered. "I was in the area and with half an hour to spare I thought I would come in to report to you personally on your new order for cotton cambric."

"Well come in, come in, my dear fellow," Jack Abrahams replied.

He was about the same age as Carl but where the Olivers could trace their family back for generations, Jack was the son of Jewish immigrants who had arrived in England in the middle of the previous century to carry on their previously Frankfurt-on-Main based textile business. Manchester, at that time, was the world centre for cotton textiles and hence attracted business men from all over the world to settle there and expand their businesses.

Both Carl and Jack were totally dedicated to their firms and apart from their families had just one other interest in common and that was cricket. They rarely had times to attend games but their support for the Lancashire team was enthusiastic and unconditional.

Whenever the two men were together their preliminary chat, before 'getting down to business,' would always be on the subject of how their team was performing and today was no exception.

Eventually Carl gave Jack the news that was the excuse for the visit; the yarn had arrived for the cambric order and weaving would commence next week. There would therefore be no problem in making the deliveries in accordance with the contract.

Now the time had come to broach the subject that had brought Carl there in the first place.

"The last time I telephoned to speak to you, the phone was answered by a Mr Oliver," Carl lied. "He has the same name as me and I wondered who he was?"

"Oh, Oliver the clerk," Jack replied. "I would very much doubt if he has any connection with your family. He is a strange man and between you and me, I suspect he is a bit of a pervert. I had a complaint last week from one of the office boys but it turned out to be a just a suspicion and I had to drop the matter for lack of evidence. However, I am going to get rid of him as soon as possible."

That was all Carl needed to know. He thanked Jack for seeing him without prior notice and was informed that he was always welcome at the offices of Hartley & Abrahams.

"Always a pleasure to see you, my dear chap," Jack told him as he escorted him out of the office.

Chapter Thirty five

Injured Innocence!

Carl spent the remainder of Wednesday back at his office and Thursday was 'Change day when, like his Grandfather many years before, he attended the Cotton Exchange in Manchester to meet his clients and suppliers. This business activity kept his mind from brooding but quite understandably, Carl was dreading the return visit of his uncle Olaf. However, now, largely thanks to the clear thinking of his wife Marjorie, he had prepared a strategy to deal with the de-frocked vicar.

With the two children duly tucked up in their cots, and under the supervision of their nanny in the room adjoining the nursery, Carl and Marjorie had an early dinner. By half past seven they were sitting in the drawing room sipping their coffee and awaiting the arrival of a most unwelcome guest. Carl normally had a glass of cognac after dining but this night, anxious to retain a clear head, he refrained. As the evening passed by with the grandfather clock in the hall announcing the time every quarter of an hour, when nine o'clock struck, they were both convinced that Olaf had thought better of his plan. However, at ten past nine the front-door bell rang. The maid had already been warned that a Mr Oliver would be visiting and should be ushered into the library when he arrived. Peggy opened the front door, enquired the name of the visitor, took his coat and hat and showed him into the designated room. She then entered the drawing room to tell Carl that the 'gentleman' he was expecting had arrived and was in the library.

Carl rose from the comfort of his armchair, a trifle reluctantly, gave his wife a sad little smile and went to join his uncle.

As soon as Carl entered the library, Olaf, in an attempt at common courtesy, apologised for his late arrival. Then he launched into what was obviously a carefully prepared speech.

"Carl, my dear fellow," he began. "I am sorry we got off to such a bad start on Monday evening. I am still broken-hearted over the death of your dear father, my beloved and respected brother. No one could have known how bad his heart was and I am sure you did not mean it when you blamed me.

"As you know, I was wrongly accused by the police of some irregularities but, as I was innocent the case was dropped but not before I had spent some time in prison. However, the Bishop, with a total lack of Christian charity, believed the accusations and I was dismissed as the Vicar of St Barnabas-by-Dalethorpe. As a consequence my life was ruined and now I work as a Manager for a textile firm with whom you are well acquainted."

Carl listened to this mixture of truth, half-truth and utter lies with growing impatience.

"So did that justify you coming here on Monday evening demanding money and making threats if I did not co-operate?"

"Carl, Carl, please hear me out," Olaf replied. "You misunderstood me the other evening. All I was trying to say was that blood is thicker than water and I was hoping for a little compassion from my wealthy nephew."

"Tell me Uncle," Carl replied. "So you are a purchasing manager at Hartley & Abrahams. Is it not curious that, being good customers of mine, I never heard your name or had any dealings with you when negotiating contracts?"

"That was because you always dealt with either Mr Brian Hartley or Mr Jack Abrahams," Olaf answered.

That was not altogether true but Carl had received a telephone call earlier in the afternoon telling him that Olaf had again been propositioning one of the office boys. As a result Jack Abrahams had summarily dismissed him. He no longer worked for the textile firm in any capacity whatsoever. However Carl decided not to let Olaf know that he was aware that he had lost his job. The time had arrived to see how the wicked uncle's far more important threat could be contained.

"Tell me Uncle," Carl began again. "Who is this Dominic you mentioned on Monday? Whoever he is, do you now deny that you accused me of killing him?"

"Dominic was the main witness in my trial, the one that never happened and you misunderstood me if you thought I was accusing you of such a terrible crime.

"All I want, my dear nephew," Olaf continued, an example of the affable uncle who had fallen on hard times, "is a little short term help with accommodation, unless you would allow me to move back in here with you? And maybe a little cash, as a loan of course."

Carl marvelled at the impertinence of the man.

"So tell me again, who is Dominic and how do you know him?" Carl replied.

"I have no idea who he is," Olaf informed him. "I had never heard of him until the police said he was to give evidence against me."

"So now we have it. This mysterious Dominic was to be a witness at your trial but you had never heard of him. How then did you get the idea that he visited me and was never seen again? Who told you that?"

Olaf was beginning to squirm and Carl could see beads of perspiration forming on the older man's forehead.

"I just heard that he came here," he stammered.

"Just heard?" Carl answered. "What did you have, a divine revelation?

"If you really think I am a murderer, you should go to the police at once. In fact why not telephone them from here?"

Olaf was now standing and looking uncomfortably at the door of the library.

"I think I had better be going," he stuttered.

"Not so fast," Carl told him. "Please understand that I never want to see you again and if you make any attempt to approach me or my family in the future, it will be I who will call the police."

"Just one other thing; instead of trying to extort money from me you would be far better employed in seeking a new job and home, as far away from here as possible. Did it never occur to you that Jack Abrahams would tell me about your disgusting behaviour in the office and that you had now been dismissed?"

And that was the last time that the defrocked vicar of St Barnabas set foot in his old vicarage for many a long year.

Carl returned to the drawing-room, a broad smile on his face.

"He has gone," he told his wife, "and I don't think we will ever hear from him again."

Chapter Thirty six

1914-War Efforts

Carl and Marjorie watched anxiously as the dark clouds of war were gathering over Europe. All through the spring and summer the Manchester Guardian and the London Times, together with all the other British newspapers had carried stories about the way that Austria-Hungary and Germany had attacked first Serbia and then finally France. Russia had entered the conflict on the side of their fellow Slavs in Serbia and now Belgium in the west and Poland in the east were falling foul of the Teutonic war machine. On the fourth of August the inevitable happened and Great Britain declared war on the aggressors.

The good folk of Lancashire in company with the rest of the country were determined to be thoroughly involved in the war effort. The finest young men from the mill towns lined up to volunteer to fight the 'Hun.' In nearby Accrington large numbers flocked to the colours and were given the appellation of 'the Accrington Pals.'

Carl James Oliver was now nearly thirty-six years old and as a captain of industry had obviously received no military training. However, he immediately contacted his old school friend Colonel Bridges and told him he was ready to play his part in quickly disposing of the enemy and imposing a Pax Britannica on all of Europe. Such was the mood at the time. Most of the men now assembling to go over to France had been told that Great Britain could and would make short work out of defeating Germany and her allies and they should all expect to be home for Christmas. How tragically and terribly wrong they were!

Colonel Bridges had told Carl to go back home and await further instructions. As the days went by and the nearby towns emptied of their young men Carl wondered why he had not been called for. Then in the third week he received two interesting visits. The first was from a senior civil servant from the War office and he told Carl that rather than being sent to fight at the front, he could best serve his country by turning over the entire production of his mills to weaving fabrics for uniforms. In addition, the government would like him to take charge of all procurement of textile fabrics, needed by the armed forces, from the entire Lancashire area. Carl protested that he wanted to fight but had to agree to the appointment when it was explained how important he would be to the war effort and the morale of the forces.

His other visitor was his friend and customer Jack Abrahams. Carl knew that Jack's family had originated in Frankfurt-on-Main in Germany but that was some fifty years earlier. He told Jack that he had volunteered to join the British Army. He also explained that when he told his commanding officer that he had been brought up in a house where German was the first language, he had been told, like Carl, to return home and await further instructions.

It then transpired that Jack had received a visit from two men from the War office in London who asked him to agree to be sent over to the continent and to make his way to Frankfurt. Once there he was to contact his cousins still living there and volunteer to join the German army and become a spy for the British.

"I am telling you this in strict confidence," Jack explained. "Even my wife and children are not to know what I am doing. As far as they are concerned I am to be sent to France as an army officer to interrogate German prisoners. I obtained permission to confide in you because I want to ask you to stay in frequent touch with Amelia, my wife, to ensure that she is spared, as much as possible from the problems occasioned by my absence. If I fail to return, which is very likely, if the Germans realise what I am doing,

I know I can count on you to make sure that the family will be financially secure."

Carl answered reassuringly that he would be proud and honoured to do this.

Jack then peered searchingly into Carl's face and said, "There is another reason why I was authorised to tell you the real details of my expedition."

"And what is that?" Carl replied.

"I am afraid that must await a meeting in London with my commanding officer and which he requires you to attend with me."

A week later, Carl and Jack were on the train to London for a meeting at the War Office.

Jack's commanding officer, Colonel Henry Waterman had been born in Hamburg and as a child at school had been known as Heinrich Wasserman. When he was eight years old his parents had decided to immigrate to England and had settled in London. Like Jack, his parents were Jewish and felt that they could live a better and more fulfilling life on the western side of the North Sea.

Henry had been sent to an English public school and thence to Cambridge to read Politics and Philosophy. Like many German Jews his parents were not particularly religious and when the young Henry had said that he would like to make a career in the British Army, they were proud that he wanted to serve his adopted country in this way. Now, like Jack, his Germanic origin was to be of inestimable use. As a result he had been ordered to recruit a number of young men of German origin to return to the native land of their families to spy on behalf of Great Britain.

A pasty-faced young soldier ushered Jack and Carl into an oak panelled meeting room and asked them to sit at the end of a long table to await the Colonel who duly arrived full of apologies and affability.

Carl and Jack rose when he entered the room to be told,

"Please sit down gentlemen. Let us get down to business.

"I gather," the officer continued, addressing Carl, "that Jack has told you, in strict confidence what his mission is to be."

Carl nodded gravely.

"I must tell you that before Jack was authorised to give you any information, we were obliged to undertake some investigation of your background. However, I quickly discovered that you are to work for the British Government to organise the entire Lancashire textile industry for the War Effort. I can now tell you that this will not be your only appointment.

"Wherever possible, information that Jack and his colleagues obtain regarding the enemy, will be transmitted through a number of secret channels, to this building. However, matters relating to any German espionage groups operating in the north of England will be dealt with separately and a small group of counter-espionage operatives is being recruited in Manchester. We would like you to head this group."

"But I have absolutely no experience of military or espionage matters," Carl protested. "I am an industrialist."

"You may never be called upon, but if you are, your responsibilities would be administrative and organisational. You are the right man for the job and that is that.

"I would like you to undertake a course of training here in London. Once you have appointed assistants for your other work, I will need you back here. Shall we say in one month's time?"

CHAPTER THIRTY SEVEN

TILLY

Carl took the opportunity to visit his mother in Hampstead before returning to Lancashire. He found Olivia in good health but frantic with worry that no less than four of her sons, Carl's brothers, had joined up. As educated men they were quickly given commissions and sent over to France.

"We live in terrible times," Olivia told her first-born. "I am only relieved that you have had more sense than to participate in this madness."

"I must tell you Mamma," Carl replied. "I tried to join the army but instead they appointed me head of all textile production in Lancashire, to supply our forces with uniforms."

"Well thank God for that," Olivia exclaimed.

Needless to say Carl made no mention of his 'other' job, the one that had brought him to London.

Olivia wanted to know all about her, now four, grandchildren in Dalethorpe and regained her usual bubbling enthusiasm as Carl told the proud grandmother about his offspring.

"As soon as possible, Marjorie and I will bring them to London to see you," he promised.

The next few months were spent in a frenzy of activity as he arranged for vast numbers of looms throughout the county to be turned over to production for the armed forces.

He had explained to Marjorie that his friend Jack Abrahams had made him promise to frequently visit Jack's wife Amelia. Marjorie had instantly volunteered to accompany him and one evening each week they visited her at her home in Broughton Park, Salford.

The Standard Cabriolet that had been Carl's pride and joy was replaced by a strong, sober car, more suitable for wartime. It was the Crossley 20/25, built in Gorton Manchester. Carl knew that large numbers of these cars were being supplied to the Royal Flying Corps and he felt that if the car was good enough for the newest branch of the army, it was good enough for him.

He was obliged, nowadays, to drive himself as Carl's chauffeur Kenneth had joined up on the day that war was declared. Many of the younger male workers in the mills had followed him. As a result a significant number of jobs previously done by men were now being undertaken by women. However Lancashire's looms were churning out their orders for the war effort with their hard-working female operatives and Carl had matters well under control.

Tragically 1915 came and went and the stories of the carnage at the front were filtering back to the folks at home. It was now recognised that this was a fight to the death and that Germany and her allies would be no push-over.

Carl telephoned his mother at least once a week and was shocked to learn that his brother Lieutenant Gerald Oliver had been gravely wounded and was lying in a field hospital in Northern France. As for the other three brothers, there had been no news for months and all the family could do was to hope and pray for their safe return.

Carl had long since finished his training for his other job, in anti-espionage. It was now 1916 and he had begun to think that his services would never be required. That was until he received a telephone call from London asking him to attend a meeting that night at the Central Police Station in Manchester. He parked the Crossley nearby and entered. He approached the reception desk and told the elderly sergeant who looked as if he had been brought out of retirement, that he was there for a meeting. The phone call from London had instructed him not to state his real name and simply to tell the policeman on duty that he was Mr Weaver.

"Oh, yes Sir," the Sergeant replied briskly. "This way please."

He entered the room to find five men and one young woman seated at a table obviously awaiting his arrival. They all stood up to greet him and one of the men gestured to him to take the seat at the top of the table.

"Please sit down," he told them. "You all know who I am. Can I know your names please, the code names you have been allocated will do fine?"

The man who had gestured to him to take the chair introduced himself as Jimmy and then proceeded to introduce the others as Bobby, Johnny, Charlie and Percy. Finally he introduced the lady as Tilly.

All five people then fixed their gaze on him and waited for Carl to open the proceedings.

"My name is Clarence Weaver," he began using his code name. "I gather that you, Jimmy, have some important information for us. Please now report."

"Some time ago, the War Office counter-espionage section, obtained a job for me at Crossley Motors in Gorton," Jimmy explained. "Apart from supplying the Royal Flying Corp with their 20/12 the company has secretly been working on an armoured version with caterpillar tracks. Yesterday it was reported to me that some of the plans had been stolen. Two men working on the production line failed to report for work this morning and my investigations disclosed that they had both given the factory, fictitious names which obviously made them prime suspects. I visited the address they had supplied when they started work and discovered that neither of them was known there, either by name or description."

"Have you reported all this to the local police?" Carl enquired.

"Yes Sir," Jimmy answered. "London told us to simply say that two men had gone missing with some plans but not to say what the plans were."

"So is that it?" Carl enquired looking very concerned. *This is my first case and it looks as if it is doomed from the start,* he thought. "You have two missing men who have almost certainly stolen plans that would be most useful to the enemy and you have no way of tracing them."

"No, that is not altogether true," the lady called Tilly interjected. Carl had found that ever since he had entered the room, his eyes had kept wandering towards her. She was certainly worth looking at with her black hair, her deep brown, almond shaped eyes and her slightly curved nose. Her skin tone was Olive which simply helped to increase her exotic appearance. She must have been in her mid to late thirties, Carl decided, and he was sure that he had genuinely seen her before somewhere. He was, of course, a happily married man but that did not stop him admiring feminine beauty. However, once she spoke all manner of emotions came flooding back. That voice; he knew that voice and it awakened in him long dormant memories.

The five men around the table were regarding him with consternation. Why had he ignored Tilly's offer to supply information? He just sat there, as in a trance, until he suddenly realised that the enchanting lady had more to impart.

"Please tell us, err, Tilly, what information you have," he all but stammered.

"I work in the entertainment business and one of the instructions we have is to check out young men under the age of forty one. As you know, since conscription started, there are far less young men around. However, our agents in the pubs, music-halls and bars, on the lookout for both deserters and spies, have identified six young men who, shall we say, require further investigation. It may turn out that none of these are the Crossley men but I hope to have more information within the next two or three days."

Carl had now recovered his equilibrium and answered briskly,

"Excellent! I am sure you realise that these men must be found and found quickly, before they can take the plans back to Germany; this matter is now extremely urgent."

"Yes, of course Sir," Tilly replied.

Jimmy then reported that the police had already been supplied with descriptions of the suspects and told to keep a close watch on long-distance buses and railway stations.

Various other options were discussed and the meeting ended. Carl then suggested that they must meet again, two nights later, to review progress.

As the meeting broke-up he wondered if Tilly had recognised him but decided against speaking to her privately. She certainly gave no indication that she was aware that their paths had previously passed. Carl, however, was convinced that Tilly was in reality his beloved Rachel, the girl of his dreams who he had only met once and that was ten years ago. Now in the middle of this dreadful nightmare of a war it looked as if their lives had once again connected.

Carl was a devoted family man with serious responsibilities to his country and industry. He adored his wife and children and he was a totally different person, in every way, to the young playboy of yesteryear. As he drove home to Dalethorpe he pondered on the strange act of fate that had brought Rachel, if indeed Tilly really was Rachel, back into his life.

The second meeting was scheduled for the same venue and Carl arrived early. This time the desk sergeant had been told to expect him and greeted him by the assumed name that he had been instructed to use.

"Good evening Mr Weaver, I have a message for you. Miss Tilly will not be able to attend the meeting tonight as she is still investigating the suspects."

Carl could not help but feels pangs of disappointment. A second later, however, he heard the outer-door of the police station open and spun round to see Jimmy coming towards him, grinning from ear to ear.

"It looks like we have the bastards," Jimmy confided. "The meeting is cancelled and London has instructed us all to go to Flossie's Bar in Ancoats. Tilly is already there."

"Right then," Carl replied. He had no intention of having any contact with Tilly on a personal basis but the news that he was to see her again, filled him with joy.

"And where are the others?" he continued.

"Bobby and Johnny are waiting there," Jimmy informed him and the other two are now involved in another investigation."

"Do you have a motor-car?" Carl enquired as they left the stuffy atmosphere of the police station.

"No Sir," Jimmy replied, "but I have a bicycle."

"Well dump it in the back and come with me in the Crossley, "Carl instructed.

"Sir, it is strange how coincidences occur," Jimmy remarked. "Of all the different makes of cars, you had to choose Crossley. It is, of course a wonderful machine but when you consider we are investigating the theft of plans from the manufacturers Crossley Motors, it is indeed quite strange."

"Certainly is," Carl replied, as they made their way down Portland Street. However, Carl was also thinking of the other and even more amazing coincidence, that Rachel seemed to have re-appeared after so many years absence.

Flossie's Bar in Ancoats was in a particularly rough part of town. The sign over the front was barely legible with its peeling paint. Fortunately a gas-light was situated on the pavement just outside which enabled the two men to confirm that they had the correct venue. Over the front entrance was a sign confirming that one Flossie Flanagan was licensed to sell Beer and Alcoholic beverages. The interior of the bar was dimly lit and Carl could just make out the outline of three women perched on bar stools and downing large tankards of ale. Women on their own in pubs and bars in those days meant only one thing. They must be prostitutes he decided, waiting for customers.

Then he saw Tilly, Bobby and Johnny sitting at a table in the far corner of the room. Of the two suspects, however, there was no sign. Carl and Jimmy crossed the room with the former feeling most conspicuous in his beautifully cut suit. Fortunately, apart from the three 'ladies' and the barmaid there were none of the criminal fraternity present who would normally frequent such a place.

Carl sat down at the table sandwiched between Jimmy and Bobby and leaned forward conspiratorially,

"So where are they," he whispered.

"Upstairs," Bobby replied.

"What do you mean, upstairs?" Carl asked, looking around for a staircase.

"To go upstairs you have to go through to the back room behind the bar." Bobby explained.

"So how do you know it is them?" Carl enquired.

"Dolores," come over here, Bobby called over to one of the women at the bar.

"This is Dolores, one of Tilly's girls," Bobby said. "Dolores, this is our boss Mr Weaver. Please sit down and tell us about the two men upstairs."

Dolores was either a genuine lady of the night or her disguise as such was superb. Her hair was peroxide bleached and she was made-up with far too generous amounts of face powder and blusher with bright red lipstick looking like a blood-red gash on the lower part of her face. She was wearing a low-cut dress that emphasised her ample bosom and it was therefore something of a surprise to find that she spoke in a cultured and articulate manner.

"I have a room upstairs in this pub," she began. "Our job is to be on the lookout for any suspicious looking men in the area. As you will know, most able-bodied young Englishmen have been called-up into the army. This leaves a few men like you, who are serving the country in other ways; deserters on the run from the forces and most importantly German spies.

"These two men came into the bar yesterday morning and one of them came right over to me and offered to buy me a drink. He told me his name was Frank and that he was Scottish. He had a strange accent and one thing I can tell you for sure, he wasn't Scottish! He asked me if he could spend the night with me and then introduced me to his friend who spoke with a Cockney accent.

"I have captured deserters in the past by using myself as a decoy," she explained. "It is a dangerous job but when I think about how my late husband suffered in the trenches, it is a small price to pay to help my country. With deserters I have always managed to lace their drinks with a little of this powder," she continued, opening her handbag to show Carl what it contained. "Now the men who I think are the ones you are after, are still fast asleep on my bed after having a second dose of powder with their breakfast. I suggest that you come with me now, together with Bobby and Johnny to try and find the plans that Tilly told me they have stolen."

As they rose to make their way to the door at the back of the bar, Tilly also rose from the table and went over to engage one of the other bar 'floozies' in a whispered conversation. There are other ways of fighting the enemy than with guns, Carl thought to himself.

The four of them crept up the dusty uncarpeted, creaking stairs to the landing with Dolores leading the way. She approached a doorway at the end of the landing and gestured to the others to follow. Inside was a double bed and sprawled out on it were the semi-naked figures of two men both obviously in deep drug-induced sleep. Carl quickly signalled to Bobby and Johnny to search the men's clothing and belongings but there was no sign of the plans.

"Were they left alone up here at any time while they were awake?" Carl asked Dolores.

"Yes," she explained. "I went downstairs to get their breakfast and to telephone Tilly to let her know that I had two very suspicious characters in my room. She told me about the plans and told me that I must keep them here, come what may."

"When you came back with their breakfast were either or both of them out of bed?"

"Yes, the one called Frank seemed to be poking around in the room, over there," Dolores told him pointing towards a large cupboard. "He seemed very nervous and immediately went back to sit on the bed and thanked me very warmly for the breakfast. I thought that was strange as his attitude before that was as if I was his slave."

Carl strode over to the cupboard and opened the door. There was an odour of unwashed clothing within which made him want to retch. He steeled himself to check all the contents of the cupboard but to no avail. He then took a nearby chair and stood on it to check the shelf within the wardrobe but there was no sign of any plans there.

"I hope you two are keeping an eye on them," Carl said quietly to Bobby and Johnny, nodding towards the two sleeping figures.

Johnny nodded back and Carl continued his search. Next he got down on his hands and knees on the filthy, dust-laden carpet to peer underneath the wardrobe; again without finding what he was seeking. He dusted off his expensive trousers as he stood up and then realised that there was a gap on the far side of the cupboard where it stood near the wall alongside the window. He slid his hand in to the gap and felt a wad of paper. Quickly, he pulled it out and there they were; the plans of the new Crossley Armoured Vehicle.

The police were called in and the two men, still dazed from the double dose of Dolores's powder, were hastily bundled into a waiting Black Maria and trundled off to secure cells in Strangeways prison.

Carl decided to take the plans back to Crossley Motors at once. He had a serious conversation with the senior management about their lamentable lack of security, firstly in employing the two men without a thorough investigation of their identity and secondly he insisted that security sensitive plans should always be locked away in a safe.

Finally Carl wrote a detailed report on the whole matter that was sent to the War office in London.

Returning home he still could not forget that he had been in the company of the woman he was now sure was his long lost love Rachel and although his head told him to wish for no such thing, his heart was only yearning for another meeting with her.

CHAPTER THIRTY EIGHT

1919 PEACE, A WEDDING AND A TRAGEDY

Amid great rejoicing in Britain and throughout Europe, except, of course in vanquished Germany and her allies, the Great War, the 'war to end all wars' had come to an end in November 1918. The victorious European countries looked forward to a return to a way of life that had existed before 1914 but they quickly discovered that along with many of their nearest and dearest, this way of life had perished on the bloody battle-fields of France, Belgium and Germany.

The Oliver family had suffered grievously in the war. Carl had lost two brothers and a third was so badly injured that he could never again enjoy a normal life. His mother Olivia, the eternal optimist, had changed beyond recognition and had become an embittered elderly lady and a virtual recluse in her home in Hampstead. Even visits by Carl and Marjorie and their children failed to re-awaken any enthusiasm for life in a lady who previously was the life and soul of every gathering.

The week after the signing of the Treaty of Versailles on June 28, 1919, between Germany on the one side and France, Italy, Britain and their other European allies on the other, Carl and Marjorie resolved to once again visit his mother and try to re-kindle just a little of her former joie-de-vivre. They drove down to London in Carl's ageing Crossley and arrived to find Olivia desperately ill with the Spanish Flu that had been causing countless deaths since the previous year throughout the entire world.

Mother-in-law and daughter-in-law had always been kindred spirits and Marjorie was determined to nurse

Olivia back to full health. Sadly this was not to be as Olivia made no effort to fight the illness and simply allowed herself to sink into an untimely death. The whole Oliver clan was broken-hearted but Carl realised that his mother had been virtually lost to them ever since the end of the war and the influenza had simply finished off the process.

Four of Carl's siblings now remained in the family home in London and after the funeral, Carl and Marjorie returned to Dalethorpe to their family and to enable Carl to re-organise his business interests now that the war was behind them.

They arrived home and Carl, still reeling from the death of the mother he had adored, little knew that an even worse tragedy, if that was possible, lay ahead of him. The children were in good spirits. His oldest son, his pride and joy was Carl William, usually known as young Bill. He was nine years old and a bright, intelligent boy with an insatiable thirst for knowledge. Young Bill seemed to be fascinated by the mound at the end of the garden and although forbidden to attempt to climb its steep sides or disturb it in any way, he seemed to be constantly drawn to it and could often be found standing on the rear lawn simply staring and contemplating the strange protuberance.

Carl was a loving and gentle father but when it came to the subject of the mound he was capable of real anger if any of the children appeared to be about to disturb the strange feature in any way. In truth it was only young Bill who showed any interest and he knew better than to disobey his father. Apart from the family tradition of treating the mound with great respect and circumspection, Carl had another and terrifying reason for threatening his children with dire consequences if they ever went within more than six feet of the feature. He had buried the body of Dominic, the boy who had tried to blackmail the family, in the far side of the mound and in the midst of a loving family and highly successful business life, he knew only too well how easily all this could disappear if the remains of Dominic were ever discovered.

The day after the return from bidding a sad farewell to his dear mother, Carl James returned to his office in the factory, originally built by his grandfather Carl Joseph. His own four mills had now returned to peace-time production and in a world still reeling from the carnage of the war, he needed to ensure that the production of his looms was sold mainly to buyers abroad in the emerging countries of the British Empire. His old friend and customer Jack Abrahams had survived the war and had been awarded a medal. He had been instructed to join the German army and through a chain of other British spies to report back on all German troop movements. It was recognised that his information had led to many successes for the British on the battlefield. He had also attained the rank of Major and now proudly used his title in his business and social life.

Carl and Jack were now working more closely together than ever before. Carl needed Jack's contacts abroad to buy his cloth and Jack needed the supplies from Carl to satisfy his customers. Neither of them was aware that when the Olivers were invited to the wedding of Jack's daughter, Sarah, in the Manchester Great Synagogue in January 1920 that Carl's ancestor had received a similar invitation from his Jewish customer one Simon Levi back in 1856.

After the misery of the war, the wedding was a glittering affair. Deep down, however, most of those present were saddened by the losses of sons and brothers and the permanent absence of many of the groom's old friends was sadly felt if not articulated. Just like his grandfather Carl Isaac, over sixty years previously, Carl found the ceremony quite fascinating and the reception and ball at the prestigious Midland Hotel in St Peters Square Manchester was a welcome break for many present from the austerity of the previous decade.

Carl and Marjorie were seated at a table with a number of other well-known figures in the textile industry and after the delicious main course of Dover Sole they rose to join others on the dance floor. It was then that he saw her. She was standing besides one of the tables and chatting in an animated manner to another and older lady. Whether Carl would have acknowledged her or not was debatable but Tilly or rather Rachel had no such reservations.

"Hello, Mr Weaver," she said with a warm smile lighting up her lovely face. She was using the name that he had been allocated when working in counter-espionage. She then turned to Marjorie and gave her an equally dazzling smile. Marjorie turned to Carl with an enquiring look.

"I don't believe I have met this young lady," she began.

"No, of course not," Carl answered quickly. He turned back to Rachel and said,

"I only know you by the name Tilly from the time we captured two German spies," he explained. "To introduce you to my wife I would like to have your real name."

Once again Carl was treated to the amazing smile that had captivated him as a young man about town, all those years ago.

"Forgive me, my name is Rachel Abrahams but I only know you by your wartime name of Mr Weaver. What is your real name?"

"I am Carl James Oliver and this is my wife Marjorie," he explained.

"Carl James and Marjorie Oliver," Rachel replied, as if she was savouring the names on the tip of her tongue. "Are you here for the bride or the groom?"

"For the bride," Carl quickly explained. "Her father is an old and valued business friend."

"Ah, so you are the Carl that I have heard my brother Jack mention so frequently in the past."

"So you are Jack's sister," Marjorie interjected.

"Yes, his 'little' sister," Rachel explained. "So you must be the Marjorie Oliver who was so kind to my sister-in-law Amelia during the war."

"Well I was one of the lucky ones," Marjorie commented. "I had my dear husband Carl with me throughout the war when poor Amelia had no idea what had happened to Jack for months on end; the least I could do was to show her some support."

Carl was looking at the only two women who he had ever desired in his whole life. One had been his wife and the mother of his children for the best part of eleven years and the other the subject of his deepest fantasies for some twenty years. Now they stood together and in his eyes they were the two most beautiful women in the room. Marjorie, the fresh English rose and Rachel the sultry tropical flower.

"Dare I ask," Marjorie continued. "Are you married or is there maybe a special someone in your life?"

Rachel blushed perceptibly. "Well no," she replied. "I have carried a tiny memory in my heart for many years but alas it was not to be."

"Did you lose him in the awful war?" Marjorie enquired.

Again Rachel blushed, shook her head and with a sideways glance at Carl she responded, "No it was long before that."

Carl had endured enough. "It was lovely to meet you again Miss Abrahams," he said. "Marjorie I think we must return to our table for the desert."

For the rest of the evening Carl was uncharacteristically quiet.

Eventually Marjorie asked him, "Are you feeling a little under the weather darling?"

"Maybe just a touch," Carl replied and the pair made their adieus to the bride and groom and to Jack and Amelia and climbed into the Crossley for the drive back to Dalethorpe.

On the way home all Carl could think about was Rachel's answers to Marjorie's questions. He was sure now that he had made as great an impression on Rachel that night all those years ago, as she had made on him. However, he loved his wife and family and he knew that he must put any thought of ever contacting Rachel again, out of his mind.

"Are you sure you are alright?" Marjorie's voice came floating in to his consciousness interrupting his reverie of a night long ago.

"Yes, my dear," he answered. "I am just tired. Let me concentrate on getting us home."

Dalethorpe was a small somewhat isolated community and nestled in a valley surrounded by steep hills. It was this that had attracted Carl's erstwhile ancestor Karl Olafsen to this small piece of God's earth over a thousand years earlier. In 1920 the roads leading into Dalethorpe were little better than rough tracks and although wide enough to take motor vehicles, the road from the south, from Manchester had numerous bends.

"Carl, why are you driving so fast?" Marjorie demanded.

But the comment came too late as the Crossley skidded on the track and plunged down an embankment turning over when it hit a rock. The car came to rest against a huge tree trunk and there it lay until the following morning.

The Oliver children awoke at dawn which in Lancashire in January was at the late hour of half past seven in the morning. Normally their father would have visited them in their rooms and awoken them earlier to be ready for school. Their Nanny, a middle aged spinster by the name of Jane Jones arrived to get them dressed for breakfast.

"Well," she commented. "You are a lazy lot today. Did your father not wake you up as usual?"

Carl William, known as young Bill, was the spokesman.

"No," he responded sleepily. "I will go and bid Papa good morning."

"Oh, no you don't," Nanny Jones replied. "We have to get the four of you up and dressed for breakfast otherwise you and Mary will be late for school."

As they descended the stairs the front door bell rang. It was the new chauffeur Roger.

"Where is the Crossley?" he enquired.

This time young Bill was too quick for the Nanny, and sprinted back up the stairs, to his parent's bedroom; he flung open the door to find that the bed had not been slept in.

"Nanny," he called over the banister, "Mama and Papa are not here."

Then the telephone rang the Nanny answered it.

"Oh, my goodness," she exclaimed, after listening with an increasingly shocked expression. "Oh! Dear. What will I tell the children?"

Joshua Mottershead was a distant cousin of the Oliver clan and was the master baker in Dalethorpe. He employed a number people from the town and his wholemeal bread and delicious cakes were delivered daily to many of the grocery shops in the area.

He was on his way to visit customers in Accrington and Burnley to launch his latest range of confections when he spotted skid marks on the rough road leading out of the village.

He brought his Ford Model 'T' to a standstill and jumped out to investigate. He clambered carefully down the steep slope where breaks in the shrubbery clearly indicated the direction that the skidding vehicle had taken. It was a precarious descent, even on foot and eventually he saw the Crossley on its roof and resting against a large tree. He slid down the final few feet to the car which he instantly recognised as the property of Carl Oliver, the man universally regarded as the squire of Dalethorpe.

Joshua was terrified to touch the large car as he could see that any disturbance would cause it to move again and tumble further down the steep embankment. He peered inside and was horrified to see the bodies of Carl and Marjorie spread eagled on the inside of the roof of the upside-down vehicle. By their positions they both looked dead. He realised he needed help, lots of help and he started to scramble back up the slope. Ten minutes later he arrived back at his car and drove off to the nearest police station.

It took two hours for a team of policemen, firemen and members of the public to be assembled with ropes and other lifting tackle. Then before any attempt could be made to move the Crossley, while it was being held in position by members of the rescue team, now approaching some forty persons, the two bodies were extricated from the wreck. Marjorie lay on top of Carl and it was obvious that her neck had been broken in crash and with no sign of a pulse or breath, she was confirmed dead by Doctor Phillips from Accrington. Then Carl was gently lifted from the wreck and it looked as if he had also been killed. However, as the volunteers placed him on a blanket alongside the body of his wife, they heard a sound and then to the amazement of all present he opened first one eye and then the other.

Doctor Phillips checked him over for broken bones but apart from severe bruising, he did not appear to have sustained any serious injury.

Then Carl turned his head and seeing the body of his wife lying besides him said,

"Marjorie, are you all right?"

There was of course no reply and the doctor bent down again, took Carl's hand and shook his head.

"My dear fellow, I am afraid she did not make it."

Volunteers then carried the sobbing, broken-hearted Carl up the slope on a stretcher.

The doctor insisted on Carl being taken to hospital for a full check up but the following day he was discharged. He had miraculously suffered no serious injuries. However, the injuries to his whole way of life and that of his children were grave in the loss of a beloved wife and adored mother

Marjorie was buried a week later in the family crypt in the old graveyard alongside the church of St Barnabas-by-Dalethorpe. A large congregation assembled to bid a sad and respectful farewell to this lady who had so endeared herself to the entire population of the small town.

Carl's brother Bernard and his sister Nancy had travelled up from London by train. Virtually the entire population of Dalethorpe were there to pay their last respects to a lady loved by all and many colleagues who were leaders of the Lancashire Textile Industry had come to lend Carl their support As the funeral procession left the church to make its way to the Oliver family crypt, a large car pulled up outside and as Carl sorrowfully followed the coffin, to bid a final farewell to his dear wife, he spied Jack and Amelia Abrahams together with Jack's sister Rachel making their way over to join the long line of mourners.

At last it was all over. Three of the children had been considered old enough to attend and young Bill had bravely dropped a note into the open grave to wish his mother well in the heaven in which he knew she would now reside.

Carl was now faced with the terrible new reality of bringing up four motherless young children and running a large business with many ramifications. His remaining blessings were however also to be found in his responsibilities. The business had made him an extremely wealthy man and at least he could afford to send his children to the best schools and employ the best servants to ensure their home life was comfortable. He also lavished all of his spare time and love upon them but knew in his heart that this was still no substitute for the love of a mother, so cruelly denied. In addition, Carl felt personally responsible for the crash that had denied him his wife. If his mind would have been on his driving instead of on Rachel and what she had said to him earlier that fateful evening, Marjorie would still have been the mistress of the Old Vicarage. He could hardly blame Rachel but he resolved to distance himself from her and her family except for his business relationship with Jack.

CHAPTER THIRTY NINE

A WORLD IN TURMOIL

For the next few years Carl's entire existence centred round his family and his work. However as the decade progressed trade became more and more difficult with many of the spinning mills that had supplied his weaving sheds going to the wall. Demand for cotton textiles was declining fast and by 1929 Carl had closed one mill and substantially cut production in the others. Fortunately as this situation had ben developing Carl had the foresight to diversify and now had a large portfolio of residential properties to generate income. Many of his friends had invested heavily in the stock market which was making spectacular gains throughout most of the decade. Carl had travelled to London and had frequent meetings with his brother Bernard in which they resolved to avoid the temptations the stock markets offered and stay with property as their main generator of income. However, once the Wall Street Crash had occurred on October 29, 1929 and the world economy went into free-fall, it was a knock-out blow for Combined Lancashire Weavers and with a heavy heart Carl was forced to close the doors for ever on his remaining mills. He was particularly sad to see the end of the Dalethorpe mill, originally started by his grandfather, but what really broke his heart was the misery and desperation now evident in the lives of his old workers. They had been more than employees, they had been friends and a number of them lived in Dalethorpe.

Carl discussed with Bernard the setting up of a charitable trust to assist the families that had been hit hardest and this helped a little to alleviate the suffering. Of course it was not only Dalethorpe and Lancashire that were so badly affected by the Great Depression. Every village, every town and every country was reeling from the recession and unemployment globally was reaching unprecedented heights.

Carl's oldest son Carl William no longer cared to be known as young Bill. He had gone up to Oxford in 1929 to read politics, philosophy and economics, just two weeks before the Wall Street Crash. As soon as he heard of the closure of Combined Lancashire Weavers, he had returned.

"Look Papa," he told Carl. "I am here to help in whatever manner you need me. I can always return to my studies when things have settled down."

"My dear boy," Carl had answered him. "I cannot tell you how much I appreciate your offer but the best thing you can do is to study hard and become a good lawyer. We are not exactly on the bread-line you know."

"Are you sure you do not need me Papa?" Carl William said.

"Absolutely, but while you are here there are certain family matters that I need to bring to your attention.

"Will you meet me in the old study tomorrow morning before you return to Oxford?"

Carl William's face clouded over.

"Papa, so there is the problem? That sounds serious."

Carl patted his son on the back and assured him that the matters were historical rather than financial and he would see him in the morning.

Carl slept deeply that night in the satisfaction that he had reared a son to be proud of and after a light breakfast he made his way to the old study on the first floor.

It was many years since he had thought about the two rocks in the cupboard or for that matter the mound. Certainly he could hardly miss the protuberance when he looked out of the rear windows of the house but it was just there and had it not been for Carl's knowledge that it concealed Dominic's body, he would never have given it a another moment's thought.

What had prompted him to tell his son about the relics and the mound on this occasion, he really could not fathom. Carl William as a child had been fascinated by the mound but had obediently kept his distance from it, which was more than his father could admit.

Carl arrived in the study before his son and immediately took the two rocks out of the cupboard. He placed them on the large oak table by the window and removed the soiled wrappers. He peered at them again in consternation and wondered why he had never sent the wax-paper rubbings off to the British Museum for translation and identification.

A moment later, Carl William entered the room and strode straight over to the table.

"Good morning Papa," he intoned and then noticing what was on the table he continued, "What on earth are those rocks?"

"Have a look at them carefully," his father instructed. "What can you see?"

"Just some scratches," Carl William replied. "No, just a minute, these look like letters. Now what do they spell?"

But of course, some of the letters may have resembled their own alphabet but others were impossible to decipher.

Carl William then started to examine the other rock but the letters on this one bore no resemblance to anything he had ever seen.

Suddenly Carl James uttered a startled, "Well, I never. I do declare, that looks like the Hebrew I saw in Jack Abraham's synagogue years ago."

Carl William was still puzzling over the first rock and both father and son had to admit that this lettering had defeated them. Not that they could read the Hebrew but at least it sounded like a possible identification of the script.

"Papa, so I assume this is what you wanted to tell me about?" Carl William enquired.

"Yes, my boy. I do not know how, but both these rocks come from the mound and have some connection to our family."

"So, Papa, although we have always been forbidden to touch the mound some member of our family did so, as otherwise these rocks would not now be in the house."

"Yes, my boy, that is correct. However, I do want you to know and to one day tell your children that the mound must not be disturbed in any circumstances."

"Yes sir," Carl William replied, "I am aware of that and I will not be the one to break the family rules. However, I would dearly love to know what is buried under all that soil and shale."

"So would I my boy," Carl replied and added quickly, "but let us concentrate on the rocks. I am going to telephone to Jack Abrahams and ask him to come over this evening. If it really is Hebrew, he should know."

Jack was delighted to hear from Carl and since the mill closures they had only spoke to each other twice. He readily agreed to drive out to Dalethorpe that evening and asked if he could bring Amelia with him.

"Of course my dear chap," Carl had replied, half hoping that Rachel would also be available to visit. He had never as much as mentioned her name to Jack since the funeral of Marjorie and had long since convinced himself that she must be happily married with maybe a few offspring by now.

"Fine, we will see you about half past eight," Jack responded.

Maybe it was his German background but Jack was always a stickler for punctuality. At precisely 8.30 pm the door bell rang at the Old Vicarage and Carl himself strode quickly across the hallway to open the door. There were three people standing in the porch. Jack and Amelia and yes, a little older but still very beautiful, there was Rachel.

Once again the mere sight of her sent Carl's stomach into knots as he stammered,

"Hello, do please come in."

He called for Doris the housemaid to come and take the three visitors coats and he ushered them into the lounge.

"Will you all take tea?" he enquired as soon as they were seated.

"Doris," he continued. "Please bring tea for five and ask Master Carl William to join us."

After proudly introducing his son to his friends and explaining that he was home for a short visit from Oxford, Carl asked Carl William to fetch the smaller of the two rocks, the one that he suspected had Hebrew script chiselled into it.

While they awaited the return of his son, the men chatted about the terrible state of the textile industry. However, every few moments Carl found his eyes were being drawn into taking surreptitious glances in the direction of Rachel and each time she rewarded him with a little smile.

Then Carl William returned with the rock and placed it carefully on a table.

"What is that?" Jack enquired.

"Please come and take a look," his host responded.

Jack rose from his comfortable armchair and strode across the room.

"Good gracious," he exclaimed after peering at the letters etched into the rock, "That is Hebrew."

"There you are my boy," Carl announced, "I told you so. Now what does it say?"

"All it says is," Jack replied, "Rachel bat Yosef, Rachel daughter of Joseph."

"So where did you find it?" Jack enquired. "It looks like a crude gravestone."

"Oh it has been in our family for many years and there is another one upstairs etched with a totally different script."

"Could I see it?" Jack enquired.

"Of course, my dear fellow, Carl William, will you bring it down for us?"

The two stones were now laid side by side on the table and Jack peered closely at the slightly larger slab.

"Well," Jack gasped. "This is a night for surprises. Do you have any idea what is written here?"

"Not the faintest, old boy," Carl replied.

"Well, I do," Jack answered. "It is written in the Runic script used by the Vikings. I studied ancient scripts at university and this is one of them."

"So what does it say?" Carl again demanded of his erudite friend.

"It says 'Here lies Karl Olafsen,'" Jack explained. "Now where do these rocks come from? Come on, my old friend, you must know."

"I do know but if I now tell you, you must promise never to discuss this matter outside our family."

Jack nodded gravely. "I think you know me well enough by now to know I would never break a confidence."

"Very well, if the ladies and Carl William will excuse us, please Jack, come with me."

The pair entered a ground floor room at the back of the house from where Carl was able to point out the shadowy shape of the mound at the end of the long garden.

"That is undoubtedly where the rocks were found many years ago but we are forbidden by family tradition to make any further disturbances to the mound and I have never allowed my children to even go within a few feet of it."

"How long has your family lived here?" Jack enquired.

"Virtually always," Carl replied. "I do know that one of our ancestors was recorded as living here in the Domesday Book."

"Good gracious," Jack commented. "So while my family and my people were dispersed all over the known world and were forced to journey from country to country; yours has been here, virtually rooted to this spot on God's earth for all that time.

"Then you do realise that the two people mentioned on these rocks are undoubtedly your ancestors."

This realisation had been dawning on Carl ever since Jack had confirmed the inscriptions.

"So you are all the descendants of a Viking man and a Jewish woman," Jack continued. "Incredible! What a combination!"

"We might even be related," Carl commented with a grin, as they returned to the others in the lounge, "on my great, great, great, great...grandmother's side!"

This was undoubtedly the best evening of Carl's life for many a long year. His friend Jack had confirmed the ancestry of the Olivers and once again he had been in the presence of the delightful Rachel. He knew now that he could never again lose contact with her and resolved to invite her out as soon as possible.

CHAPTER FORTY

1933-1937

A DISASTROUS VISIT

Carl James Oliver was now fifty five years old. He had been meeting Rachel Abrahams regularly for over three years and constantly thought of marrying her. Neither of them could now be described as being in the first flush of youth but she always turned him down.

"Carl," she would explain, "I have had a special place in my heart for you since the very first time we met when I was a singer and you were a young man-about-town. However, I broke my parent's hearts by going on the stage. They always told me that this was not a career for a nice Jewish girl and were convinced I would marry a non-Jew and disgrace the family. I, for my part, was determined to prove that I could be a singer and still not marry out of my faith. Then came the war and I was approached by the War Office to organise a band of pretty young women, mainly chorus girls, to make themselves available to possible spies and deserters. You knew all about this and saw my girls in action on a number of occasions.

"Once the war was over I gave up the stage and allowed myself to be introduced to a number of eligible young Jewish men but none of them interested me. Possibly my life had been too exciting to face the prospect of being just a little Jewish wife. And then there was always the memory of you, Carl, in the background. My parents have been gone now for years and I am reduced to being the spinster aunt to Jack's children. I desperately want your friendship but to marry you would cause us both far too many problems."

Carl always dismissed her reservations but the lady was determined to deny herself the person she most wanted in the whole wide world. And so the relationship drifted on. They attended theatre and concerts, and all manner of social events together and saw each other at least three times each week. But after each meeting they returned to their respective homes.

The Abrahams family had lived in Frankfurt-on-Main for centuries. They were successful business people and pillars of both the Jewish and general community. They lived quietly and only those who had benefitted from their generosity knew of their many charitable deeds. When Jack and Rachel's father had decided to move to England, he had left behind one brother named Franz. It was his children, who were of course Jack's first cousins, who had given hospitality to Jack when he had arrived in 1914 to join the German army as a spy for the British. They of course never knew, although they might have suspected why, when the two countries were at war with each other, their cousin Jack had suddenly arrived and pledged allegiance to his father's country of birth. Now in 1937, Jack's cousins were in their sixties with grown-up children of their own. And suddenly, after being good German citizens for generations they were faced by the virulent Anti-Semitic laws known as the Nuremberg Laws that were destroying their entire way of life. Magda, a first cousin of Jack and Rachel wrote to her trying to describe the restrictions under which they now lived. Rachel discussed the letter with Jack who found it hard to believe that the position of old Jewish families in Germany could have deteriorated to such an extent. Jack wanted to go over to ascertain the position personally, but with all the problems in the textile industry, he was obliged to keep postponing the visit. In the end, Rachel said she would go and telephoned cousin Magda to expect her in two weeks time.

Carl was more than a little concerned to learn of her intention.

"I have heard the Nazis are making life very difficult for German Jews," he said. "I think it is far too dangerous for you to go."

"I think you are forgetting that I am British and I know these Germans from the war. I am certain they will not mess with a Briton, Jewish or non-Jewish."

Carl tried and tried again to dissuade Rachel but she was determined.

So on the nineteenth of August 1937, Carl drove Rachel over the Pennines and on to the port of Hull to board the 'Imperator', a Hapag-Lloyd luxury liner that would take her to Hamburg. He escorted her on board and saw her comfortably settled in one of the best cabins. After bidding him farewell and watching him return to his car on the quayside she went below as the huge ship slowly made its way out of the port area. On arrival in Hamburg she had to go through German immigration where she noted the strange looks she encountered when the official checked her British passport and saw her name to be Abrahams.

"Enjoy your trip to Germany," the official said with exaggerated courtesy.

She purchased a first-class railway ticket and took the train to Frankfurt where a rather shabby-looking Magda was waiting for her. They had only met on one previous occasion, some fifteen years earlier from when she remembered Magda as an extremely elegant woman.

Much to Rachel's surprise, Magda picked up Rachel's suitcase and made for the tram-stop.

"Why not take a taxi?" Rachel enquired.

"Jews are not allowed to take taxis," Magda told her.

"Well I am." Rachel replied. "I am a British visitor and we will take a taxi."

Magda gave her cousin a fearful glance but followed her anyway.

Rachel deliberately spoke to the cab driver in English which seemed to satisfy him that she was not a German Jewess. She told Magda to give the driver the address and they both climbed into the car. On the way Rachel was shocked to see many shops daubed with the Star of David and the word 'Jude.' Already she was beginning to see that Magda's letter was no exaggeration. Could this be the Germany that her parents had loved and only left to further their business interests?

They were greeted in Magda's modest apartment by her husband Bernd Kaufmann, a distinguished looking academic who told her that he had been a professor of Mathematics at the University of Frankfurt but was dismissed because he was a Jew. During her stay she saw numerous examples of the way that Nazi thugs were attacking Jews in the street, often with the active collaboration of the police. Rachel told Magda and Bernd that she feared for their lives and begged them to come back to England with her when she returned.

"We are Germans," Bernd told her. "This Jewish persecution will end. It is just the Nazi party trying to find a scapegoat for Germany's economic woes."

Rachel pleaded with them and other members of the family to leave while they could and she and Jack would look after them in Manchester until they had settled in and found work. Tragically her pleas fell on deaf ears and she left alone. She took the train back to Hamburg but was stopped from boarding the ship to Hull as she made to ascend the gangplank,

Three men in long black leather coats barred her way. The oldest of the three was a tall blond man in his forties.

"You are Fraulein Rachel Abrahams?" he said.

Rachel was determined not to answer in German and said,

"I am Miss Rachel Abrahams from Manchester, England. I am a British subject and I demand that you let me proceed to this ship at once."

One of the other leather-clad men replied in faultless English.

"We know exactly who you are and we just want to ask you a few questions."

"I must tell you that you have absolutely no right to stop me boarding this ship. I have no business with you, whoever you are, and you have none with me. If you do not let me go at once I will report the matter to the British government on my return."

The older man produced an identity card emblazoned with the swastika that now appeared on all official German documents.

"I am Kriminalinspektor Heinrich Muller of the Gestapo. We will not detain you for long, Fraulein, but there are certain matters relating to your visit to Frankfurt that we would like to clarify."

The request was made with courtesy and seeing that these men were some sort of policemen Rachel decided that resistance would be futile and it would be better to co-operate.

"Gentlemen," she said again in English. "The ship leaves in one hour so if we can conclude our business, whatever that may be, quickly in say half an hour, I will be pleased to help."

There was a customs-shed nearby and the men then escorted Rachel there and asked her to be seated in an office that had a large swastika on the door over the name plate *Kriminalinspektor Heinrich Muller-Gestapo*.

"Please sit down, Fraulein," Muller said, settling into the large leather chair on the other side of the desk. "Fritz and

Wolfgang please sit at the side here and I want you both to take notes."

"Now Fraulein, please confirm that you are Rachel Abrahams, a German citizen currently living in Manchester England."

"No," Rachel answered. "I am Miss Rachel Abrahams of Manchester and a British citizen."

"You may have a British passport but our records clearly state that you were born in Frankfurt-on-Main on the twenty third of May 1878 which makes you fifty nine years old."

"No," Rachel replied, "I was born in Manchester some years after my parents had left Germany."

"Fraulein, I am sorry to say you are wrong. Your parents returned to Germany to spend a few months with their family in 1878 and you were born right here on the soil of our beloved Germany. It is all documented. After that your parents returned to England. Your father might have decided to tell the British authorities that you were born there but that is incorrect."

"Anyway, I am still a British subject," Rachel answered. "So what do you want with me? I have a ship to catch and all this talk about my birth is rather academic."

Suddenly the demeanour of Inspector Muller changed. "Academic, did you say academic? Fraulein, I must inform you here and now that you are German and subject to the laws of the Third Reich."

"That is enough," Rachel countered, suddenly feeling very insecure. "I am British and I demand to see the British Consul here in Hamburg."

"That is impossible," Muller replied. "You have broken German law and you will be returned to Frankfurt for further questioning as that is where the offences occurred.

"I must also tell you that like many members of your race, your loyalty to Germany is sorely wanting. We are not idiots here, we know all about the activities of you and your brother during the war. We Germans have long memories, Fraulein."

Rachel was now really frightened and realised that the intention of Muller and his men had always been to return her to Frankfurt as a prisoner. Without another word the two lower rank officers stood up and grabbing one of Rachel's arms each, they attempted to drag her out of the chair. Rachel however, was not prepared to give them the satisfaction of seeing her upset and arose in her usual dignified manner and walked with them out of Muller's office. She was then locked in a small cell where she agonised on what fate may await her in Frankfurt.

CHAPTER FORTY-ONE

THE OLD 'BLACKSHIRT'

Carl had property in Leeds and decided to stay there at the Queen's Hotel while Rachel was away and then return to Hull to meet her back from her trip to Germany.

He arrived at the quayside a good two hours before the liner was due and went in search of a light lunch at a restaurant with a view of the docks from where he could see the ship with Rachel on board, returning home. He had missed her company and lively conversation and wondered what news she would have to report of Germany under the rule of the Nazi party.

The ship was due to arrive at half past three in the afternoon and Carl returned to the area outside the customs shed, through which all arrivals were processed, to watch the huge liner docking. He was surprised to see a group of some ten men all wearing dark suits and black shirts, waiting just near where he was standing. He wondered at first if they were German Nazi's as they all had a small badge on their lapels that looked from the distance like a swastika. He could however, overhear their conversation and quickly realised they were English and speaking in a variety of working-class accents. Carl realised that they were members of the Blackshirts, a fascist organisation led by Oswald Moseley and whose ideology was similar to that of the Italian Fascists and the German Nazis. He then decided that they must be a welcoming party for some German official.

The ship had now docked and from his vantage point Carl could see the steady stream of people disembarking down the gangplank. He tried to identify Rachel without success and he watched with increasing anxiety as most of the passengers left the ship and ultimately joined friends and relatives waiting to greet them. Eventually only Carl and the group of ten Blackshirts remained. There were still one or two stragglers coming down the gangplank and then he heard the Blackshirts saying to each other, *"there he is."* Carl watched as an old man with a walking stick, escorted by two crew members, made his way down. Once on the level he increased his speed and a few minutes later he emerged from the Customs Shed to greet his welcoming party. Carl was sufficiently interested to glance at the face of the old man as he and his friends walked within a few feet of him. Carl was deeply worried now as to why Rachel had not appeared but the sight of the face of the old man, smartly dressed in a tailor-made pin-stripe suit, sporting a lapel badge like the others and a Black shirt, came as a horrible shock. There was no doubt that he was looking at the face of his uncle Olaf, the long-ago defrocked vicar of Dalethorpe. To Carl, if the man had ever had any redeeming features they were gone, and he resembled nothing more than the evil that he now represented.

Olaf passed by Carl, almost near enough to touch but his thoughts were all about the report he had to make to his party cell.

In the meantime Carl thought, *to hell with him,* as he realised that no more passengers were now disembarking and it was Rachel who was his real concern.

He went into the office of the Hapag-Lloyd steamship company and approached the enquiry desk.

"Was a lady called Miss Rachel Abrahams on board the 'Imperator,'" he asked the clerk. The young man produced a list of passengers skimmed through it and informed Carl that no one of that name had been aboard.

Carl was shattered. He could see no useful purpose in staying in Hull and returned to his car to start the long drive back to Dalethorpe. It was eleven o'clock at night when he arrived and he realised it would be after midnight in Frankfurt. After a sleepless night he arose and asked the operator to contact the telephone number in Germany that belonged to Rachel's cousins. He spent the next hour pacing up and down the study until the telephone rang. He grabbed the receiver and without listening to the voice at the other end demanded to speak to Rachel Abrahams. Then he realised that what he was hearing was the voice of the English operator who told him that the Frankfurt exchange had reported that the number had been disconnected.

Carl was now frantic to discover what had happened to Rachel. He telephoned her brother Jack who was shocked and deeply worried to hear the news of her non-return. Carl decided to telephone the foreign office in London. He had a contact there, Richard Selby-Thomson, from his days in counter-espionage during the war. It took some two hours to contact Richard who asked a number of questions about Rachel's background and then promised to send a message to the British Embassy in Berlin to ask them to investigate.

"These are very difficult times in Germany," Richard told Carl. "Ordinary Germans, unless they are members of the Nazi party, are feeling the squeeze and Jews are subject to more and more acts of persecution and daily indignities."

"I am aware of that," Carl answered, "but Richard, Rachel is British and of course the holder of a British passport."

"I do not want to add to your worries but you told me she is from a German-Jewish family, "Richard replied. "If the Nazis discover this, I am afraid she may be in great danger."

Carl thanked Richard and hung up the earpiece feeling even more concerned. He had to find Rachel but how?

CHAPTER FORTY TWO

INSPEKTOR SCHMIDT

Rachel had been driven in a Mercedes police car along the newly opened Autobahn to Frankfurt. There she was bundled out of the car by the officers who had accompanied her on the drive. Again she shook off their attempts to drag her into the building and told them that she was quite capable of entering if this was where she must go. Rachel had noticed this grey structure a few days earlier as it was near the railway station. The only colour it exhibited to the passing world was the red background of the huge Nazi flag that hung over the entrance.

Inside she was taken to a reception desk where a Gestapo official demanded her name and then said,

"Ach, Yah, Fraulein Abrahams, we have been awaiting your arrival."

She was then escorted into a small dimly lit room and told to sit down at the desk. Then she heard the key turn in the lock and she knew she was a prisoner. For an hour or more she sat there. She was understandably terrified and she wondered what had become of the suitcase and handbag that had been taken from her before leaving Hamburg. Then she heard the sound of the door being unlocked and in came two men. One was dressed in Gestapo uniform and introduced himself as Kriminalinspektor Wolfgang Schmidt. The other was an old man dressed in a smart business suit and Inspector Schmidt told her his name was Herr Gruber. Schmidt seated himself behind a desk and told Gruber to take a seat at the side of the room.

"Ach, so," Schmidt began. "You are Fraulein Rachel Abrahams?"

"Yes," Rachel replied. "I am Miss Rachel Abrahams and I demand to see the British ambassador."

"I am afraid that will not be possible," Schmidt answered. "You are a citizen of the Third Reich and as such you are under our jurisdiction."

Rachel could not let this go unanswered and repeated what she had told Schmidt's colleagues in Hamburg; namely that she was British.

Schmidt ignored this information and told her that she had to answer a number of charges that involved, as a Jew, breaking various ordinances of the Nuremberg Laws relative to racial purity of the German people, during her visit to Frankfurt.

"However," he continued, "the most serious charge relates to treason against the German people during the war. Herr Gruber," he said, "please come and stand besides my chair and tell me, after having a good look at this woman, if you have ever seen her before?"

Rachel, of course, carefully scanned the face of Herr Gruber to try to decide if she had ever seen him before. Was there a vague familiarity from some time, long ago or was she imagining it? Gruber for his part stared long at hard at her and then turned to the Inspector and said,

"Yah that is she. She was the Madame who introduced me to the whore who seduced me in Manchester and who stole the plans of a secret vehicle the cursed British were developing, during the war."

"You must be dreaming," Rachel interrupted. "I have never seen you before."

She then turned to the Inspector, having decided that attack was the best form of defence.

"For this you arrested me when I was about to return to England? Do you think a court of law will take seriously the testimony of this old man?"

"We will see about that when your trial takes place," Schmidt answered. "Anyway, we have enough on you to detain you in respect of your illegal activities as a German Jewess. That is all."

Schmidt pressed a bell push and two young Gestapo men entered the room.

"Please make arrangements for **Miss** Abrahams to be detained as our guest," he said heavily emphasising the title Miss.

Rachel had known that she was in serious trouble from the moment she had been arrested before boarding the ship. She was, however, determined not to give the Gestapo the satisfaction of showing any fear or concern.

"**Herr** Schmidt," she told the inspector, emphasising his civilian title as he had just done with hers, "You will be in serious trouble with the British Government when they hear how I have been treated."

"Really, Fraulein," the Inspector replied with deep irony. "You have me really worried."

Rachel expected to be locked up in some kind of cell in the Gestapo building but instead was taken immediately to a large prison truck waiting outside the building. A number of other prisoners were already locked inside the vehicle. As soon as the doors were firmly closed she heard the engine being started. She looked round the dimly lit area and could see that of the dozen or so prisoners on board only two looked recognisably Jewish-the others seemed to be Germans and by their manner of dress, people of culture and refinement. The man sitting next to her was probably in his late forties. He was dressed in a tweed sports jacket and well-pressed navy trousers. He had the earnest thoughtful look of an academic and turning to Rachel he gave her a sad little smile.

"I am Claus Reinhardt, professor of history at the University of Frankfurt," he said.

"I am Rachel Abrahams from Manchester, England," she told him. "What is to become of us?"

"We are on our way to Dachau Concentration Camp. I was there in 1934 for criticising the Nazis and released after just six months without a trial. I just hope that this time we will be as lucky."

The conversation had taken place in German and now Herr Reinhardt spoke to her in English.

"Why are you here, Miss Abrahams? Dachau is a prison for German political prisoners although the Nazis have just started sending a few Jews there."

It was a long drive, some 300 kilometres, from Frankfurt to Dachau and Rachel had plenty of time to tell her story to Claus Reinhardt. Eventually she asked him if he knew her cousin's husband Bernd Kaufmann, who had been a professor of Mathematics at the University of Frankfurt.

Claus looked shocked,

"Yes, of course I knew Bernd," he answered. "He was a lovely man and a brilliant mathematician."

Rachel studied Claus's face. "Why do you speak of him in the past?" she asked, dreading the reply.

"He and his wife Magda were shot yesterday, resisting arrest," he told her. "The whole university is shocked to the core and it was as a result of my speaking at a protest meeting that I was arrested today."

For the first time, Rachel showed her feelings and wept. She knew that if she had not visited her cousins, they would still be alive. What had happened to the Germany that her father used to talk of and what, she wondered, would now be her fate in the already notorious concentration camp at Dachau?

CHAPTER FORTY THREE

MISTAKEN IDENTITY

It was about half past seven on the evening after Carl's return from Hull when the phone rang. He lifted the earpiece to hear the voice of Jack at the other end.

"This is an outrage," Jack said. "I have been in touch with the Foreign Office and they said they will try to find out what has happened to Rachel."

"I did the same this morning," Carl told him, "And they promised to let me know as soon as they have some news."

"Goodness knows what is happening over there," Jack replied, "and our government seems to think we can be friendly with these monsters."

"They should be listening to Winston Churchill," Carl commented. "He has the measure of these Nazis."

"Listen Carl," Jack continued. "I am going to go over and find Rachel. It is the only way. I don't think HMG is going to try very hard to find her, do you?"

"Look Jack, it would be absolute madness for you to go," Carl responded. "You are a Jew and you know from the newspapers that they are blaming your people for all Germany's ills. For all we know they might have arrested Rachel because your family were originally German. And you were there during the war as a spy. They would really love to get their hands on you. No, I will go. I am British through and through, they can't touch me."

Jack reluctantly agreed and Carl prepared to drive back to Hull to board the first ship he could find bound for Hamburg.

The voyage was uneventful and the immigration officials surprisingly welcoming.

"Enjoy your trip to the Third Reich, Herr Oliver," they told him.

He caught a train to Frankfurt-on-Main and was impressed by the cleanliness and punctuality of the rail service.

A taxi driver recommended the Frankfurter Hof as the best hotel in town and indeed it turned out to be comparable with similar hotels in London and Paris.

Carl left his suitcase in his room and immediately returned to the lobby of the hotel where a porter called a taxi for him.

"Where do you wish to go?" the porter enquired.

"I will decide the best route with the taxi driver," Carl informed him. He was taking no chances and the less people knew of his movements the better.

Carl instructed the taxi to leave him two streets away from the Kaufmann's apartment and ensured the cab was out of sight before starting to walk over to his first port of call. The area was obviously a Jewish area and many of the shops were daubed with the word *Jude* and Stars of David. The streets in the district seemed unnaturally quiet, particularly in comparison with the busy town centre which he had left just fifteen minutes earlier.

The address was apartment 5, Weberstrasse 27 and Carl entered from the street through the large double-doors that opened with just a gentle push. Number 5 was on the first floor and the half open door was clearly visible as Carl climbed the wide staircase. He called out *Guten Morgen* and entered to find the place deserted and signs of a struggle and sudden departure in the inner hallway. He checked every room and then, very concerned as to the fate of the occupants, he decided to try the neighbour's doors. From numbers 3, 7 and 9 there was no reply to his knocking so Carl ascended to the next floor to number 11. There the door opened enough for him to see an elderly man peering out but with his safety chain prudently in place.

"Who are you? What do you want?," he demanded in German.

Carl's German was seriously limited but he understood the questions and responded,

"Ich bin Carl Oliver."

"Ah, so you are English," the old man replied in perfect English. "What can I do for you?"

"I am looking for Professor and Frau Kaufmann from number 5."

The door closed and Carl heard the chain being removed. Then the door opened again and the old gentleman ushered Carl into the apartment.

"Please sit down," the occupant of the apartment said. "Can I offer you a cup of coffee or English tea?"

"No, no thank you," Carl replied. "Do you know what has happened to your neighbours?"

The old man nodded sadly,

"I am afraid I have some very bad news for you. It is hard to believe of such gentle people but the official version is that they were shot resisting arrest."

Carl looked at him in shocked silence.

"By the way, my name is Friedrich von Brandenburg and I am sorry to meet you in these circumstances. Did you know the Professor and his wife well?"

"No, sadly I never met them," Carl explained. At this point alarm bells began to ring. Who was this charming old gentleman? His surname indicated he was a Prussian aristocrat and possibly anti-Nazi but dare he take a chance and ask him about the real reason for his visit, to locate his beloved Rachel?

Friedrich seemed to be surveying him and then at last he spoke.

"They had a charming English cousin with them last week and invited me in to meet her. Her name was Rachel but what was her surname? A Jewish name, I believe. Why yes, it was Abrahams. Do you by any chance know her?"

Carl decided to take the plunge.

"Actually, I do know her from England and was hoping to see her while I was in Frankfurt. Now I am really worried what has become of her."

Friedrich nodded. "I heard she had been arrested," he said.

"But why?" Carl almost screamed.

"I have no idea. They do not normally arrest foreign visitors, even Jewish ones," Friedrich commented. "However, after what they did to my friends the Kaufmanns, I fear for all German Jews. Rachel however, was English was she not?"

Carl nodded.

"Do you know where they would be holding her?" he enquired.

"No," Friedrich shook his head sadly. "Try the central police station but I suspect that this all sounds far more like a Gestapo operation."

Carl rose, thanked Friedrich and bade his farewells. *It just goes to show,* he pondered, *not all Germans are like the Nazis.*

There were no taxis on the streets in this neighbourhood, so Carl took the tram to the central police station. There he was told, after an officer checked the list, that they had never heard of an Englishwoman called Rachel Abrahams.

"If you wish, you could try the Gestapo headquarters," the policeman told him.

Carl approached the building with trepidation. If the Gestapo had arrested Rachel, what would become of her? There had already been a number of stories in the English press about German academics, Communists and social Democrats who were now imprisoned without trial for simply opposing or criticising the Nazi regime. And then there was the unremitting flow of anti-Semitic propaganda that the Nazis were unleashing.

Carl approached the reception area manned by two black uniformed men.

"I am trying to locate a friend from England," he said in English. "We were supposed to meet here in Frankfurt but she seems to have just disappeared from the face of the earth."

"We do not speak English here," one of the men replied in German. "Please have the courtesy to address us in our language while you are a guest here."

Carl fell back on his very limited German to explain his mission. The Gestapo officer seemed to understand and as soon as he said Miss Rachel Abrahams, he reacted.

"What is your name?" he demanded.

"My name is Oliver, Herr Oliver," Carl replied.

"One minute," tha man replied and went off somewhere in the depths of the building.

He returned within a couple of minutes and to Carl's surprise addressed him in English.

"This way please, Herr Oliver."

He was then escorted to an office with the name *Kriminalinspektor Heinrich Schmidt-Gestapo* on the door.

His escort then told him to enter and sit down and that Kriminalinspektor Heinrich Schmidt would be with him in a few minutes.

The office was sparsely furnished and consisted of a large empty desk and chair, a filing cabinet and some seats for visitors. Carl sat down to wait on a chair behind the door and after about five minutes he heard the sound of someone coming in and a male voice saying in English,

"Ah, Olaf, my dear fellow, you are back again so soon?"

Then the man saw him. "You are not Herr Oliver," he said.

"Indeed I am," Carl answered. "My name is Carl Oliver."

The man who Carl assumed was Kriminalinspektor Heinrich Schmidt actually looked flustered as he realised that he had quite possibly made a mistake.

"Who are you and what do you want?" he snapped.

Carl's head was in a whirl. He had only discovered earlier that week that Olaf was involved with Moseley's Blackshirts and their Nazi friends. Now he was in the office of Inspector Schmidt of the Gestapo, obviously one of Olaf's Nazi friends.

"Who are you and what do you want?" the inspector repeated.

"My name is Carl Oliver and as I explained to the officer on reception, I was trying to locate an old friend who I was supposed to meet while we were both visiting Frankfurt."

"And what is the name of your friend?" Schmidt enquired.

"Miss Rachel Abrahams of Manchester," Carl replied.

"Ah, so," the inspector replied, as if this was a standard reply to most enquiries about missing persons. "I am sorry I have some tragic news for you. The Fraulein was meddling in matters that did not concern her. She became involved with a group of communist agitators and was shot resisting arrest."

Carl had no idea if he should believe this story or not. However, Friedrich von Brandenburg had told him a similar story regarding the fate of Rachel's cousins. Could it be that his beloved Rachel was really dead? He decided to test the veracity of what the inspector had just told him.

"I would like to take her body back to England for burial," he said feeling that he was on the point of bursting in to tears.

"I am sorry sir," the inspector replied. "That is impossible as all dissidents and rioters are buried immediately in unmarked graves."

Carl rose, still not knowing if he could believe this story or not.

"By the way, Herr Oliver," Schmidt added. "I think you should leave Germany at once and not come back as the Third Reich does not welcome trouble-makers or their friends."

Before returning to the Frankfurter Hof, Carl decided to make one last attempt to, at least, set the wheels in motion, to see if his beloved Rachel was really dead. He walked over to the British consulate and asked to see someone regarding a missing British person. After a short wait he saw a Vice-Consul who told him that they already had a report from the Foreign Office on the subject of the disappearance of Miss Abrahams but there were a number of similar cases on the books and they had to tread very carefully so as not to upset their German hosts. Carl then told him of his interview with Inspector Schmidt. The Vice-Consul was sympathetic and assured him that if Miss Abrahams was alive, they would inform the Foreign office and he then brought the interview to a close.

"Go home," Mr Oliver, "the Vice-Consul told him. "You can do no more here and could easily find yourself in a very dangerous situation."

There was just one other possible avenue of enquiry open to Carl and that was in England. He must track down 'Uncle' Olaf.

Chapter Forty four

The End of an Era

The ship ferrying a broken-hearted Carl arrived back in Hull the following afternoon. He immediately set off for Dalethorpe and arrived just before midnight. The house was in darkness and Carl crept in so as not to disturb the sleep of his two children still remaining at home. Carl William, his first-born, was now living in London and was a successful actuary. He was betrothed to Muriel Garside, the daughter of Montague Garside, who had a chain of drapery shops in the home-counties. Their marriage was scheduled to take place the following April (1939) in the parish church of Saint Luke in the small Hertfordshire village where the Garside family now resided. Carl's daughter, Elizabeth, was already married to Charles Winterbottom, from another of the old Lancashire mill families. They too had taken up residence in the capital where Charles was a stockbroker.

The following morning Carl telephoned Jack Abrahams.

"Oh Carl," Jack said, "It is such a relief to hear your voice. Are you home? Is Rachel with you? Are you both alright?"

The questions came tumbling forth, in hot pursuit of each other. Jack, quite understandably, was a deeply worried man but sadly Carl had no good news to offer.

"Yes I am home and 'no' Rachel is not with me. In fact I do not know if she is alive or dead?"

He then related the entire story of his trip to Frankfurt.

"Carl, I have or had, just one sister, and I love her very much. What do you think is the truth?" Jack asked in a voice strangled by emotion.

"I have to tell you," Carl replied, "I just do not know what to believe. However, there is one possible area I want to explore that may give us some answers."

"And what is that?"Jack asked. "Please, anything you can do, anything, I know you love her as much as I do."

"I need to find Olaf Oliver," Carl explained.

"Not that uncle of yours who liked young boys and who I sacked years ago?" Jack demanded.

"The same," Carl told him and proceeded to explain how he had seen him at the port of Hull and how the Gestapo inspector had assumed that he, Carl, was Olaf waiting to see him.

"Do you need some help in tracing him?" Jack asked. "Anything I can do, anything, just tell me."

"Leave it to me," Carl replied. "I have one or two ideas and I will report back to you as soon as I have some news."

The obvious starting point was with the British Union of Fascists (BUF), commonly known as Moseley's Blackshirts. They had small offices in a number of Lancashire towns and Carl easily found their local phone number. The telephone was answered by a rough sounding man and Carl had no choice but to tell him his business.

"Yes, I do know the old gentleman," the man replied. "He ain't here now but I can give him a message."

Bulls-eye! Carl thought. Should he leave a message or see if there was another telephone number where Olaf could be reached? The response to that was to the effect that the man who had answered the phone was not allowed to give out members details.

"Very well," Carl answered in desperation. "Tell Mr. Oliver to contact his nephew Carl James Oliver as soon as possible."

"Are you a member?" the man then asked.

Carl felt like telling him that he and his party disgusted him and he could never be a member of such an organisation but instead he just answered,

"No, not at the moment but please tell Mr. Olaf Oliver to contact me urgently on family business."

Carl then phoned Jack again and told him that his quest to find Olaf appeared to be working. Then, he decided to try and work on his plans for a new housing development in south Manchester. This was easier said than done as all he could really think about was what had happened to Rachel. Suddenly he realised that he had not spoken to his two younger children since his return and on enquiring where they were the housemaid Bessie told him that they had both gone down to London to spend some time with their older siblings.

He spent the rest of the day awaiting the phone call that never came. Three times the telephone rang and each time it was a business matter. *Why did the old devil not return his call?* Carl wondered irritably and a little unreasonably. The cook had prepared a delicious dinner for him but his appetite had vanished along with his beloved Rachel. He managed to force down just a few morsels and had just decided to pour himself a single malt whisky when the front-door bell rang.

Bessie answered the door and came to tell him that there was a Mr. Olaf Oliver wanting to see him.

"I don't think you will want to see him Sir," she commented. "He seems to be one of those Blackshirts who have been causing so much trouble."

"Bessie," Carl snapped back. "If you don't mind I will be the judge of whom I see and whom I don't see. Show him in to the library."

It was almost like a replay of Olaf's last visit so many years ago. The difference was that Olaf was now an old man with a walking stick and wearing the uniform of the BUF. And Carl was a decidedly middle-aged man himself who had experienced a life of great business success but against a backdrop of considerable personal tragedy.

Again Olaf was playing the kindly old uncle just as he had on the last occasion.

"My dear Carl," he began. "How are you and your family? They must all be grown-up by now."

"Please sit down," Carl replied coldly, getting straight down to business. "I believe you know Inspector Schmidt of the Frankfurt Gestapo."

"What on earth made you come to that conclusion?"

"The man himself mentioned you when I saw him just two days ago. In fact, before he saw me he thought that I was you, visiting him again. Now listen to me carefully Uncle Olaf," Carl continued. "It is pay back time. My late father and I put up with a great deal of embarrassment and aggravation years ago and now you can do me a favour."

The old man smiled but it was not a friendly smile; it was more the smile of a predator about to catch its prey.

"So, what can I do for you, dear boy?" Olaf replied.

"A very good friend of mine, Rachel Abrahams has disappeared while on a trip to see relatives in Frankfurt."

"Abrahams, Abrahams," the old man interrupted. "Would that be any relation of Jack Abrahams the Jew-boy who sacked me from his business and left me almost starving?"

"Do not dare to speak of my friend Jack in such terms. I can see your utterances match well the uniform you are wearing. Anyway," Carl continued. "I went to see your Inspector Schmidt to see if he could help me find Rachel."

"So, what do you need me for, after all these years?" Olaf answered. "As it happens I know all about your floozy

Rachel. She is locked up in Dachau. I am surprised at my high and mighty nephew consorting with criminals and Jewish criminals at that," he added.

How Carl kept his temper, he never knew, but somehow he managed to answer this detestable man calmly.

"I must tell you that your Nazi friend Schmidt told me she was dead, shot resisting arrest. He never mentioned anywhere called Dachau. I assume it is some kind of prison."

Olaf was winding himself up into a rage.

"If she is not dead yet she soon will be, and it serves you right, and your money grabbing Jewish friend Abrahams, for the way you both treated me. Hitler is right the Jews are ruining Germany and England as well. The sooner they are all disposed of the better."

Having completed that diatribe he jumped out of the chair and started to put his arm up in the Nazi salute.

"Sieg Heil," he shouted and then suddenly clutched his chest and fell to the floor.

Carl bent down and picked up a limp arm. He felt for a pulse and listened for a heartbeat but there was no doubt, the old devil was dead.

Carl telephoned the police and ambulance service and explained that the old man had become very excited and suddenly collapsed.

Carl was no nearer to finding out the truth about Rachel. All his efforts and those of Jack through the Foreign office, the German Embassy and other contacts came to nought. Carl was convinced that Olaf, in his hatred of both Jack Abrahams and himself, was very likely to have had a hand in her fate. He had the motive and the means.

Carl flatly refused to have any part in Olaf's funeral and simply told the authorities to dispose of his body as they saw fit.

A few months later, with the Nazi war machine goose-stepping its evil march across Europe; Great Britain, despite the 'valiant' attempts of Prime Minister Neville Chamberlain to appease Hitler, was about to declare war on the Third Reich. Carl Oliver, a broken-hearted man, in the early stages of dementia, made ready to close the Old Vicarage at Dalethorpe. His intention was to go and live in the other Oliver family home in Hampstead.

He locked the front-door with the large iron key and decided to pay one last visit to the mound at the end of the long back garden. He stood gazing at the huge protuberance and then decided to walk round to the far side; the side that was never visited and could not be seen from the house. Carl, by now, was a sick demented soul and what he discovered there was enough to ensure that the time left to him on earth would be of very short duration. As he made his way, on the rough earth behind the mound, he saw a shape that looked like a bundle of old rags. He bent down to discover an emaciated human body and he flung himself to the ground hysterically as his fists flayed the earth. He lay like that sobbing until it was dark and then, by the light of a full moon, being of far from sound mind, he fetched an old shovel from a garden shed and buried the body in the side of the mound. This body now lay in close proximity to Dominic who he had accidentally killed all those years ago.

He then climbed into his car, still sobbing, and miraculously managed to drive all the way to Hampstead without incident but in a far from sound state of mind. As he drove through the night just one thought went round and round in his mind, *how oh how, did Rachel's body get to Dalethorpe?*

Then, just a month later, as the conflagration that was to destroy the lives of countless millions continued, Carl James Oliver, at only sixty two years old, surrendered his soul to his Maker, still mourning with almost his last breath, Rachel, the love of his life.

And so the Old Vicarage at Dalethorpe fell deeper and deeper into a sad state of disrepair and the mound behind the house still kept its secrets.

CHAPTER FORTY FIVE

2010

RETURN TO DALETHORPE

Carl Oliver sat in his study at his home in Hampstead. He was alone in the large house and in deep despair. What had possessed him to ruin his career and destroy his family for the sake of minimal financial gain? It was greed, pure greed and of course lust, he realised, that had destroyed his reputation.

He had been the member for the constituency of Broadfield in Bedfordshire for some ten years. He had watched with considerable satisfaction the fast diminishing popularity of the governing Labour party, especially since the present Prime Minister Gordon Brown had taken over. Carl was not in the Shadow Cabinet but at last, he was beginning to be noticed by his senior Conservative party colleagues, having served with distinction on a number of parliamentary committees. It was January and a General Election had to be called within the next three or four months. He had hoped after this to be offered at least a Junior Ministry appointment but that was until it was discovered that he had been claiming expenses for a flat in Mayfair which was, in fact, occupied by his mistress, Nicole. Now both his career and his marriage lay in ruins.

Carl and Amanda had one son, Carl Robert Oliver, a twenty three year old with a First Class honours degree in Economics. He had recently taken up a graduate appointment in a Merchant Bank. He looked forward to a successful career as a banker and had been horrified when the disclosures about his father became public. It was he who had ensured that his mother Amanda immediately left the matrimonial home and they had both taken up residence in Amanda's parent's house just outside the town of Esher in Surrey.

Carl's local constituency party had made it clear that he should not re-apply to be their candidate in the forthcoming election, not that he had any intention of embarrassing himself and his family any further by doing so. He had now parted from his long-time girl-friend Nicole and their luxurious love-nest in Mayfair, was placed on the market. The Hampstead family home was owned by the Oliver Family Trust and had been so for many generations. Apart from a huge portfolio of investment properties that gave the Olivers their wealth and security he knew that there was another ancestral home in Lancashire in a place called Dalethorpe. Neither Carl nor his father Carl Winston Oliver, during his lifetime, had ever visited and to the best of their knowledge the place was just a ruin. Indeed Carl's grandfather, Carl William had hated to even hear mention of Dalethorpe and the Old Vicarage and used to say that the place was cursed. There was just one thing about this place that had long provoked Carl's curiosity. According to instructions in the Trust deed of the Oliver Family Trust there was a strange mound behind the house and this was considered to be some kind of shrine and must never be disturbed.

As Carl sat at his desk in Hampstead surveying the self-inflicted ruins of his life, he decided to pay a visit to Dalethorpe and to see for himself the Old Vicarage and the mysterious mound.

The following morning he reversed the Jaguar out of the garage at the rear of the house, threw in an overnight bag and set off for the north. The traffic on the M1 motorway was horrendous and it took him nearly two hours to reach the junction with the M6 which would take him all the way to Lancashire. As he crawled along at 30-40 mph he kept asking himself what had possessed him to make this journey. The car was capable of at least 120 mph although the legal limit was 70. If only he could actually reach the legal maximum, he decided, how wonderful that would be.

It was half past one in the afternoon when he arrived and he parked the car a couple of hundred metres outside the perimeter of the small town. He had found a map with the deeds that told him that the Old Vicarage was the first house on the right and approaching it on foot enabled him to take in many of the exterior details. As he neared the building he marvelled at its size and was relieved to see that although sadly in need of repair it was certainly not a ruin. There were the remains of a gate hanging off the wall on one hinge and this gave access to a heavily overgrown driveway. To the left was what had probably once been a cultivated garden but now with shoulder-high weeds, plants and shrubs it resembled nothing more than a jungle.

Carl had to take great care in navigating his way to the front steps that led up to a glass-panelled front-door. Where the tiles had cracked on the steps wild vegetation had also established itself but somehow Carl arrived on the wide top step, fished in his pocket for the large metal key and opened the door. Everything in the house was of course, covered in thick layers of dust and even inside some impudent weeds had managed to gain a foothold or rather a roothold.

Carl entered the first room on the right and was astonished to see bookshelves floor to ceiling containing hundreds and probably thousands of leather-bound volumes. He had not come all the way from London just to have a peripheral inspection and he toured every room in the huge house taking in the details of all features of value that would bear restoration.

Next Carl, after carefully locking the front door, descended to garden level and made his way to the back. Again there was a long garden, now in an inevitably overgrown state. And then he saw it; the huge mound. It must have been twenty feet high and at that time of day it cast a dark shadow on the garden to its east. He made his way over towards it and stopped some ten feet away. There was something strange and special about this mound and although a matter-of-fact person, not given to emotional flights-of-fancy, he shivered in the un-seasonally warm mid-afternoon sun. The mound had stood there from some long distant past and he could well understand that it must remain. It was part of Dalethorpe, the Old Vicarage and of his family.

He resolved there and then to have the house restored to something approaching its former glory. He had far more money than he and his son would ever need and if it cost a few hundred thousand to make it into a habitable residence, so be it. However, he decided he would employ a designer and with strict instructions to salvage as much as possible of the original interior, the house would become his residence, as far away from London and disgrace as possible.

It would soon be dark but before returning to the south Carl decided to take a brief walk through the village. There were about ten detached houses and then rows of terraced cottages. Unlike London, every house showed that it was maintained with loving care. Of course, property was a fraction of the price in the capital and quite understandably, with much lower mortgage re-payments, people could afford to spend more money on their homes and gardens.

He came to a village store and noted that it sold postage stamps but all other postal services necessitated a trip to nearby Accrington. Then after passing more terraced cottages he arrived at the church with its rather grand title of St Barnabas-by-Dalethorpe.

Carl wondered if there would be any evidence of members of his family being buried there and a brief stroll round the churchyard led him to the Oliver family crypt. He read the long list of names of his ancestors whose remains had been deposited there and was astonished to discover that he was far from being the only Carl James Oliver although many of his forbears had other middle names.

That is it! He decided. *I belong in this tiny village. I too will be one of the Olivers of Dalethorpe.*

On the long drive home Carl felt happier than he had been at any time since his two misdemeanours had been discovered and brought to the notice of the world. He decided he would rent the house in Hampstead to suitable tenants. His second resolution was to try and re-build a relationship with his son. As for his wife, they had been far from happy before he had even met Nicole and he liked to use this, if only to himself, as justi for his affair.

Of course the sole justification he could find for the dishonest claiming of expenses was that he was far from alone in this type of behaviour. Hadn't a substantial number of his fellow MPs been caught out, some of them for far worse abuses of the system? At least, unlike some of them, he did not face legal proceedings; but his parliamentary career and his marriage had sunk together.

The following day he contacted a well-known interior designer, in fact the man who had decorated and furnished his love-nest with Nicole. He gave him full details of what he wanted to achieve with the Old Vicarage, presented him with the large Victorian iron key and told him to prepare a scheme.

CHAPTER FORTY SIX

RE-UNITED

By August the old house was ready to welcome its new occupant and Carl ordered a removal firm to take his personal effects to Dalethorpe. He then drove up to Lancashire to start a new and very different life. He needed staff to run the large house; a cook, a housekeeper and a maid. This was only a fraction of the servants employed by his ancestors but then there was usually a large family to look after, not just one lonely man.

He advertised on the internet and in the area's newspapers and received plenty of applicants for the positions. In a time of recession, domestic work had become respectable and well paid. The positions were filled and Carl looked around for a way to occupy his time.

His first contact with neighbours had been unfortunate to say the least. He had been tense after coping with his self-inflicted public disgrace, his broken marriage, estrangement from a son he loved dearly and the move to Dalethorpe. It took some weeks to repair the damage caused by his rude outburst to the Mottersheads but, eventually they became firm friends.

It was Roger Mottershead who suggested to Carl that he should write a history of the Oliver family of Dalethorpe and Carl started the project with enthusiasm. He was excited to discover from parish records that a kinswoman of Roger had become a great, great, great, grandmother of his, on marrying a Carl Joseph Oliver back in 1853.

He decided to call the history *The Dalethorpe Chronicles* but was unable to discover the original roots of the family. Going back to the Domesday Book was no small achievement but he still wanted to know how and why the Oliver family had settled there in the first place. And then he discovered the stone grave-markers.

Carl had been telephoning and texting his son Carl Robert for some weeks without receiving any response. His emails were also ignored and Carl decided that he must visit his son in London and beg him, if necessary, to resume contact. At the same time he would take the stone tablets he had just found, locked away in a cupboard, to the British Museum, for identification. He could not understand why anyone would take what looked like two worthless pieces of rock and wrap them up in filthy old lengths of cloth then leave them in a cupboard built in to a wall. There was some kind of writing chiselled into each of them but to Carl they were indecipherable. Also in the cupboard were the crumbled remains of some large sheets of paper and these he chose to ignore.

He emailed his son once again and told him he was coming to London on important family business that concerned not only Carl but the entire Oliver family, past, present and future. This brought a response.

You broke my mother's heart and embarrassed me with all my friends and associates. Where are you? and what do you want?

At least he had a reply. Now he had to persuade his son to meet him and the stone tablets were the perfect excuse.

I emailed you a few weeks ago to tell you that I have taken up permanent residence in the old family home in Dalethorpe, Lancashire. Since I moved here I have found two stone tablets locked away in a cupboard with some kind of writing on them. I would like you to see them before I take them to the British Museum to see if they can decipher them. Will you meet me? How about the car park at Kenwood House? On a weekday, at this time of the year it should not be too busy.

Much to Carl's relief, his son agreed and a date and time were decided upon. Carl carried the two stone tablets to the car, placed them carefully in the boot and set off for London. It was September and the English weather had been very kind; warm and sunny. Carl Robert arrived just ten minutes before his father and when Carl pulled on to the car park his son came up to the driver's window.

"Hello Father," he said, somewhat coldly. "I suppose you would like a coffee after your long drive?"

"Yes, that would be nice," Carl answered stiffly. It was some time since he had seen his son and he knew that he must take any attempt at reconciliation very gently.

He climbed out of the car and the pair walked round to the rear of Kenwood House to where the café was situated.

They found a table outside and without any preliminaries Carl James said,

"Right, so what is this all about?"

"The stone tablets are in the car and as soon as we have had our coffee I will show them to you," Carl senior explained.

As they sipped their drinks they both tried to make conversation on inconsequential subjects in the manner of men who have just met. They discussed the weather and the new coalition government but without enthusiasm. Carl was almost relieved when the drinks were downed and they made their way back to his Jaguar. There are benches alongside the wall of Kenwood house facing the amazing views of the spacious grounds where the stately home is situated; hard to believe that this was in London. They carried the two stones round to the benches and there Carl showed his sons the chiselled markings.

"Hmm," Carl Robert said. "This is certainly some kind of writing but don't you think they both look like totally different alphabets?"

"Yes, I thought that. Strange isn't it? Look would you like to come with me to the British Museum tomorrow? After all they belong to you as an Oliver, just as much as to me."

Somehow the discussion on the subject of the stone tablets broke the ice. Now both father and son had the same agenda; to discover the origin and meaning of the chiselled stones. They chatted more easily as they returned to the car. Neither of them suspected that the stone tablets had come from the Mound; indeed Carl Robert was only vaguely aware of the existence of the strange feature and that from being present at the reading of his Grandfather's will, just two years earlier.

The visit to the British Museum had answered some questions and raised many others. The two Carls now both knew that the larger tablet was written in the Runic alphabet used by the Norsemen and the smaller one in Hebrew. They had also been told that the stones were obviously some kind of burial markers and they now knew the names of the people whose graves these stones had been intended to identify. The Runic one was for Karl Olafsen and the Hebrew one for Rachel bat (daughter of) Yosef.

Back in the car with the stones lying safely in the boot, Carl turned to his son and commented,

"These people must be our ancestors. We know that throughout our family history the oldest son has always been called Carl and maybe this Rachel was his wife and a Jewess."

This conclusion was hardly rocket-science but then Carl continued,

"How did these stones come to be in the house? I am beginning to suspect that they came from the mound."

"What is this mound?" Carl Robert wanted to know.

"All we know," his father explained, "is that it should never be disturbed. These instructions were written into the Oliver Family Trust deed many, many years ago."

"Father," Carl Robert enquired pensively. "When do you intend to return to Dalethorpe? I have some holiday time to take and I would very much like to come with you to see this mound and, of course, the old house."

Far from cursed, the old house is blessed, thought Carl Joseph. *It is bringing my son and me together again.*

And so the following Sunday found the two Carls, father and son, driving up the motorways towards Lancashire and possibly to discover more of the ancient history of the Oliver family. But neither of them could have known what other sinister secrets would be learned.

CHAPTER FORTY SEVEN

A GRUESOME DISCOVERY

The drive to Dalethorpe could best be described as a voyage of discovery or maybe re-discovery. Now that an identity of purpose had been established, the pair could talk far more easily on other subjects. Before they had lived together with Carl Robert's mother under the same roof but went about their own everyday lives with scarcely a thought of the other. When the son was growing-up Carl had played, with absolute sincerity, the role of the doting father and they spent many hours together on outings and joint pursuits such as following their favourite Rugby team. All that had changed some twelve years ago when the boy was sent off to boarding school. In the meantime Carl's parliamentary commitments and extra-curricular activities with Nicole kept him away from home for long periods. As a result, father and son drifted farther and farther apart. Thus, when Carl's scandalous behaviour became known, the son had taken his mother's part. Now as they drove north together Carl Robert was finding that his father had many good points and that they could resume a close relationship.

On arrival that evening the pair dined together on a delicious menu devised by Carla, the new Italian cook. They then sat in the library, a room that fascinated them both.

"I am sure these walls and these books could tell us many a tale from the past, if only they could speak," Carl Robert commented.

They were both up bright and early the following morning and while waiting for breakfast Carl Robert removed one of the hundreds of leather bound volumes from the library shelf. He had no idea why he should have taken down that particular book; it could only have been divine providence. He opened it to discover an unsealed envelope, containing a letter, had been inserted inside the cover. The envelope was addressed to a Miss Rachel Abrahams at an address in Manchester and as it had obviously been there for many years he carefully extracted the letter and began to read,

Rachel my darling, my one true love,
Where are you? And what has become of you? I do not know if you are alive or dead and if it is the latter I pray that I can die soon so that our souls may be re-united for eternity. I addressed this letter to the home of your brother Jack, my dear friend, but of course you cannot be there or I would know you were home safe and sound. The only thing I do know is that I have loved you to distraction from the first moment I set eyes on you, forty years ago. Please, oh please come back to me.
Your ever adoring,
Carl.

He had just finished reading the letter for the second time when his father entered the library.

"What have you got there?" he enquired.

Carl Robert wiped his eyes as he handed the letter and envelope to Carl senior.

Carl Joseph read the letter and replaced it in the envelope.

"That is so sad and poignant," he said. "I wonder who this Rachel was. One of our ancestors obviously loved her very much."

It was a fine day and as soon as breakfast was over, father and son walked down the newly laid garden path, passing the beautifully manicured lawns and rose garden towards the mound. Neither was aware that the other was experiencing a strange tingling sensation down their spine as they approached. They stood there staring at it from some ten feet away until Carl Robert said,

"Can't we go right up to it and touch its surface. Surely there is nothing wrong in doing that?"

"Yes, why not" his father agreed as the pair approached the mound, both with a certain degree of trepidation.

"What is on the other side?" the son then asked.

"I have no idea," Carl Joseph answered. "Come on then," he suggested, "let us walk round it."

The far side of the mound was almost identical to the front. That was until Carl Robert saw something white sticking out of the shale just a few inches off the ground. He bent down and then jumped back as if he had received an electric shock.

"My God," he said. "It is a part of a bone. It could be from an animal but from what I remember of my biology at school that is the end part of a Tibia."

"Are you sure?" Carl Joseph replied. "Don't you think it could be a bone from a dead sheep or cow that a dog had left here at some time?"

Carl Robert bent down and started to remove some of shale and soil surrounding the bone.

"No," he said. "This is human. We must call the police."

Within half an hour five police vehicles all carrying the crest of the Lancashire County Police had arrived.

The senior officer was Detective Inspector Crabtree and after hearing their story, including some background information about the mound, he told father and son to wait in the house while the area was cordoned off and further investigation undertaken.

At six o'clock in the evening the pair was still waiting for news from the police. They had separately been to peer out of the rear windows of the house but the police had erected a high plastic curtain labelled 'CRIME SCENE' to obscure the view. Then there was a ring on the doorbell and Carl saw his new friend and neighbour Roger Mottershead standing next to the constable on the top step. He opened the door to be addressed by the constable.

"Do you know this gentleman? He says he is a friend of yours."

"Yes, of course," Carl replied. "Roger, please come in."

He escorted Roger into the library and proudly introduced him to his son.

"What on earth is going on here?" Roger said.

"We found what Carl here thinks is a human bone embedded in the mound in the back garden-so now we find ourselves swarming with members of the police-force."

"And what have they told you?" Roger enquired.

"Precisely nothing," Carl answered.

"Well," Roger continued, "we realised something was amiss when we saw all the police cars on the lane so Rosemary sent me down to ask you to come over for dinner."

Before Carl could respond to the invitation there was a knock on the library door and Detective Inspector Crabtree entered.

"Might I talk to you on your own?" he asked eyeing Carl Robert and Roger.

"Certainly," Carl replied. "We will go into the drawing-room."

"Please sit down," Carl said. "What news do you have for me?"

"So far we have found the remains of two people," Crabtree informed him.

"However, our forensic experts tell us that both have been dead for a minimum of sixty to seventy years, so if there is any evidence of foul play, I would say that puts you and most of the local population outside the time-frame.

"I gather this house has been in your family for many generations," the detective continued.

"Yes, in fact my family lived on this spot from as long ago as the Domesday Book," Carl explained. "You say you have found the remains of two bodies. Can you tell me any more than that? Are they male or female? Are they young or old?"

"Please understand that our forensic team must carry out a thorough examination but I can tell you that the preliminary findings indicate a young male, probably only thirteen or fourteen and a female of at least sixty years of age and maybe more."

"Thank you for that," Carl replied. "Our friend who is in the library with my son has invited us to dinner at his house just down the lane. Will it be alright if we go?"

"Of course," the DI replied smiling. "It is soon going to be dark and we will then leave just a couple of policemen on site over night. We will see you in the morning and enjoy your dinner."

Nice chap, Carl decided and returned to the library to tell Carl Robert and Roger the news.

Chapter Forty eight

Fiona Mottershead

Considering the gruelling day that the two Oliver men had experienced, dinner was a resounding success. This was partly due to the fact that Rosemary was an excellent cook but the contribution of the Mottershead's nineteen year old student daughter, Fiona was also of considerable significance. It was obvious that Carl Robert and Fiona were more than little impressed with each other and this provoked telling smiles between the three parents.

They had been seated next to each other at table and on the way home Carl Robert confided to his father that he had arranged to take Fiona out for coffee the following afternoon.

"Where are you thinking of going?" Carl Joseph enquired smiling.

"Oh, Fiona tells me there is a lovely tea shop over in Whalley," he explained. Then after a pause he continued, "However, my car is in London. Could I possibly borrow the Jag?"

Carl Joseph was only too pleased to agree. *We have come a long way in a short time*, he thought as he reminded himself that his son would not even speak to him just a week ago.

Before going to bed the two Carls discussed the events of the day.

"I keep wondering who these two poor people could be."Carl the elder wondered out loud.

"The whole thing seems so bizarre," the son replied. "Maybe the remains are much older. Could they be the bones of Karl Olafsen and Rachel?"

"I doubt it," Carl the father replied. "There is a very big difference between sixty or seventy years and a thousand years and more, when the Vikings were writing in the Runic alphabet."

The police returned in force at eight o'clock the following morning.

The Detective Inspector told them that they hoped to have more information on the identities of the remains by the afternoon and in the meantime they would be carrying out further investigative work on the mound.

"I am afraid we are going to have to undertake more excavations. I know you told me this whole mound is very old and considered sacrosanct in your family but we could be dealing with a serial killer here. There may be more bodies to be found. I am sorry, this must be done."

The father and son spent the morning together as Carl Joseph worked on the family tree he was constructing on his PC. Carl Robert was fascinated and they both wondered which of the old Carls had written the heart-breaking love letter that they had found.

At lunchtime Carl Robert suggested that he should postpone his date with Fiona until another day but his father insisted on him going and after their light meal he handed the keys of the Jaguar to his son and told him to go off and have a lovely afternoon.

"Just keep your mobile switched on," he told him, "just in case there is any more news."

Carl had copies of the Parish records for the last two hundred years and the more he delved into them the more absorbing and fascinating they became.

It was four o'clock when Inspector Crabtree returned.

"I can tell you that the boy was killed by a blow to the head. He had also received a number of other injuries of the type that could have been caused by falling down stairs. We have no idea however of his identity and we are still looking for clues. The tattered remains of his clothing, buried with him, give us absolutely no leads. The forensic boys think that he died years before the woman, probably at the very beginning of the twentieth century, so over a hundred years ago.

"They tell us," He continued, "that the woman was about sixty years old and appeared to have died from natural causes. The state of her bones indicates a period of severe malnutrition. They also place her death as occurring in the late 1930s."

The Inspector smiled a triumphant smile. "We found a temporary travel document; badly stained but quite legible. Curiously, it was issued by the British Consulate in Hamburg in 1939, just a few months before the war. As a result we have a name," he said. "Have you ever heard of anyone called Rachel Abrahams?"

Carl rose without a word and went over to the book containing the love letter. He handed it to the Inspector in silence and waited for him to read it.

"Yes," Crabtree finally said. "Very interesting and where did you find this letter?"

Carl explained and the DI then promised him that they would try to trace a family called Abrahams who might know of a long-lost relative called Rachel. He assured Carl that the police would check all public records to enable them to make a positive identification.

CHAPTER FORTY NINE

1939 DACHAU-DALETHORPE

Claus Reinhardt, professor of history at the University of Frankfurt, was a man of considerable influence or he had been until he was incarcerated in Dachau. At that stage, before the outbreak of war, the inmates were, of course, treated appallingly in this, the first of the many concentration camps that were built by the Nazis. The prisoners were virtually starved and used for slave labour and although many lost their lives as a result of their cruel treatment, the organised slaughter of millions of people on an industrial scale had not yet commenced. It was also possible for the Nazis to release prisoners if they felt there was some benefit to them in doing so. Claus Reinhardt somehow managed to convince his interviewers from the Gestapo that he would be prepared to join the Nazi party and help to assuage the strong opposition of the German intelligentsia to their regime. This was not Claus's first period in Dachau and he knew that if he did not gain his release again now, there would certainly be no third chances. However, his real plan was to leave Germany and try to alert the world to the evil that was being perpetrated there by the Nazi government.

Whenever the opportunity presented itself he talked to Rachel and told her of his plan to gain his release and she began to formulate a plan of her own. Her appearance was skeletal although nothing could take away the beauty of her face. She was working twelve to fourteen hours every day in the textile factory inside the camp. Once her plan was clear in her mind she told one of the guards that she had some important information for the camp commandant. Incredibly, her plan worked and she was marched into his office.

"You have something to tell me," he demanded.

"No, but I have something important to tell the Frankfurt Gestapo."

"So, what is it?" the commandant snapped. "I have better things to do than to gaze at a scrawny English Jewess."

"I cannot tell you," she replied amazed at her own daring. "It is a matter of national security and can only be told to Kriminalinspektor Wolfgang Schmidt of the Frankfurt Gestapo."

Suddenly there was a change in the commandant's demeanour. A camp commandant is an important man and probably would have just dismissed Rachel's request except for the fact that his path had crossed with that of Kriminalinspektor Wolfgang Schmidt three years earlier. At that time he had been investigated by Schmidt for converting valuables stolen from Jewish homes and considered to be the property of the third Reich, to his own personal benefit. As a consequence he decided that discretion would be the better part of valour and he arranged for a guard to take Rachel back to Frankfurt. He had no desire to be in Schmidt's bad-books again.

He telephoned Schmidt in Frankfurt who told him that the release of Rachel together with other trouble-making foreign nationals had already been authorised, providing they left the country at once.

It then transpired that Claus was also to be released into the custody of the Frankfurt Gestapo so the two prisoners were given rather decent clothing to wear outside the camp, each handcuffed to a guard and taken to the railway station.

Rachel had no idea that she was to be released anyway and spent most of the journey plotting how she could escape from her guard. However at the Frankfurt railway station she was transferred to another guard who told her he was taking her to Hamburg where she would be expelled from the Third Reich as an undesirable alien. She said her goodbyes to Claus and then travelled on towards freedom.

In Hamburg she was taken on board a ship bound for Hull and her handcuffs were removed. A member of the Hamburg British Consulate staff gave her a travel document and enough money to purchase a railway ticket from Hull to Manchester and a change of clothes. Her time in Dachau, however, had left her weak and suffering from tuberculosis. She tried to eat the meals that the steamship company provided but this only resulted in bouts of nausea and vomiting. She was more than happy to be free but her general state of health precluded her from enjoying the situation.

On arrival in Hull, she attempted to telephone her brother and his wife, who were away in London, still trying to locate her in Germany, through yet another visit to the Foreign Office. She could not remember Carl's telephone number and in desperation she took the train to Accrington. From there she hired a cab to Dalethorpe, all the time feeling weaker and weaker. Carl was not at home and the house appeared to be closed so she decided to walk round to the back to see if there were any lights on in the rear facing rooms of the house. This proved to be negative. However, she could see the dark shadow of the mound against the night sky and felt a compulsion to walk slowly down towards it. Carl had long ago told her of its special place in the history of his family. She knew about the other Karl (the Viking) and the other Rachel (the Hebrew slave-girl) of long, long ago and felt that her ancient namesake was calling her to visit the mound.

On the train journey from Hull she had decided that if Carl still wanted her, she would agree to marry him and she felt that circling the mound would, somehow bind her closer to his family. With every step she took, she felt weaker and weaker and at the back of the mound she was forced to sit down on the damp clay. She was trembling and had a terrible pain in her chest. She broke out in a cold sweat and she was forced to lean back on the mound itself as she fought for breath and for life itself. She thought she heard a voice coming from the mound saying to her, *Rachel! Rachel! It is time to come home.* Her weakened heart stopped beating and she drifted into eternal sleep.

CHAPTER FIFTY

2010 THE MOUND'S SECRETS

Inspector Crabtree seemed to have taken a particular liking to the Oliver family or maybe he was intrigued by the various facets of the investigation. During the subsequent three weeks he was hardly away from Dalethorpe but he was able to put the Olivers, father and son's, minds at rest regarding the initial discoveries, although one of the skeletons implied another type of 'skeleton in the cupboard' from the past.

His quest to find an Abrahams family in north-west England with a lost relative called Rachel Abrahams had produced a quick result. A remarkable old lady, Diana Jackson, now eighty five years old and living in an apartment in Bowdon, Cheshire, remembered that her grandfather Jack Abrahams had been heart-broken at the disappearance of his sister Rachel Abrahams on a trip to Germany, not long before the second world-war. Census and birth records confirmed that they were indeed brother and sister. Diana was also able to confirm that the address, on the love letter that was never sent, had been that of her dear Grandpa Jack. The poor lady, Rachel, had died from natural causes and it was assumed she had been visiting her gentleman-friend Carl James Oliver, had been alone in the house and suffered a massive heart-attack while walking behind the mound in the garden. The body was released to the family and Diana's son Paul Gilbert was able to arrange a quick burial, in a Jewish cemetery.

There was more of a problem with the second body, that of the young boy. There was no doubt of the cause of death, a severely fractured skull. Whether this was accidental or deliberate foul play was impossible to establish. That was until the Inspector decided to run the names 'Oliver' and 'The old Vicarage, Dalethorpe' through the records of local Police forces; his own Lancashire County Police; Cheshire and Greater Manchester. As a result he was handed the entire un-savoury story of the unfrocked vicar of St Barnabas-by-Dalethorpe, Olaf Oliver. However, whether the recently discovered body of the lad was the missing Dominic and whether he had been murdered by a long dead forebear of the present Carl Oliver, was impossible to prove. Inspector Crabtree was fairly certain, but enough police time had been spent on this investigation and the file was closed. The remains of Dominic, if that was who this was, were re-interred in an unmarked grave maintained for this purpose and in close proximity to where the bones of Olaf lay, although the authorities had no idea that possibly this was an inappropriate location.

Carl Robert had now returned to London to pursue his career in banking and telephoned or emailed his father daily for news of the police investigation. Carl Joseph, his father was delighted that they had forged a strong family bond and was determined to visit London regularly and spend time with his son. However, it soon became apparent that this would not be necessary. Carl the younger had his own reasons for frequently visiting Dalethorpe in the person of an extremely attractive young lady called Fiona Mottershead.

Then came the final police report!

"We have been employing thermal imaging equipment on the mound," the Inspector told Carl, "and there were sixteen more bodies buried inside there. The latest of them proved to be at least one thousand years old and the earliest probably two hundred years earlier. We are happy to reinter them in the mound if that is your wish. However we have a number of stone tablets with strange markings that we had to remove before examining the bones and I believe these to be your property."

Carl followed the Inspector into the back garden and saw three stones containing large amounts of text written in the Runic alphabet. And then he saw that the fourth one was in Hebrew.

Carl thanked the police Inspector for all his help and made ready to visit the British Museum once again with the four new tablets.

The first three tablets were deciphered and the story on the Runic stones started as follows:

It was said of Karl Olafsen that he was forced to leave the settlement becoming known in the Norse language as Wid Næss, (wide promontory) as a result of his dalliance with a slave girl....

The Museum produced for him an English translation of the whole story ending with the death of Karl Olafsen. It was a story of the love and devotion that a man and a woman of totally different backgrounds could bestow on each other. It was also the story of how a Viking worshipper of heathen gods, could learn to believe in the one true God.

The Hebrew stone tablet contained a shorter story. It had been written by her son, who had followed her religion and finished up with the ancient Jewish statement of commitment to the Lord,

Shma Yisrael, Hashem Elokaynu, Hashem Echad

Hear oh Israel, the Lord is our God, the Lord is One.

With the assistance of his son Carl Robert Oliver, Carl Joseph Oliver finished his history of the ancient Oliver family, *The Dalethorpe Chronicles*. A leather-bound copy was presented to Carl Robert on the occasion of his marriage to Fiona Mottershead and the Oliver family faced the future, however turbulent it might turn out to be, with faith and with confidence.

End